NIGHTMARE CITY

NIGHTMARE CITY

Jack Conner

For my mother. One tough chick.

Chapter 1

Katya fled through the streets of Upper Lavorgna, her heart pounding wildly.

Faster, she told herself. *Faster*.

Shadows and fog swirled around her, and one of the three moons glared down from above. She was more terrified than she could ever remember being.

He was after her.

She'd lost sight of him some time back, but she knew he was there, somewhere. Hunting.

Lightning blasted overhead, startling her, and a deluge began to pound down. *Great, just when I thought it couldn't get any worse.*

She had no place to go, not even a damned umbrella. Rain plastered her hair against her scalp, but she pulled her black leather jacket tighter about her, feeling her jagged rings against her fingers, and pushed on, choosing alleys and main roads, never any one for very long. Sedic had an auto.

"Got you, bitch."

A hand reached from the shadows and grabbed Katya's shoulder, spinning her around. A narrow, tattooed face peered out at her from the darkness, eyes bloodshot and lips hard, blue and fish-thin; he was infected, then. A victim of the Atomic Sea.

"Thought you could filch and flee, eh?" he said. "Sedic'll pay good money to see you get yours, girl. Where's the loot?"

"Had to ditch it." *Damnit.*

His fishy lips stretched in a ghastly smile. "Guess I'll have to search you to find out for sure. *Thoroughly—*"

Katya punched him in the throat. Her jagged silver rings bit into his flesh, and he gagged and reeled backward, eyes wide. Before he could recover, she turned and ran. Her heart nearly exploded out of her chest. *Dear gods.* Lucky that idiot had been high and stupid. He'd be after her soon enough, though.

Autos rattled past, then a horse-drawn carriage. A few homunculi stalked the shadows, blackened things in the shapes of men. A great steam-man stomped by, vapor squirting from his upper reaches, but those were relics from another age and there was only the one, dented and rusty though it was.

Bombs dropped during the war (still ongoing in other parts of the world) had cratered some of the roads and collapsed a few of the buildings, largely unrepaired. This was the Uppers, after all. *Support the Brotherhood*, one scuffed poster read. *Good luck*, she thought.

Wet and exhausted, she found Aggie at the corner of Navvers and Trilston.

"Thank Magnar!" Katya panted. "I was afraid you'd be out on a date."

"Damn, look at you, hon."

Aggie pulled her under the overhang, where several other prostitutes lounged, stinking of cheap perfume. One was blatantly infected, and she resembled a living anemone, orange tendrils waving in defiance of gravity.

The corner they'd picked was one of the busiest in the Fifth Ward, but at this time of day and in this weather only a trickle of traffic rumbled by. Two homunculi listed against the wall, seemingly lifeless. Only their eyes moved, rolling in their black sockets. Their eyes were the only things human on them, and they creeped Kat out. Still, she knew the creatures provided protection for the girls. *And me, hopefully.* They were one of the reasons she'd come here.

"H-have a cigarette?" she asked, teeth chattering.

Aggie unslung her tiny purse with the red frills and dug out a pack of smokes. Menthols, but Katya didn't complain as Aggie put one to her lips and sparked it for her.

"What happened?" Aggie said. "Don't tell me you got the law after you."

"Worse. Sedic."

"The loan shark? He's bad news. Hear he crippled Cinda last week."

"Paralyzed her. Thought I'd get him back. Use the loot to pay her bills. Didn't work out so well, though. He got sick at dinner—bad clams or something—and doubled back. Caught me right in the act of finding his stash."

"Rotten luck, girl."

"Now I've got him and his pack on my trail."

"He's killed, like, nine people this year that I know of. And what he does to girls like me . . ." Aggie shook her head. "How can I help?"

"Just give me cover till I can think my way out of this."

The other prostitutes glared at Katya. Likely they didn't appreciate the thought of more competition. *As if.*

"More bad news," Aggie said. "Mala saw a haunt earlier."

"Not another one," Katya said.

"She was goin' down an alley after a job and saw this-- well, shadow, I guess--fly up into the sky. She heard a scream and went ahead. Found an old lady kneeling over some bodies. Mala said their skulls were *smoking.*"

"Shit."

The haunts had been terrorizing Lavorgna for months, and no one even had a guess at what they were.

"Just be careful out there," Aggie said.

Katya sucked in a hit and shivered as the nicotine fired her bloodstream. The menthol tasted terrible, but it was worth it. She blew out the smoke and stared up into the storm-tossed night. Here and there between the clouds scudded two of the three moons, one pale and white, one greenish and misshapen.

"Hey, look what crawled in," Aggie said.

A long black limo squealed up to the corner, sloughing water. A dirty spray splashed Katya's legs.

"Watch it!" Aggie called, approaching the vehicle. "Look where you're goin'. Can't you see it's rainin' out here?"

Sudden fear for Aggie made Katya call out, but the redhead ignored her. Four homunculi stood on the limo's running boards, two on each side, chains linked to spiked collars around their necks. The creatures' gangly black frames glistened in the rain. Like guard dogs, Katya thought. Except that they looked like blackened human corpses, only their eyes undamaged.

The limo's chrome grill shone like silver teeth, and its bulbous headlights stabbed into the darkness like swords. A Boss's car, or one of his lieutenant's.

As Aggie sashayed toward the limo like she was the Empress of Qar, Kat felt a swell of admiration for her. *She should've been a thief like me, not a whore.*

"What the fuck do you think you're doin'?" Aggie asked whoever was in the limo. "Sprayin' water all over my girls? We ain't made of sugar but that don't mean we like gettin' gutter water hosed all over us."

The back window rolled down. Darkness gaped.

Aggie ducked her head into the interior, and Katya half expected black hands to grab her and haul her inside, for the auto to roar off and vanish into the night, Aggie's screams on the air. Instead Aggie laughed and fingered her wet clothes.

"Naw, it's slower than a Returner's come," she said, and continued talking to the occupant of the limo's cabin in low tones. Her pimp?

Sudden movement down the street. Katya snapped her head to see the low, curving lines of Sedic's auto, prowling like a tiger in the shadows. One of his goons drove, and she thought she saw Sedic himself in the passenger seat, a terrifying waste of a man whose addiction to alchemical substances had turned his veins yellow and caused most of his hair to fall out. A chill swept her. She looked back to the limo.

This is my chance. She moved toward the vehicle.

"I think I'd like an introduction," she said.

Aggie looked surprised. "Alright, then. Jack, Katya Ivreski. Katya, meet Death's Head Jack."

"Come in if you want to talk," said a dry, crackly voice from the car. "I always have time for pretty young women in need. But I'm kind of in a hurry and don't have time to sit here and chat all night."

With a rueful smile, Aggie opened the limo door for Katya. The darkness inside looked *very* dark.

Katya hesitated as her eyes fell on the homunculi. *Suck it up, Kat.*

She cringed at the proximity of the creatures, which leered down at her from either side (Aggie patted her on the back and said "Good luck") and ducked into the interior of the limousine. It smelled of incense smoke and chemicals and was so dark she couldn't see. A hand guided her, and she fell back into plush leather. It was more comfortable than anything she'd ever known. She hoped she didn't ruin it with her wet clothes.

The car doors slammed shut, locking her in darkness. Tires squealed, and the limo shot off.

Someone lit a match, and light flared across the face of the only other occupant of the cab, the man who must be Death's Head Jack.

Katya opened her mouth and screamed.

When the thing sitting across from her didn't lunge for her and tear out her throat, Kat forced herself to stop screaming. *Courage, girl.*

It wasn't easy. The thing was quite literally named. Death-black eyes glittered out of a decayed, withered face. The head had to belong to a corpse—yet when he spoke the flesh bunched and moved, surprisingly mobile.

At her fear and fascination, Jack laughed.

She tucked her legs under her and crawled as far away from him as she could get. She understood what the smoke was for now—to hide the stench of rot. And the chemicals must issue from Jack himself.

"Are you a Returner?" she asked.

Amused, he shook his head. He put his cigarette to his lips, and as he did she saw—her eyes adjusting to the dimness—that his hand was normal. That is, he had the hands of a living man, while his head was undeniably that of a dead one. And that just couldn't be, not if he was a Returner. Returners were *all* corpse—in fact, they were usually composed of pieces of several. Besides, Returners were normally just mindless slaves. Reanimating the dead was a tricky process and mostly the brain was too far gone by the time it was brought back to life. It was said that only the mysterious and reclusive Dr. Reynalt could perform the procedure successfully.

"No," Jack said, his withered lips curling around his cigarette. "I'm not a Returner, not precisely. But let's leave that for now. I know *my* story. I don't know yours. Do you want to join our little family—start working for me?"

Katya stared at his rotting head. She knew Jack could, if he wanted, slit her throat and throw her corpse from the car, and even if it landed at the feet of the most honest cop in Upper Lavorgna no one would lay a hand on him. Bosses' men, especially the high ones, could get away with anything.

"We'll see," Katya said.

Smoke curled up from his cigarette. "You are pretty, I'll give you that—wet and bedraggled and all."

"I don't need to be pretty."

"No?"

She bit the inside of her cheek. "Listen, Jack. It's been a rough night. It's just, that's not why I'm here. I didn't want to meet with you to become, you know, a working girl."

"Why then?"

She made herself sit up straight. "I want to meet with Boss Ravic."

His eyebrows, what he had of them, shot up. "Oh?"

"Yep."

"Well, as it happens, I was just on the way to the Factory to pay him a visit."

She kept quiet for the rest of the trip. They moved east, away from the sea; Lavorgna was a port city, sprawling like a smoking, cancerous mass along this section of the Atomic Sea, but the Fifth Ward was deep inland, far from the water. When Katya was feeling bold sometimes she would climb a skyscraper and stare out toward the mad, boiling sea with its lightning erupting upward and noxious fumes oozing from its crashing waves.

Soon enough, more normal lightning flickered across the night, silhouetting the three thick towers of the Factory that jutted up proudly, belching smoke into the black sky. Katya knew the smoke was red, not black, and that it was just for looks, a constant symbol of Ravic's power.

"Ever been inside?" Jack said.

She shook her head.

It wasn't a real factory, of course, she knew, not since the fighting. A great hulking monstrosity, the building stood in a wasteland surrounded on all sides by bombed-out buildings. It too had been bombed, reduced to rubble, but Ravic had taken it over and rebuilt it to his own specifications. Now it was more castle than anything else, a huge mountain of metal and stone, and the hairs prickled on the nape of her neck as she approached it.

Ravic's lair. She'd grown up in the Fifth Ward, the underworld of which he ruled with an iron fist, and all her life she'd heard stories of him and his barbaric ways. Now she was going to meet him.

Jack's limo threaded through the bombed-out ruins. Bonfires blazed under jagged overhangs, and gangs of disreputable-looking people gathered around them for warmth, swapping bottles. They eyed the limo admiringly.

It pulled into the wide parking lot that surrounded the Factory. The only windows that looked out from the building were on its top floor; red light flooded out from them. A thousand autos and carriages cluttered the parking lot, and drunken rabble drifted to and from the Factory's great hangar doors.

"We're really going in?" Katya said, staring at that huge, red-lit doorway, like a portal to the hells.

Rough-looking people walked past the limo, some staggering drunkenly. They glanced at the homunculi and gave the vehicle a wide berth.

Jack smiled. "Scared?"

Katya hadn't been aware of it, but the front compartment of the limo was equally as large as the rear, and four large bodyguards occupied it. One stayed behind the wheel, but three others emerged, one opening the door for Death's Head Jack.

Jack wore a fine suit marred by a garish teal tie, and a black sable robe cascaded from his shoulders. He gathered it about him, placed a fedora on his head—it had a matching teal band around it—and left the cab. As he did, one of his bodyguards snapped a black umbrella open, and Jack stepped right under it just in time, as if by clockwork. Not a drop of rain hit him that Katya could see.

He turned back to her. "Well?" He stretched out a hand—a perfect, living hand, well-formed and long-fingered.

She mustered what threads of her courage remained and stepped outside. She wasn't as smooth as Jack, or maybe the bodyguards didn't care to accommodate her, and rain hit her. She hadn't realized how much she had appreciated the warmth and dryness of the cab until it was gone. She shivered and huddled close to Jack.

He placed a hand around her shoulders, and for a moment she wondered if she should play the helpless maiden, but then she shrugged him off.

He marched toward the great gaping hangar doors, and Katya hastened to keep step with him, and his umbrella. More rough-looking people passed them, and some gave her interested glances.

At the doors, people paid the tattooed doormen and -women cover charges to get in. One man tried to sneak past, and a doorwoman unleashed one of her pet homunculi on him. It tackled the man to the ground, and screams filled the air. A handful of patrons gathered around to watch, screening the victim from Katya's view—a blessing as far as she was concerned.

The doorpeople waved Death's Head Jack in with a respectful nod, not asking for a cover charge, and his company, Kat included, passed through and into the Factory. Instantly heat enveloped Katya, and she shuddered in release. How long had it been since she'd felt *warm*? She couldn't remember. Her crappy apartment, back when she'd had one, had never really kept away the chill, and she relished the Factory's heat.

People pressed tight all around, and the bodyguards made way for Jack. What was more, once people saw who he was, they gave him space. Many nodded to him, almost bowing. Despite herself, Katya stood straighter at his side. If nothing else, she would be safer from Sedic now.

Most of the people here were normal—that is, for the Fifth Ward—but a few were infected. Mutated by the sea. Special processors cleansed the seafood caught in the Atomic Sea, but some people were too poor or desperate to afford properly processed food (or they swapped bodily fluids with someone who had eaten it), and these could fall ill and die ... or become infected. Mutated. Most mutations were subtle, a reducing of the nose, webbed fingers, fish-like striations across parts of the body, but some were extreme. Katya saw a man with a crab-claw for an arm, a woman whose flesh looked like seaweed, a man with huge black fish eyes staring out of a warped, bulbous, fish-like head, and more.

Around her people talked and laughed, and vendors circulated, selling peanuts and trinkets. One vendor, an infected fellow with jellyfish-like skin, claimed that the strange-looking objects he sold hailed from the Below, that great system of caverns that honeycombed the ground beneath Lavorgna.

"Genuine artifacts from the Elders!" the vendor said, moisture (probably recently applied) glistening on his half-translucent skin. "Get your Elder artifacts here! No one knows where they came from or where they went, but you can own a piece of them for a copper!"

Katya ignored the man. Real artifacts from the Elders would be ridiculously expensive.

It smelled like food in here, of roasting peanuts, dripping meat on sticks, peppers stuffed with spices and beef, and suddenly Katya realized she hadn't eaten in hours. Her mouth watered, and her belly rumbled.

She bought a hotdog off a vendor and lathered it with relish and mustard. Without a moment's hesitation, she bit into it eagerly, and the flavors burst in her mouth. Hot. Delicious. She gulped it down, bite after greasy bite, then licked her fingers and scoured her lips for errant mustard. When she finished, she caught Jack staring at her.

"See anything you like?"

He didn't answer. By this time they'd reached the lip of the Pit, and she gazed down into it, fascinated and repulsed. The Pit Room was a vast chamber, encompassing the whole ground level of the Factory, with a high, lofty ceiling wreathed in smoke. The smoke drifted around large electric lights far overhead, sometimes obscuring their illumination, sometimes diffusing the light into a golden glow. The great furnace blazed in a corner, and Ravic's men threw alchemically treated rectangular objects that looked like blocks of crimson concrete into its gaping mouth. Kat didn't know why they bothered; it was night and no one could see the red columns of smoke anyway. She supposed it was just tradition. Those red fires had been burning since before she was born. Some of the fire-tenders were steam-men, clanking and issuing vapor. Katya didn't see many of those around anymore; they were relics from the Age of Steam, which had ended some years ago, but of course this was Upper Lavorgna, where everything old and broken down ended up eventually.

Thousands of people in the room pressed around the lip of the Pit, and many more sat in the seats below. The Pit was a great arena carved out of the earth in the center of the massive chamber. Tiered seats encircled the earthen floor, and Kat had heard that twenty thousand people could sit in those seats, with more standing above.

As she watched from the edge of the bowl, people down below swept aside body parts from a recent fight, clearing the arena for another round. In the intermission, swarms of spectators placed bets, ordered drinks, and engaged in criminal dealings. Katya knew the Pit was in some ways the heart of the Fifth Ward—black and bloody, corrupt and brutal. In the floors above, more entertainments and services could be enjoyed, or so she'd been told. A casino vied for business with a brothel, contract killers could be bargained with at the bar, loans could be taken out (with steep interest and harsh penalties for non-payment), and more. Ravic's own private apartments could be found at the very top. It was his chambers that blazed with the red light Katya had seen from outside.

Her face must have betrayed some of her thoughts, or maybe it was her fidgeting hands. Jack said, "Feeling a bit over your head, are you?"

"Not a bit of it." She took a deep breath, let it out. "Have a cigarette?"

A bodyguard produced one, and another flicked a silver cigarette lighter for her. She took a hit, then a second, and blew the smoke in Jack's face. That only seemed to excite him. It was weird to look into a dead face and see *randiness* there, but that's what she saw. Well, she supposed, at least his lower parts would be normal. It was only his head that was dead.

"Ever been to the fights?" he asked.

This time she blew the cloud of smoke to the side, out of the corner of her mouth.

"No."

A horn blew. All attention turned to a tall, curvaceous figure striding into the blood-stained arena below. It was a buxom woman in fish-net stockings, tight short black leather skirt and low-cut top, tattoos up and down her arms.

"Perhaps we should linger for a moment, then," Jack said. "Increase your cultural perspective."

The woman below held a microphone. "I hope you've been enjoying yourselves!" she called, her voice ringing clear and loud. The audience responded lustily, hooting and hollering, banging beer bottles together, stamping feet. The wave of sound hurt Katya's ears. She pressed her palms over them. Yet, at the same time, she felt a smile creep over her face, and a jolt of fire flushed through her veins. "Well, as it happens," the woman continued, "the man himself would like to entertain you!"

More hooting and hollering, even louder.

"That's Vivia," Jack said, speaking through cupped hands directly into Katya's ear. "An interesting woman. You might get to know her."

"Would you like a show?" Vivia roared. She thrust the microphone outward, toward the crowd, and the crowd responded wildly.

"Is Ravic really going to fight *himself?*" Katya said.

"I'm sure he'll fight other people," Jack laughed.

"Well, with no further ado, *welcome to the darkness!*" Vivia said.

The overhead lights flickered out, plunging the Pit Room into utter blackness save for the furnace in its corner, though even its light was mostly hidden by the ranks of spectators. As soon as darkness fell, the crowd hushed, except for numerous excited whispers. Kat held her breath. Seats creaked as people leaned forward . . .

Without warning, a great gout of flame shot high into the room, roaring out of a hole directly in the center of the arena. Katya gasped and jumped back. The spurt of flame licked so high she feared it would incinerate the overhead lights. Then, instantly, the flame shut off. As soon as it did, a dozen smaller fires erupted from the circumference of the Pit. They flickered sullenly at first, then, as one, they surged upward, throwing light on the middle of the arena, where a broad-shouldered figure stood, a man that could only be Boss Ravic.

By the light of the flames, Katya saw a tall, thick-chested man with bristly beard and long curly hair. Boots covered his feet and ragged pants his legs. His big chest was bare, and a long fur coat of some kind depended from his shoulders. Fire-light glistened on his many scars.

And in his hands, he held some object, large and phallic . . .

Katya stared.

A chainsaw.

Ravic wasted no time. He pulled a chord, and the chainsaw emitted an industrial-sounding roar. A dozen trapdoors exploded open in every direction around him. The crowd screamed as a Returner scrambled out of each one and flew at Ravic, like starved dogs on a piece of meat.

Ravic stepped forward, swung his weapon—

A head bounced to the floor.

Another Returner reached for him. He waved the chainsaw. Hands flew through the air. More and more of the reanimated, patchwork dead fell on him, gnashing their teeth and raking at him with their nails, and he cut them down, piece by piece. Arms and legs flew, and half-clotted blood sprayed him. He tore through them like a bull. His chainsaw cleaved and chewed. Gore sprayed from it in fountains. To Katya he almost looked like he was dancing, weaving and ducking and spinning, lit by fire and savagery . . .

Part of her wanted to cheer. Part of her wanted to retch.

Finally all the Returners flopped in pieces on the ground. Ravic switched off his chainsaw and raised his bloody arms to the crowd. They stood and screamed out their love and awe.

Then, just as suddenly as he had appeared, Ravic vanished. The fires died and the lights flickered back on, stinging everyone's eyes, and when Katya could stand to look back into the arena, Ravic was no longer there.

Tattooed men began sweeping body parts to the side of the Pit.

"Wow," she said. "What a showman."

A touch of jealously entered Jack's voice. "Oh, yes, he is many things."

Katya looked at him with new respect. "How long have you worked for him?"

"A long time."

Below, Vivia strutted back out into the Arena as men broomed aside the last of the body parts. "Now for some more fun," she said into her microphone. "Let us introduce our lucky contestants."

Doors opened in the side of the Arena, and gladiators strode out. Katya knew that the rest of the night would involve willing men and women fighting each other and

Returners, homunculi or steam-men, to the death (or destruction, in the case of the latter), for money and fame.

"This is horrible," Katya said. "Why do you people do this?"

"Ask Ravic," Jack said.

"Ask me what?" said a voice from behind.

Katya whirled. A large, burly figure was materializing out of the crowd. He must have taken some tunnel under the arena. Bodyguards surrounded him, pushing back the throng. Upon seeing him, the people cheered and would have surged forward to greet him were it not for the guards.

Boss Ravic stepped toward Jack and Katya, and she saw that he was older than she'd thought. Gray streaked his hair and beard, and lines crinkled the skin around his eyes. Thick chest hair bristled from every inch of his front, and scars shone through it like knotted worms. Even his chest hair was more gray than not. Still, he was an impressive figure, huge and broad-shouldered. The whole effect was bestial, which, Katya supposed, was the point. This was a man that needed to be feared and respected. If she'd had any doubts, the show he had just put on would have dispelled them.

"Why are you letting those men kill each other?" she demanded, stabbing a finger in the direction of the Pit.

Ravic took her in, then hooked an eyebrow at Jack. "What's this, a new filly?"

Jack shrugged. "Katya Ivreski. She says she wants a word with you."

"Does she now?" Ravic stroked his beard. "Interesting." He regarded her for a moment longer, then returned his attention to Jack. "My men saw you arrive. You have news?" There seemed to be some significance to this statement that was lost on Katya.

Grim, Jack nodded. "I do."

"Then come."

Ravic marched off, clearly expecting them to trail in his shadow as if he were some magnet, and like shards of graphite Katya and Jack followed. The army of bodyguards shoved people out of the way as Ravic led them all to one corner of the Pit Room. Katya saw that in each of the corners, except for the one with the furnace, there stood some sort of metal contraption, and a scaffold-like device that ascended to the smoke-wreathed ceiling high above.

"Oh no," she said, too low for any to hear.

She'd heard of elevators but never thought she'd ride in one, and the sight made her hesitate.

Vivia waited for them at the lift. Beautiful and with high red hair, she slunk over to Ravic and threw her lissome arms about him. She had long legs, an elegant neck, and emerald green eyes. She seemed sleek, tiger-like—half as bestial as Ravic.

"You did *brilliantly*," she said.

The Boss encircled her in his arms and lifted her off the ground. She squealed in delight. They kissed, and Katya wanted to gag.

While this was going on, servants held open the elevator door for them. Ravic and Vivia ended their affections, and the big man entered the compartment. Vivia followed, her hand in his, yapping on about his show. Katya tuned her out.

Jack entered next.

On the threshold, Katya paused.

"This is your last chance to back out," Jack said.

She paused, then looked back at the throng of revelers. Any one of them could be an agent of Sedic.

She stepped over the elevator's threshold, and the doors slammed shut behind her. The noise seemed very loud.

Chapter 2

An engine roared, and the elevator lurched upward. The tight space stank of grease, unwashed bodies, vomit, smoke and sex. Graffiti scrawled along the walls, some of it scratched into the metal itself. Obviously the elevator had been in use for many years, and the Factory's patrons had made good use of it. Jack explained that it used to be a public elevator like the other two that would take patrons to the casino or brothel on the levels above, but in recent years Ravic had appropriated it for his own private mode of transportation between floors. Katya wished he'd put in a new unit when he'd done it. She could barely tolerate the stink, although some of the graffiti looked interesting.

Ravic, grinning and plainly on fire with adrenaline, seemed to take up most of the space, but Katya wasn't sure if this was really the case or if his personality simply sucked up all the room by itself.

His eyes glittered savagely and he pressed close to the doorway, staring down at the Pit and its throngs, a giant gazing out at his empire.

Below, the gathering about the base of the elevator shouted, "RA-VIC! RA-VIC! RA-VIC!"

"Fools," he said, but he said it warmly.

"Oh, but who could resist you?" Vivia purred. She ran her hands up and down one of his tree-trunk arms.

He sighed, and there was a trace of lament in the sound. He said nothing, and Katya wondered if he doubted Vivia's affection. Katya sure did.

She turned to give Jack a look and found him already watching her. He didn't seem embarrassed by her catching him at it, though. Katya wasn't sure if she was relieved when he looked away or not. She really was in over her head, he'd been right about that much.

She pressed back against the far wall, not willing to look down into the depths as they shrank below. Her stomach twisted, and she tasted bile in the back of her throat. The world heaved and spun around her. *Don't upchuck*, she told herself. As first impressions went, that would be a bad one. Maybe a fatal one.

The elevator climbed, ticking with every inch. At last Ravic finished with Vivia and turned hard gray-green eyes on Jack.

"So what's the news?"

"It's not good," Jack said. "Our friend is behind the attack on the Gin-Cat Club, just like we thought."

"Shit."

"And it doesn't get better. I have it on good authority that he'll strike again, and soon."

Ravic slammed a fist into the palm of his hand. "I wish I could throw *him* into the Pit. What could he want? Is it war? Does the stupid bastard want another war?" Katya could see his large jaw bunching even through his beard. "I'll give it to him, by the gods, see if I won't. I've got one more big fight left in me."

Jack shrugged. "I don't know what he wants."

"There's the problem. Only a fool would start a war now, and he's no fool. If only . . ." He turned about once again. This time Katya didn't think he was staring down into Pit Room, but off into the distance, somewhere unseen, maybe unseeable. She wanted to ask him about the men in the Pit, to demand he account for their deaths, but sensed this wasn't the time.

Ravic spat, and with the gesture he seemed to switch gears. A new worry shone in his eyes. "What about last night's haunt attack? The one on Gaether. Is there a body count yet?"

"Seven this time. One survived and had to be institutionalized after he tried to bash his brains out on the sidewalk."

"Magnar on a stick, this has got to end. Just what are they, anyway, the haunts?"

Jack had no answer. The elevator reached the casino floor and Katya saw the banks of gambling machines, green tables around which men and women gathered. Dice flashed. A groan went up. At another table an obese woman threw down her cards with a laugh and proceeded to rake in the colored chips in the middle of the table.

Tick, tick, tick went the elevator.

It ascended past the brothel floor. Katya saw what had been one of the three lobbies back when this elevator had been open to the public but was now just an empty room from which a velvet-lined hallway led. A pretty, tired-looking girl led a man by the hand—they'd been coming from the other direction—and together they disappeared into a doorway spanned by a bead curtain.

The elevator passed this level, then another, probably the (authorized) loan shark level. At last a chime sounded, and the elevator lurched to a stop. Katya staggered and fell back against the rear wall. Jack attempted to steady her, but she evaded him.

Ravic emerged into a dark hallway, Vivia hanging from his arm like an ornament. A leech.

"Come on," Jack told Katya, and followed his master.

Kat wished she had another cigarette. She supposed she would have to get her own pack at some point. She pried herself out of the elevator and followed the others down the dark hallway. Almost immediately she noticed the strange smell. Chemicals and herbs. Almost like—

A hand snatched at her hair.

She yelped. Jumped forward. Another groped at her ankle. She screamed and stomped down on it. A hand snatched at her hip. She twisted, bounding forward to catch up with Jack. The floor of the tunnel was spongy, and she noticed the shape of the tunnel was not rectangular but *round*, and the space was hot, moist . . .

"What the hell?" she said, slapping another hand away.

Jack chuckled. "Look and see." He flicked a cigarette lighter, illuminating a patch of wall.

Katya jumped back. Then, when nothing attacked her, she craned her head forward.

"Is that really . . . ?"

"Yes, indeed."

A human eye stared back at her from the wall. A fold of dark flesh-like material eclipsed it, then slid back. It had *blinked*.

"What the hell?"

Jack steered her forward. Ravic and Vivia had already vanished from sight.

"Homunculi material," Jack explained. "Really a big homunculus, one with many eyes and appendages. They don't have to look human, you know. Alchemists can sculpt them to look like anything."

"Yeah, but a hallway . . . ? I mean, I'm all for fancy architecture, but Magnar!"

"A security measure. The homunc hallway is trained only to admit Ravic, his lieutenants and anyone that they deem safe, or who's accompanied by same."

"And if they're not accompanied?"

"And Ravic hasn't taught the hallway to let them be?" Jack shrugged. "They don't make it to the end of the hall, then, do they?"

When the two passed out of the hall, Kat breathed a sigh of relief. The homunculi material did not extend around the bend. A normal, rectangular-shaped hallway stretched on—well, normal except that it was composed of large stone blocks. Torches mounted on brackets stuck out from the walls.

"What is this, a castle?"

"Sort of," Jack admitted. "Ravic really does have a love of the medieval. Obsession, some say."

The hallway emptied out into a largish room, floor, ceiling and walls all composed of the same sort of stone blocks. Torches flared along the walls, and a great stone fireplace dominated the middle of the chamber.

"Damn," Kat said. The fireplace was big enough for Ravic to have stood in without stooping. The flames roared, bright and hot. *This is what makes the red light in the windows.* Embedded in the stone walls between the torches glimmered the thick glass of the windows themselves. Passing the Factory on numerous occasions she'd wondered what went on on the other side of those windows, and here she was about to find out.

Jack led the way around the great fireplace and Katya saw what had been hidden by the gray bulk of the chimney. What could only be described as a throne perched near the far wall. Made of stone, it reared over the room, mounted at the head of a short flight of steps. A *dais*. There Ravic was just sitting down, sighing wearily. A beautiful young woman in silks and jewels placed a goblet of what was probably wine in his hands, and he gave her a pat on the rump as she turned away. Vivia shot the girl a glare and slid into Ravic's lap with the grace and proprietorship of a tigress. For all that, he held her only half-heartedly.

As he drank from his goblet, wine sloshed over the rim and trickled into his beard. He drained it all in one go. Burped.

"Ahh."

The young woman refilled the goblet as Jack and Katya approached. Katya wasn't sure if this had been such a good idea. Maybe she shouldn't have gotten into that stupid elevator after all.

"About what we were saying—our friend still doesn't suspect?" Ravic said.

"Not a whiff," Jack said.

"Good. That gives us one edge, at least. Would that we had more." The Boss drained this goblet of wine, too.

"He's mainly striking from the east, from the Hollows," Jack said.

"Perhaps it would be prudent to fortify our positions there. We'd have to draw men away from the other areas, principally the west, but it might be worth it. We can't let it continue like this."

"Shall I summon a war council?" Jack said. "I could have the other lieutenants here within an hour . . ."

Ravic shook his head. He stared around Jack into the leaping flames. Smoke ghosted upward. "He might be trying to draw me out," Ravic said. "He might *want* open war."

"You think all this has been in an effort to provoke you?"

"It's possible."

Katya wished she knew what they were talking about. She wanted to leap in with some witty remark, gain Ravic's respect before she hit him up.

Vivia stroked the Boss's beard. "It'll be all right, my love. Whatever it is, Vivia will make it better."

He grunted. "Go on. I need my peace."

"What—?"

He thrust her off his lap, and she stumbled down a stair before she could right herself. Ravic chuckled a little. Vivia made a moue of pique, turned her back on him and stormed off, disappearing down a side hall concealed by a scarlet tapestry. A similar tapestry hung behind Ravic's throne, and Katya supposed there was another hallway there, leading to Ravic's bedchambers.

Ravic's attention turned to her.

"You," he said, adjusting himself in his seat, and Katya started. "What are you doing here? Come to join the wait staff?" His gaze flicked to his scantily-clad serving girl, then back to Katya. "You're a mite rough around the edges, but you're pretty enough. I could make do."

She opened her mouth to speak. A squawk came out. She tried again. "I am not a . . . waitress. I'm a—"

He smiled, his face crinkling up. "A thief, I know."

"You've heard of me?"

"Of course. I like to keep up with what's going on in my district, and I've heard plenty of rumors about the young woman who burgles the stashes of thugs and pimps and other lowlifes she thinks deserve it."

Sweat beaded her forehead. "There *are* a lot of assholes out there. I, uh, you know, just take them down a peg."

"I'd say good for you, but some of those assholes work for me."

Shit. "Well, then you have bad taste in goons."

Studying her closely, Ravic seemed to realize something. "*That's* why you're here. You're on the run!" He laughed. "You chose the wrong asshole to steal from, didn't you? Who was it?"

Fuming, she said, "Sedic."

Ravic's expression darkened. "Well, in that case, I *could* help you. Technically. He's an independent operator, and I owe him nothing but a place in my arena." At her reaction, he added, "That's what passes for justice here, Katya Ivreski."

"Execution by Returners," she marveled, though of course she'd heard of it. "That's . . ."

"Terrible? I know. But it is what it is. It'll keep other shitheels like him in line, or at least give them pause before they step outside of my authority, or beat up on some girl. And yes, I've heard of Sedic's reputation. If it wasn't for that, I wouldn't be so happy to toss him in the Pit." He rubbed his hairy cheek. "The problem's that all my men are tied up in resisting . . . well, I have some tension going on right now with a certain party. I can't deal with Sedic's gang right now. I'm sorry, Ms. Ivreski, but I'm not able to help you. So, if that's all you came for, I'll ask you to quit stealing from my people and send you on your way. One warning, though, then—"

"The Pit?" Before he could dwell on that point, she plowed on. "If you send me back out there, I'll die. If Sedic doesn't get me, someone else will."

"I certainly don't want that to happen. I'm not sure what I can do for you, though."

She took a deep breath. *Now's the time, Kat.* "I . . . I want a job."

"A what?"

Even Jack was looking at her with surprise.

Kat held her ground. "Things are rough out there. What with the haunts, and the gang war last year, well . . . the whole district's falling apart. Even my apartment was condemned. I'm tired of scrounging for crumbs. Plus, if I worked for you, Sedic would have to leave me alone. Even he wouldn't dare attack one of your people."

Ravic studied her. "You want to be a thief for the big leagues, eh?"

"That's right."

"I don't need a thief."

She clenched her teeth. "Well, then something else, damn it."

Ravic shared a glance with Jack. "What do you propose to do, girl? I have plenty of janitors. Perhaps my attendants .

. ." Again he looked to his serving girl; he seemed keen on the notion of Katya in that get-up.

"Never!"

"Well, then? *What can you do?* I can't send you to crack bones for me, now can I? I need killers, not waifs."

"I am not—" She suppressed her anger. "I have a very special skill set, Mr. Ravic. Getting in places where I'm not supposed to go. Learning things I'm not supposed to know. Surely you have a use for someone like that."

A long silence passed. Then, slowly, he nodded.

Hope surged through her. "So you mean it, you'll really take me on? I mean, you'll hire me?" If he said yes, she had found her place. No more barely getting by, no more living on the streets. It's what she had wanted long before today. Sedic had just given her the impetus to seek Ravic out.

Ravic did not say yes, however. "It depends," he said.

"On what?"

"Give her a drink," he told one of his people, and seconds later Kat was sipping expensive whiskey, the finest she'd ever had. She couldn't enjoy it, though. *This isn't a good sign.*

"I have an enemy, Katya," Ravic said. "Well, I have many enemies. But there is one that particularly concerns me."

"This the guy you have tension with? The one you and Jack were talking about? You're 'friend'?"

Ravic smiled mirthlessly. "Loqrin Mars is no more a friend to me than the President. Although things did not used to be so sour between us. Hells, a year ago I thought we'd patched things up. Finally."

"You mean the big gang war between the Bosses?"

"Some of us, yes. Especially Loqrin and myself."

Katya remembered it vividly—shootings, bombings, stabbings. It had gotten messy. She took a long sip. *What have I gotten myself into?*

"Well, I thought it was behind us," Ravic said. "We'd signed a peace accord. The Archminister of the Guild of Alchemy himself acted as witness." He snorted. "Might as well have signed toilet paper. Loqrin has been striking at me for the last few months, firebombing my clubs, mowing down my men, and it just doesn't make sense. We've already proven neither one of us can out-wrestle the other. War between us only loses business—business which goes to the other Bosses, you should know." He ran a hand through his thick hair. *"It makes no sense."*

"Yeah, you said." The drink was making her unsteady. There was a richly upholstered chair sitting nearby. She dragged it out a few feet—it was heavy—and sat down.

Thunder cracked overhead, and rain flung against the windows, making her jump.

Ravic hardly seemed to notice. "He's been hitting me, and hitting me hard. Attacking gambling dens, brothels. He's even been abducting citizens, regular people of the Fifth Ward. *My* people."

"Why would he kidnap regulars?" She'd heard about the killings, but not the abductions.

"Ask *him*. And the timing of it! With all this haunt business . . ."

"What are they, anyway?"

"Who knows? They appear and disappear, killing people wherever they go. All across the city. They've killed near a hundred people by now. That we know of."

"Monsters," she said. Of course, this was Lavorgna, home of homunculi, Returners, steam-men, strange cults and worse. Haunts seemed so abstract, though. Loqrin Mars was a threat she could understand. "So what do you want me to do?"

"That depends on you, Katya. I need something done about Loqrin Mars. With that skill set you were bragging about, you can get closer to him than I can."

She felt a chill. "You want me to what, kill him?"

He took the last sip from his glass. "Bosses killing Bosses only causes trouble. His territory will rip itself apart finding a new Boss, and the new Boss will aim his sights on me to rally his troops. Revenge is a good unifier. And the Fifth Ward . . . well, if I die this place really will go nuts. All my lieutenants will fight over my seat and who knows how many folk will get mown down in the crossfire. It's my job to prevent that. I'm the Boss of the Fifth Ward. I'm the sheep dog, and they're the sheep, and over there is Loqrin Mars with his wolf pack." He eyed her urgently. "What I need is someone who can wear a wolfskin, go over to his pack, and see what he's up to. Whatever it is, it ain't good, and it ain't normal." He paused. "And, yeah, if it comes to it, an' he needs killin', then that's what I need you to do."

"I . . ."

What he was asking her to do was madness. She saw how important it was—not just to him, but the whole Ward—but she was no spy, no matter what she'd told him.

Before Kat could answer, a sound like thunder ripped the night, but it was not thunder. It came again, and again.

Ravic bounded to a window. Breathlessly, Kat and Jack joined him.

Below, in the parking lot, the thinning crowd of patrons was stirring madly. Gunshots pierced the night. And screams.

"Come," Ravic said. "Let's hurry."

Chapter 3

Rain drenched Kat's hair and ran between her shoulder blades all over again. She pulled her leather jacket closed to cover herself. Around her the crowd swept in from the parking lot. Something outside had frightened the patrons departing the Factory, and they were rushing back inside, taking shelter. In their fright they did not seem to notice Ravic striding against the tide.

Ahead, people screamed. Horses tied to posts whinnied and reared up, trying to break the ropes that bound them.

Ravic had rounded up half a dozen of his men and women. They jogged before him in a loose wedge, scattering Fifth Warders as they went. They carried repeating rifles with magazines that jutted up from smooth, blunt shafts—ugly, industrial weapons for an ugly, industrial age.

Ravic carried a large revolver, nothing else. He panted hard beside Katya. Her lungs burned, and the whiskey turned her legs to rubber. It was all she could do to keep up. Where had Jack gone?

At last the crowd thinned, and Katya and Ravic reached the edge of the parking lot. Gas lamps lit the perimeter in broad, glowing green-white arcs. Beyond lay the dark, jagged ruins of bombed-out buildings. Katya saw fires guttering in a barrel under an overhang that had once been the ceiling of a first floor antechamber. It was one of the fires she'd seen earlier with bums and drifters gathered around it, seeking warmth and liquor, but now several shapes that must be bodies sprawled across the ground.

Ravic's gunmen ran into the mostly-collapsed structure, disappearing from sight. As soon as they did, shrieks issued from within. Gunfire. Katya's breath caught in her throat. She could no longer feel the rain. Her footsteps lagged.

Ravic ran forward. One of his men emerged from the building and fled past him, gibbering. As the man reached the circle of the gas-lamp Katya saw that his face was white with fear.

As Ravic disappeared into the ruin, there came a great noise, at once liquid and leathery. Then a monstrous shape took flight, sweeping up out of the ruin. Katya saw unnatural wings silhouetted against the lightning, almost like bat wings but far larger, and an impossible, gelatinous shape, with stars just visible through it . . .

She entered the building.

Ravic stood in a broken room, rain pouring down on him, firing his gun at the disappearing shape. Beside him stood two of his men, emptying their guns as well. Another slumped against the wall. Two more littered the ground.

The *thing* vanished into the storm-tossed night. Gradually the men stopped firing their weapons. The air stank of gun smoke.

Katya felt like she was sleepwalking. Her mouth slack, she stepped to Ravic's side and stared up into the night. "Was that . . . ?"

"A haunt. Had to be."

"Shit," said one of the men. He was short, broad and infected; fish scales glimmered on his face. "I've never seen the like. I've sailed from Tivis to Morundai, and I've never seen anything like that."

The other gunman's voice was grim. "I have."

"What do you mean?"

"Burnig," the man said. "It was Burnig. I saw it when the lightning flashed. There was a shape inside. A man. I'd know him anywhere."

"A *man*?"

"Yeah."

"Burnig," Ravic repeated, after some thought. "*Bob* Burnig?"

"The very same."

"The one who runs the club over on Tidmoore?"

The taller man grunted. "Was."

Ravic turned to Katya. "Burnig was one of the men Loqrin abducted when his men attacked the Gin-Cat yesterday."

She stared at him. His face was in darkness, but still she could feel the intensity of his gaze. In a whisper, she said, "You really think Loqrin has something to do with all this?"

"He must. The haunts only started appearing about the time he began his move against me."

"Son of a bitch," added the infected man.

The taller one let out a surprised grunt. He was staring at the man slumped against the wall. Katya had thought him dead, but now he staggered forward. Lightning lit him briefly: slack jaw, glazed eyes. But what caught Kat's attention, and surely everyone else's, was the fact that steam—*steam*—wisped up from his head.

"Fedrik!" said the infected man. "What's happened?"

Fedrik opened his mouth even wider, as if to answer, and steam poured out of it. He didn't go two more steps before he toppled to the muddy ground right beside the other corpses. Mud splashed Katya's shins, but she barely felt it. Her heart hammered inside her, a mile a minute. *Their heads were smoking*, Aggie had said earlier. Katya had hardly believed it then. She believed it now.

Ravic knelt beside the fallen man, feeling his pulse. "Dead," he confirmed. He moved to the other bodies. "Dead. Dead. Dead.". He felt the last one's skull. Instantly he drew his hand back and sucked in his breath. "Hot." He stared down at the corpses.

Katya, despite herself, laid a hand on his shoulder. "At least we're safe."

"Safe!" spat the infected man. "Didn't you see that thing? The tabloids may call 'em haunts, but if that's a ghost I'm a fairy princess!"

Ravic turned his face up. "Then what was it, Gunnerson?"

The fish-man threw up webbed hands. "Hell if I know. But mark me, Boss, that was no thing of nature, and it wasn't no damned spirit neither."

Katya studied the bodies. Several hissed as their burning skulls smoldered in the muck.

"Why are their heads . . . *hot?*"

The tall man spat. "When I got here, the thing, that haunt, it had its . . . I don't know, like cords . . . they were spread out from it, each through the head of one of the bums. Then it got Fedrik and Jons and Signon. I can't believe Martin turned yellow."

"He always did have a weak liver," Gunnerson growled. "I ought to wring his neck."

"Leave him be," Ravic said. "We were the fools for staying. He was right to run. Guns didn't hurt it."

"Then why did it go?"

Ravic's broad shoulders rose and fell. Gesturing to the scattered corpses, he said, "Reckon it was full." Gingerly he felt the skull of the man in front of him. "There's no holes. If those cords went in like you say, Syd, they didn't leave a mark."

"That's impossible," Katya said.

Syd cocked an eyebrow at Gunnerson. "Still don't believe in ghosts?"

The rain was thinning, and Katya began to see stars overhead, and, for a change, all three moons. She kept expecting to see a strange, gelatinous winged shape sweep against the stars, but there was nothing. On the air she thought she detected lingering aromas, sulfur and ammonia and other, weirder things. What had that thing been? It hadn't been a ghost, on that much she agreed with Gunnerson. If nothing else, ghosts wouldn't smell.

Footsteps. Katya spun to see two dark shapes, a tall man in a suit and a fedora, and another man holding an umbrella over his head. The man in the fedora lit a cigarette, and flame lit his withered, corpse-like face.

"Jack!" she said. For some reason she felt an unlikely rush of warmth at seeing him.

Jack nodded to her, his face hard. By the light of the newly emerging stars, Katya saw that his face was somehow less withered than before. It was smoother, less wrinkled. He looked around at the bodies lying in the filth and said, "This one hit close to home,"

Ravic rose slowly. "The next one will be in the Factory itself at this rate. Maybe in my fucking lap."

"You think that's deliberate? You think the haunts are targeting you?"

Ravic didn't answer. He turned his attention to Gunnerson and the tall man. "Could you go and gather some men to see to these boys? They deserve a funeral of some sort."

"And the bums?" asked Syd. "Shall we throw 'em in the furnace? Or maybe they'd be more amusing brought back as Returners . . ."

"Bury them, too," Ravic said. "Now go. Give us a moment."

They moved off, hunkering their shoulders under the thinning rain. When they were some distance away, Jack said, "Did you get a good look at it? The haunt?"

Ravic let out a breath. "No. But Syd said he saw something. Some*one*. Burnig Big-Top."

"Bob Burn? But he disappeared. Loqrin took him . . ."

Katya felt a large, rough hand on her shoulder, and she jumped. She looked up to Ravic's face, framed by starlight. He looked old. "What do you say now, girl? We need you."

She crossed her arms over her small chest. She felt cold, wet and tired. "First of all, you're insane. Second . . . you want me to spy on someone that might be doing *this*. Third . . ."

"Yes?"

She sighed. "Tell me about him."

Ravic and Jack exchanged glances.

"I didn't say I would do it," she cautioned. "But, I mean, if I were inclined to, how would I get close to him? Join his organization?"

"I don't think he'd hire you for a gunner or enforcer," Ravic said. "You're too small, and I doubt you know which end of a gun to fire. But mainly Loqrin's old-fashioned. He only hires men as enforcers. Between that and his harem—"

"Harem?"

"What is it?"

She snapped her fingers. "That's it. That's how I get in."

"I thought you didn't want to be a working girl," Jack said.

"Oh, I wouldn't let him touch me, of course. I'd play hard to get."

"Bad idea, Kat," Jack cautioned. "He's a monster. Treats his harem toys, like, well, like toys—if, that is, they were owned by a kid that liked to take them apart and recombine them."

Ravic blew a plume of smoke at the stars. "Of course, if you did do it, I think you'd be safe at first. He likes to make the new ones watch, build up their fear. Of course, I don't really know. I don't want to lie to you."

Her gaze fixed on the corpses. Steam still rose from Fedrik.

"You really think Loqrin has something to do with all this?"

"I'm sure of it," Ravic said.

The storm was moving off, and a cold breeze rustled Katya's short dark hair. She wanted nothing more than a hot shower and dry clothes. And maybe another sip of that whiskey.

"Okay," she said. Her voice was small but determined. "The Fifth Warders are my people, too. I'll do what I can. But I swear if he lays one finger on me I'll gut him."

"Thank you," Ravic said.

"Just remember our deal," she said. "I do this, I'm part of your organization. And you'll keep Sedic off my back."

"If both you and the organization are still in one piece at the end of this, no problem. But . . . if you fail, there might not be any organization left."

She steeled herself. "So—how do I get an introduction to this creep—Loqrin?"

Ravic pointed at Jack. "Jack's your boy. I'd use him if I were you."

"Use him?" She looked at Jack. "What does he mean?"

Jack inhaled on his cigarette, then blew a long plume. "He means that I'm a spy. And I didn't get all dressed up for nothing. You see," he added, leaning forward and speaking in a conspiratorial whisper, "I'm on my way to meet with Loqrin right now."

Katya felt dizzy. With some effort, she straightened, looked Jack in the eyes, what she could see of them, and said, "Then I'm coming with you."

As the car rumbled along, Katya enjoyed the smell of leather and taste of tobacco smoke on her tongue. She played her free hand over the plush seats and lolled her head against the soft headrest.

"Nice, isn't it?" Jack said, seeing her enjoyment and maybe liking it a little too much.

She blew a cloud of smoke out of the window.

"It'll do."

The truth was she felt a thousand times better. They'd allowed her a quick shower, given her a change of clothes and put some more food in her belly. It had only been onion rings and a stuffed pepper, but it had tasted delicious. She still had the flavor of grease on her tongue.

"I'm so glad you approve," he said. "However grudgingly."

"Hey, just being honest." Earlier when she'd ridden in his limo, she hadn't been in a mood to enjoy it much. Now, refreshed and employed, she loved it. This thing was fricking amazing.

Fear still gnawed at her. They were on their way to rendezvous with Loqrin Mars. *About to meet the enemy, Kat-o-mine. Look sharp.*

"What's he like, Loqrin?" she said.

Jack grimaced. "You'll find out soon enough."

"You really think he's behind the haunts?"

"Someone is."

She tapped the cigarette against the window. A stream of ash and sparks trailed into the night.

"Fine," he said. "What do you want to know?"

"Well, how long's he been Boss?"

"He's been in power about ten years. Before him was Seqrin. Before him Reqrist. Before him . . . Meqrith, I think."

"Similar kinda names. Related?"

"No one knows where they come from. There's a long line of them. About the time one vanishes, he'll appoint an heir. When the Boss retires, the new one steps in. They've performed the dance so many times it's seamless by now, and all his lieutenants seem to accept it. At any rate, they have no choice. All the Bosses share similar . . . peculiarities."

"Like what?"

He gestured vaguely. "You'll see."

She sucked on her cigarette and stared out at the Fifth Ward. There were the usual sprawling tenements, bombed-out buildings, squat temples, belching factories. By the lights of street-lamps she saw rough-looking men and women with too much make-up stroll from bar to bar. The clubs roared with music and neon light. A man exploded through a tavern window and hit the sidewalk. He picked himself up, dusted himself off and threw away his cigar. As he did, another man climbed through the window, rolling his shirtsleeves up as he went. The limo swept on by before Katya could see any actual fighting.

There were lots of taverns in the Fifth Ward, some owned by Ravic. The men in the Ward were tough, their lives hard. Many slaved away in the factories, which in turn were often owned by the dreaded Guild of Alchemists. The Guildsmen treated their employees like shit, Katya knew.

Beside her, Jack remained silent. She sensed something was on his mind, but he didn't talk about it. Was he worried for her? Part of her wanted to believe it, that someone actually gave a damn about her, but she'd rather there not be any reason to worry in the first place.

As the limo headed east, the buildings changed. Katya saw new streets, strange roads she had never seen before. The one she was on sloped up, hit a crest, then sloped down. Unconsciously she tensed, drew her legs up under her and pushed herself back into the seat.

"Nervous?" Jack asked.

"First time I've ever been out of the Fifth," she said, trying for offhand. *Never show weakness*, her mother had taught her. Not that her mother had been particularly good at it.

"Really? I figured you'd seen it all, worldly lass like you."

"Screw you."

His smile dropped. Katya thought she saw a twist of guilt cross his face. All at once she realized it: he thought he was driving her to her death. Suddenly she began to feel queasy. When she took the last drag on her cigarette and flicked it out the window, sparks flamed and died in the night. Jack's silence continued. She distracted herself by looking out, and what she saw amazed her.

"The buildings . . . they're *leaning* . . ."

The buildings the limo was passing visibly listed, all in a uniform direction: east. Great shambling tenements, crumbling and cracked, striking high into the night, slightly curved, their tips stretching eastward so that shadow fell on the streets below. Row after row, like sunflowers turning to the sun.

"What in fuck?" she said.

"Haven't you ever heard of the Hollows?" When she shrugged, Jack told her, "That's Loqrin's territory. And his territory's centered around the Sink."

"The Sink?"

"Some blame it on the war, on an Octunggen bomb. Some blame it on a sinkhole. Some both. I don't know which is true, or if something else did it. But sometime during the war the land gave out. That's where we're going: the Sink. A great hole. Some say it goes down to the Below itself."

"Really?" All her life she'd heard about the Below, the network of grand caverns and black abysses under the city. They said a city of the Elders perched on the chasm walls down there, the buildings huge and ancient, having existed long before man shook off the slime and crouched on two legs.

"Really," Jack said. "This area was built out over a chasm, and part of it collapsed—because of the bomb or what-have-you. You can see what it's done to the local architecture. Probably an improvement. At any rate, Loqrin's the Boss of the Hollows—and he should be very close now."

"How're you gonna introduce me to him?"

"Guess I'll just, you know, say you're one of my girls, and he'll take a liking to you, and . . ."

She snorted. "I thought you were the brains of Ravic's operation."

"You have a better suggestion?"

She pressed a button. "Driver, pull over."

"What are we doing?" Jack asked.

Katya didn't answer.

The driver braked and Katya stepped out onto a cracked sidewalk to find that the rain had stopped, but everything still glistened with moisture. The sidewalk was pitted and scarred, and muddy puddles dotted it. Few lights blazed in the nearby buildings, and the weird towers twisted overhead, leaning downhill as though reaching out toward a lover. They looked even stranger and more sinister when she was on foot looking up at them.

Jack followed her, and his goons in the front compartment came, too.

"What's this all about?" Jack said.

Katya looked from him to the homunculi. The gangly automatons just stood there. Alchemists made them from earth and herbs and other, more occult items. Rain had soaked into the four, making them seem to shine under the starlight. None of the nearby streetlights worked. The homunculi were just tall black shadows with human eyes, opening and closing their claw-like hands, glimmering subtly by the light of stars and moons

"I've got a plan," she said.

Chapter 4

Cursing under her breath, Katya fled down the sidewalk toward the east.

Behind her, two homunculi gave chase.

Shitshitshit, she thought. She should have come up with something better. Anything, really.

The road she ran down sloped, first gently, then sharply. The buildings looming above her seemed to sag more precipitously. Laundry lines strung from one window to another across dank alleyways, clothes flapping like pigeon wings. Drunks and criminals slouched in the shadows.

Breathlessly, Kat ran.

Behind her came the scrape and shuffle of homunculi feet.

Fuckfuckfuck.

People ahead. They lounged against a dirty wall covered in graffiti and posters. One read: *Fight the 'chemists! Join the Underground Brotherhood today!*

The people that loitered on the street were pale and strange. Fear lurked in their eyes, and numerous scars covered their hides. One scrawny, pasty woman may have been a prostitute, judging by her skimpy attire, but Kat didn't have time to ask, only whipped past the bystanders and ran on.

Behind her the locals screamed and scattered, spooked by the homunculi.

Katya ducked down an alleyway. A man stepped out from behind a dumpster, knife in hand.

"Well, hello little girl, what have we—"

Scrape, shuffle behind her.

The man bolted. Kat followed.

She turned left at the next alley, continued east down the slope. Buildings with cracked walls listed on either side. It stank of shit and garbage. A fat man in a fourth floor apartment leaned out his window and dumped a bucket into the alley below. Kat ducked under it, hurt a splash, and smelled something foul. She hoped the homuncs would slip in it, but by the continued scraping and shuffling she judged they hadn't.

She spun left at the next alley, right at the next, left again. The sounds of the homuncs faded. A little.

Her heart hammered inside her ribs. Sweat coursed down her face.

Jack Jack Jack, she thought. *I'll fucking MURDER you!* She'd told him to give her thirty seconds head start before sending two of the homuncs after her, but either he hadn't listened or else they hadn't. That was a frightening thought. The homuncs could only think and reason to a small degree, just enough to follow simple instructions. They might not differentiate between *chase* and *tear into a thousand chunks.*

At last the buildings ended. Katya ran across a wide, cobbled road. A horse-drawn carriage nearly ran her down. The driver cursed her. She wanted to curse back but couldn't draw enough breath. Her lungs burned.

The wide road made a huge circle around . . . some sort of hole ahead. *Could it be?* The hole was massive, maybe two hundred yards across or more, a huge pit plunging down into darkness. On the other side of it the roads sloped up and the buildings leaned west, not east. All of the roads in the area sloped down to the great pit, and the buildings listed toward it. *The Sink,* she thought. *The sinkhole. Stupid.*

A prominence overhung the black pit, a visitor's platform. Two limousines parked in front of it. Men with large guns stood in tense arcs, one for each car, while two well-dressed men shook hands in the center.

Furious, Kat ran toward them.

The goons noticed her. One barked something. The two men in the center turned to her, apparently surprised. She heard laughter.

Then another sound—scraping, shuffling. It would have been reassuring to hear the labored breath of a human hunter, but there was little human about the homunculi. They did not need to eat, sleep, shit, speak, nor laugh. They were just *things*.

Katya ran toward the men, now close enough to see Jack. Gas lamps ringed the circumference of the Sink, bathing his face in a phosphorescent glow. She saw tenseness there. Concern.

"Girl!" he shouted, as if he didn't know her. "Duck!" Hastily he barked an order to his men.

Katya thought she saw what he wanted. Gritting her teeth, she threw herself to the ground. The cobbled road had ended. Pavement scraped her palms, her knees, rasped her cheek.

Gunfire erupted. *Rat-rat-rat!* Bullets whined over her head. When it tapered off, she smelled gun smoke.

Breathless, her mind spinning, she glanced back to see her pursuers. The homunculi lay in the middle of the road, steaming black puddles of mud and goo. She thought she saw a single claw twitch, then go limp. She breathed a sigh of relief.

Shoe-falls, coming toward her.

Wearily, suddenly on the verge of fainting, she turned to see a man approach. At first she thought it was Jack.

A hand gripped her upper arm, helped her gently but firmly to her feet.

"Thank you," she said. She didn't have to feign her breathlessness.

"Why, it's no trouble at all," the man said. "Allow me to introduce myself. I'm Loqrin Mars."

He stepped back, giving her space. Light fell on him, illuminating his wide, even smile. At the sight, Katya's heart caught in her throat. Loqrin Mars was the most handsome man she'd ever seen.

He had medium-length blond hair that swept back from a high, aristocratic forehead. The rest of him was thoroughly non-aristocratic, though. Broad shoulders, athletic arms and legs, muscles straining against the lines of his tailored suit. Beautiful features with a strong jaw, bold, straight nose, and twinkling eyes. It was too dark still to tell what color they were, but Katya thought they were blue.

"I . . . I'm Katya," she said, hearing the awe in her voice. "Katya Ivreski. Th-Thank you. Sir." She added this last bit hastily. The part she supposed she was playing was that of a woman raised in the Hollows. She would hold Loqrin in reverence, just as the people of the Fifth Ward held Ravic. In the chaos of Upper Lavorgna, mob bosses kept order, and the people appreciated it.

"Well, that was quite an escape," Loqrin said, sounding amused.

"Indeed," Jack said, stepping forward as if to take custody of Kat.

Loqrin beat him to it. Taking her arm, he led her away from the ruins of the homunculi. Truly grateful now, she leaned against a balustrade and found herself staring down into the depths of the Sink. The hole stretched down and down into darkness so rich and deep she could well believe it descended into the core of the planet itself. It wouldn't surprise her at all if it penetrated through to the Below. A warm wind gusted up from the abyss, streaming her hair back behind her. Still, the pit made her nervous. Despite herself, she pushed herself straight and tried not to look over.

Jack didn't seem to notice her discomfiture. "I thought they had you for sure," he said.

Katya resisted the urge to shoot him an angry glare. "S-so did I." Involuntarily she glanced at the road to reassure herself that the homunculi hadn't congealed into their old shapes and begun after her again. They hadn't. She looked back to find Loqrin eyeing her kindly. He reached out a muscular hand and tucked a strand of hair back behind her ear. The gesture was oddly tender. Was this really the man that was terrorizing the Fifth Ward?

"May I ask how you came to be chased?" His voice was gentle, concerned. He stared right into her eyes as if trying to comfort her. He reached out his hands and held one of hers. He patted it as he spoke.

For a moment her mind blanked. Then, hesitatingly, remembering what Jack had told her to say, she said, "A man . . . a man with an eye . . . uh, a tattoo of an eye . . . It was on his forehead."

Loqrin scowled. "Reddin! He's been trying to poach girls for too long."

"Poach?"

He smiled. "Well, you know who I am. You must know that I constantly have to fight independent operators. People who would, among other things, run their own, ah, escort services. As Boss, it's my right to tax them, or disband them. Some, most notably that fool Reddin, persist in trying to exist outside my authority." A cold look came over him, and for a moment Katya could see something terrible inside him. "I will deal with him, oh yes." Then it passed, like a dark cloud on a sunny day. He brightened. His gaze wandered up and down her, weighing, judging. Behind him Jack tensed again. When Loqrin spoke next, it was calculating, coaxing. "I don't suppose a girl as pretty as you would mind . . . accompanying me . . . for a while. I will be sure to make it worth your while."

Gotcha. "I-I don't know. I'm not . . . I mean to say . . ."

"Oh. Of course." Loqrin looked embarrassed. "Why couldn't I see it? You're a girl of class. I didn't mean to offend." His voice was nervous, conciliatory, but underneath it there was something else.

"Oh, uh, none taken," she said, thinking, *Don't make this TOO easy for him.* "I mean, I'm honored, but—"

"But you're not that kind of girl. Understood." His manner started to become brusque. He dropped her hand, started to turn to Jack.

Katya touched his arm.

"Yes?" Loqrin said.

"I wouldn't mind, you know, maybe having dinner with you."

A new look came over Loqrin. "Oh? Well, good. I was just on the point of—well." He giggled. "Men, show her to the car." To her, he said, "I'll join you in just a moment."

As casually as she could, she glanced at Jack, who swallowed nervously. His eyes were eloquent, deeply apologetic, but he could obviously not help her.

Strong arms steered her into the interior of Loqrin's car. Dimly she heard Loqrin and Jack speaking. At first she paid little attention, but then she heard something that caught her attention:

"And he doesn't suspect?" Loqrin said.

"No," Jack said. "Not at all."

"Excellent. And you've done what I asked?"

"To the letter. He believes you're trying to weaken his positions in the east and he intends to fortify his establishments there. In all other directions, particularly west, he will be vulnerable."

"Well done, as usual."

"It was your attacks that did it. I just color information."

Loqrin laughed. "Well, your coloring does more for me than a thousand bullets, and then some."

That lying double-crossing bastard! Katya thought. Jack had been playing Ravic for a fool all along.

Maybe Jack was just playing his part, she thought. Playing the spy. That would make sense, wouldn't it? But no. She had heard the report Jack had given Ravic and understood that what he'd just told Loqrin circumvented Ravic's response to it. Jack was well and truly a traitor.

At last Loqrin left Jack standing beside the abyss and made his way over to the limo, where with a smile he slid in beside Katya. His door closed. She was locked in with Loqrin Mars. Jack the traitor seemed very far away. The auto's engine roared into life.

"Well, now," Loqrin said, eyeing her eagerly, "this should be a fun night, shouldn't it?"

"Ah . . . sure."

He pressed a button. "Driver, go."

Loqrin babbled amiably as they drove along, but, distracted by Jack's treachery and her own vulnerability, she hardly listened. They moved uphill, away from the Sink. Half-collapsed tenements listed downward, some of the roofs almost touching. They drove past a row of mountainous rubble that seemed to stretch on and on.

"That's the Domino," Loqrin said. "Near the end of the war—well, at least in these parts, and we only saw enough to scare us from entering the wider conflict, which is why Octung bombed us in the first place—well, near the end of their campaign, an Octunggen bomb hit one building, knocked it over. It hit the next building, and it hit the next. They collapsed one by one, the last one falling into the Sink itself, which had been made just a few years prior."

"Oh?" Why was Loqrin telling her this? Didn't he believe she was a local girl? It occurred to her that he was simply out of touch with the common people of his territory.

The car neared the lip of the hill created by the Sink, and Katya saw weird buildings ahead like nothing she'd ever seen before. It looked like at some point in the past there had been a line of connected structures, each one forming something of an inverted U shape, curved at the bottom. The apex of each one must have been uniform, and the ones she could see were about fifty or more feet high. In its day, the series of structures must have resembled a snake's back, or maybe a dragon's, undulating across the landscape. But Octunggen bombs had destroyed most of the strange arches. Jagged end-pieces stood up here and there with masses of rubble heaped between them. Only three of the great arches remained. The car drove toward the central one.

Loqrin must have seen her interest. "That's Horqrin's Arch," he said. "My home. They're ancient Qaran ruins, built two thousand or more years ago, before their empire fell. Did you know that some say the Qarans worshipped the Elders? There are even Qaran ruins underground, as if the Qarans aped the ones they worshipped, or simply wanted to be closer to them, and it's said only the nobles lived in such lairs. It seems a backwards culture, doesn't it, with the nobles living like moles underground and the peasants living above?"

The limo pulled to a stop at the base of Horqrin's Arch. Several men had already gathered there. One held the door open for Loqrin, and he climbed out smoothly. She heard him take in a deep breath of the night air. He beckoned for her to follow.

I still have my rings. She could rip her way through these assholes. She could get clear of this whole mess and be back in the Fifth Ward by morning. *But what about the haunts? The abductions?*

"Come!" Loqrin barked.

She took a deep breath, let it out, and climbed out of the auto.

Loqrin marched forward, into the Arch.

The first thing she noticed was that the men who'd come out to greet Loqrin weren't really men at all. Well, maybe they had been at some point, but they were walking corpses now. They wore nice suits and nodded to Loqrin politely, but they were rotting on their bones and gave off a horrid stench. Katya wanted to ask about them but didn't. She assumed the Returners were genuine Reynalts, but it was hard to be certain. Dr. Reynalt was the only Awakener Kat had ever heard of who could reliably bring a corpse back to life with all its mental faculties intact, and these seemed to possess theirs.

At any rate, the mystery provided her with something to think about as Loqrin led the way into the interior of the Arch. The Returners grouped around, stinking and strange.

A large set of doors made of beaten brass led inside, into a foyer with once-fine brass railings now covered in dust and long, curving couches, likewise coated. A few decrepit Returners lounged on the couches cleaning guns or just staring and slowly rotting, thinking their wormy thoughts. That was it.

Katya had expected a long, curving ramp that led into the upper reaches, but instead saw that the arch was arranged in tiers. There would be a broad level, usually with chambers on either side, then a short flight of stairs, then another level. It had all been radically remodeled since the Qaran days, she was sure, but much of it seemed quite old and out of date, and everywhere there were Returners, some about various errands, some just leaning against the wall, staring into space. Cobwebs spanned from some of them to the nearest surface. A few she didn't even see until she had nearly bumped into them, and then she'd start violently. The whole place stank of mildew and corpses, and it turned her stomach. Loqrin marched on, oblivious. They mounted level after level.

She began to see that some of the Returners were not really Returners at all. Metal appendages stuck out from them, and through visible ribcages she saw *gears* turning inside their chests. *Tick. Tick. Tick.* They were clockwork! She stared, fascinated. Clockwork-driven zombies. She'd never heard of anything like this.

Loqrin saw her interest and smiled. He did not volunteer to give away his secrets.

At last they reached what must be the highest level, where the stairs ended at a set of thick metal doors, like those of a bank vault. Loqrin spun a dial, the mechanism inside clicked, and the door swung open. Here the Returners paused, but Loqrin stepped forward.

Reluctantly, Katya followed. Loqrin slammed the door closed, and the heavy thud resounded throughout the apartment. It was a beautiful suite, she had to give it that. While dust and grime coated the lower levels, this place absolutely gleamed. Polished brass fixtures, gleaming granite counters, mirrors that sparkled like diamonds. Young men and women sprawled on the handsome couches or lounged in expensive leather chairs. A few stood at the bar, mixing drinks. They wore silks and furs, and not much of them.

"Meet your new playmates, the members of my harem," Loqrin said. "That's Anna over there. That's Billy, that's . . . oh, what's your name? And you, I forget . . ." He snapped his fingers, as if trying to recover the memory, but he did it in mock. "Well, no matter. They're charming lads and lasses all. I'm sure you'll get along famously."

Loqrin wore his look of what Katya was coming to suspect as perpetual amusement. The lights in the apartment were bright, and she got a better look at him than she had before. Earlier he'd seemed so handsome. Now she saw strange lines on his face, and his veins bulged blue and throbbing. A manic light lit his eyes, and his mouth twitched spastically. Something was unnatural about him. His body was so perfect, his face that of an angel, but his mind . . .

"Come," he said. "I'll show you something I think you'll enjoy."

She followed Loqrin out onto the balcony. Wind blasted her, and overhead two moons floated. One was far and white and round. The other was closer, larger, greenish and misshapen. Astronomers said the near one was a planet or moon that had drifted through space for uncounted eons and finally been captured by this world's gravity field. *Lucky us.*

Loqrin gestured to the Qaran arches on either side of his. The night was dark, but Katya could clearly make out the high dark curves erected so long ago by the Qaran Empire, separated by mounds of rubble. From here Katya could see the landscape spread out before her. The ridge that surrounded the depression led down to the Sink, the arches curving over it. Mansions and nice brownstones crowned the ridge, along with a few rearing factories, while the crumbling tenements crowded together below, drooping down toward the Sink miles away. Down in the bowl-shaped depression she could imagine the huddled, misshapen, disease-ridden throngs that Loqrin ruled over. Just what had he *done* to these poor bastards? They had looked awful, Katya remembered from her flight.

"Do you want to see something fun?" Loqrin said.

Katya didn't answer.

He pulled a small device from his breast pocket, unfolding a stalk-like antennae. It seemed to be some sort of radio emitter.

"You see the other Arches?" he said. "Well, inside them are a few of my friends. They help keep order around here. Usually I let them out to play earlier, but I could not let them interfere with my meeting with Gentleman Jack. Oh, no. He is helping me, you see."

"How?"

Wind blew his gorgeous blond hair away from his high, noble brow, and a blue vein throbbed under the skin. "Never mind. But enough of that. I want you to meet my friends." His finger hovered over a button on the transmitter, then stabbed down.

Instantly, alarms began to blare through the night. Kat jumped. As soon as the alarms sounded, she heard screaming coming from below. The people of the Hollows were scared. Of what?

"I like to be sporting," Loqrin said. "Sometimes. *Sometimes* I don't give them any warning, though. It's fun to see them hop."

"I don't—"

"Shut up!"

He backhanded her across the jaw, and she spun about. The world tilted, and she tasted blood on her tongue.

"There," Loqrin said. "You made me do that."

She didn't know what to do for a moment, her brain was that shocked. One hand went to her cheek. *Bastard! I should—*

She waited for some of the harem subjects to come to her aid, but none did, and looking through the glass at them she saw them still at their drugs and drinks. They evinced no interest toward her or the goings-on on the balcony.

Loqrin's attention returned to his device. "And now . . ." He pressed another button.

A clanking, grinding noise issued from one of the Arches, then the other. It sounded as though large, rusty doors grated open. Katya peered out. It was too dark to see much, but she could discern a tide of ragged, hunched figures streaming from the base of one of the Arches. She turned to the other. The same.

There were hundreds and hundreds of figures. Maybe thousands. Had they been caged in the Arches? At first she thought they must be prisoners.

"Oh, look at them go!" Loqrin said. He clapped his hands in glee.

The ragged horde descended on the Hollows. Katya heard savage cries and idiot hoots. Screams drifted up to her ears as the horde surged through the streets. Lights in some of the homes flickered off, and vague figures fled for doorways, with strange, misshapen figures at their heels.

Loqrin laughed. "Isn't this fun? But I guess you're used to it, aren't you? The scream of the siren, the mad rush to get behind locked doors before the dead ones fall on you and rip you to pieces." He shivered in excitement. "You must have wondered how I train them. Well, you see, each of my children has a small device attached to its brain. If it strays beyond my territory, a radio transmitter causes that device to send electric shocks throughout its nervous system and it turns back. Everything else is fair game. If it catches someone in the open, well . . ." He gestured expansively.

She felt her gorge rise. The things in the arches were *Returners*. *Swarms* of them. Looking at the streams of misshapen wretches slipping through the streets and alleys of the Hollows, she realized that Loqrin was utterly insane.

"But why?" she said. "Why sic Returners on your own people? I've … always wondered."

"It started off as a curfew device, then expanded. Now my flock never knows when the alarm will ring. It could be noon, it could be now."

"But . . . where did you get so *many*?" Jack had told her Loqrin had only been in power for ten years or so. It did not seem sufficient time to amass so many Returners.

When he didn't answer, she said, "I've seen enough." She tasted her own blood on her tongue. *Well, Jack did try to warn me.*

"So soon? Ah, well. Some things are wasted on the young."

There was something about that comment that struck her as odd. "*You* don't look so old." He looked in his late twenties, maybe early thirties.

He withdrew into his apartment, again without answering.

Katya relished the wind on her cheek for one more moment, but the screams of Hollowers and the mad hooting and shouting of Returners caused chills to run down her spine, and she followed, slamming the sliding glass door shut behind her. When she turned around, she saw Loqrin cross to the far side of the room, opposite to the one they'd entered by. Another thick metal door stood there. He spun a dial. Click. The door swung open. He lightly stepped into the next room.

She felt a sudden burst of apprehension. "No, wait—"

He slammed the door, locking her in the harem.

In the distance, Hollowers screamed in fear and pain, and the wind shrieked outside, rattling the glass wall of her prison.

Katya moved to the steel door Loqrin had vanished through. Banged on it. No response. She slumped her back against it and stared around at the pathetic harem. The girls and boys sprawled like broken dolls throughout the living room.

"Hi," Kat said lamely.

Some stared back at her. Glazed eyes, half-parted mouths. One placed something on her tongue. Another inhaled on his hookah. A particularly ambitious girl, the one with honey-blonde hair, waved feebly at Kat, then went back to her long black cigarette on a long black cigarette holder. Faintly phosphorescent smoke drifted up. *Ah*, thought Kat. Alchemical drugs. The same crap the Guild used to keep the aristos in line. Commoners couldn't afford the stuff, and the Guild needed them relatively sober to work the factories. The gentry of the nation, however, was kept passive through pricy designer drugs like that one. Loqrin evidently had access to such things, and he kept his little harem fully supplied. They in turn doped themselves to the gills to avoid thinking about when Loqrin would show up next.

They weren't members of a harem, really, Katya realized. They were sex slaves. Prisoners.

Now she was, too.

In that moment Kat was tempted to stroll over to her fellow inmates and take a good strong hit of whatever was handiest. She was cold, wet, tired and sore. Her cut cheek still throbbed, as well as the scrapes on her knees and elbows. She wanted nothing more than to inhale something strong, curl up on the floor and vanish into dreamland.

Instead she found herself wondering what Loqrin was up to, locked away in his private quarters. He had hinted that some important business remained for him to do tonight. Perhaps she should find out what. If she didn't start her spying now, then when? Only when she'd found what she needed could she plan her escape, and she wanted that to be ASAP.

But she was so tired . . .

There was a cure for that. She stormed over to the dolls, and they stared up at her vacantly. One boy of maybe seventeen wearing nothing but silk briefs leaned over a silver plate on the floor and inhaled a fine gray powder through his nose by way of a short straw. He sank back, an idiot grin on his suddenly red face. Kat recognized the drug. Azcui. *It'll do.*

She gently thrust the boy aside, took his straw, and snorted a long line of Az. A thunderbolt hit her brain. Fire rushed through her veins. She'd had it before, once or twice, but it had never been this pure.

She felt her cheeks burn, a smile plaster itself across her face and her eyes light up. Something burned inside her. It was kind of painful, and completely invigorating.

Aflame, she ventured outside. Wind blasted her, and in the distance the moans and howls of the Returners rolled over the Hollows. She ignored them. She stared from this balcony to the adjacent one, the one that must be Loqrin's; it was actually a few feet higher. She had thought the harem level the ultimate level, but apparently it was the penultimate. Her mind buzzing, she calculated the distance, or tried to. She had energy now, but her mind didn't work quite the same.

About fifteen feet, she thought. Fifteen feet sideways, another five up. She could tie some bed sheets together . . .

She leaned over the edge of the balustrade. Her stomach churned. Instantly she reeled backward. It was a *long* way down. And in her present condition the thought of shimmying the gulf on bed sheets knotted together with her trembling fingers did not appeal.

She tapped her chin. Wind gusted, knocking her backwards. She staggered, and as she did she glanced up.

"Shit!" she said happily. "Motherfucker!"

The roof was only about ten feet overhead. Seashell-like shapes undulated across its top, glistening from the recent rain.

It might work. It was insane, but it just might. Without another thought she ran back inside, limping down one hallway, then another. Luxurious bedrooms stretched everywhere, most occupied by several sleeping and completely doped-up young people. Others nested on the floors, some beside pools of their own vomit. Kat didn't want to have to go through the trouble of emptying the beds, so instead she searched for a linen closet. There!

With her fingers trembling from the Az, it took some effort to knot together three sheets, then test the strength of her knots. Toward the end of it, her high began to fade, and extreme weariness seeped throughout her limbs, anchors tying her down. She staggered back to the living room and snorted another gray line. Fire coursed through her again, and sparks exploded behind her eyes.

Whoa. She'd better be careful with that stuff. She didn't want to end up brain-fried like these poor bastards.

On her way back to the sheet-rope, she came across the shoe rack. After some study, she picked a lime-green calf-high number with six-inch heels made in Amandie, a country famed for its craftsmen. It looked both gross and adorable. Quickly she tied it to one end of her rope.

Marshalling her courage, she returned to the balcony and threw up her rope four times before the shoe snagged around one of the seashell shapes. She tugged on it, and it wedged firmly between two of the mounds. She hoped the shoe could bear her weight; she'd chosen it because it looked sturdy. Hopefully the Amandian craftsmen were as good as their rep.

She wrapped her hands around the sheet and hauled herself up, but she must not be as strong as she thought she was, because her arms screamed with the effort. She only weighed about a hundred and fifteen pounds, it shouldn't have been that hard. Wind slammed her against the side of the building, then blew her sideways, and she stifled a scream. When the wind calmed, she resumed climbing. At last, arms aching, she neared the edge of the roof, flung a leg over the lip and half pulled herself up. A quick heave and a roll to the side and she lay on her back, gasping and staring up at the stars. They blazed across the sky, closer and clearer than before. With the wind in her hair and the stars twinkling above, she smiled drowsily. Her fire had faded once again, quicker this time.

She needed more Az. Exhaustion weighed her limbs.

Too bad, kiddo. Up you go! She strained against the roof. It seemed to suck at her like glue. Every fiber of her muscles screamed. An itch in her nostrils craved Az. *Fuck that. I am NOT getting hooked.*

Suddenly she heard a great *whoosh*. At first she thought it was the wind—and it was. But not a natural wind. A *created* wind. The gust nearly knocked her aside.

Something roared. She heard taut fabric creaking. The whip of propellers. Then, to her shock, a massive dark shape eclipsed the stars, and every ounce of weariness she felt drained away, replaced by a surge of adrenaline. At first she thought she was looking at another haunt and she had half a mind to leap from the building to her doom rather than have the thing do whatever it did to people's brains, but almost immediately she realized it wasn't a haunt. The thing overhead was huge, a great blob blotting out the stars.

"Oh gods," she said, scrambling to her feet. Vertical now, she felt the wind tug at her with even more strength.

The great shape wheeled overhead, slowly, almost seeming to drift. What could it be? As she stared at it, observing its torpedo-like silhouette against the stars, the truth dawned on her, and she laughed.

"A zeppelin!" she said. "A fucking zeppelin!"

From time to time she'd see one drifting over Lower Lavorgna, docking with one of the great skyscrapers there, picking up a group of aristos for travel or pleasure tours. Seeing their silver shapes gliding amongst the towers had always seemed like a dream to her, and she'd longed to get a closer glimpse of one, even take a trip in one someday if the fates were kind. Well, this was as close as she was likely to get. Hells, she could practically reach out and touch it!

She stared, fascinated, as it drifted down to the other side of the Arch. Her heart thumping madly, Kat hunkered low and scurried up the gently curving slope of the structure. The wind pummeled her, bringing tears to her eyes and wrapping her briefly in the stink of some nearby factory, but she pressed on. At last she stood over what must be Loqrin's apartment. On the east side jutted his balcony, the one that was adjacent to his harem's, and on the other jutted what must be a zeppelin dock, an addition to the original building. Even as Kat watched, the zeppelin's gondola came to rest against the docking bay, something snapped, a door was thrown, and through the windows she saw the tall, stately form of Loqrin Mars pass into the airship.

Then, as if they had practiced this maneuver countless times before and were not about to waste a moment, the zeppelin disengaged from the dock and drifted away. Kat caught a glimpse through the windows of Loqrin, in what must be the ship's bridge, surrounded by strange machines, some spitting sparks, with misshapen hunched creatures that must be Returners all around him, and then the massive airship angled, not upward, but down.

"What the hell?" Kat whispered the words, as if she might be overheard.

The zeppelin moved downhill, nearly touching the roofs of the tenements that listed toward the Sink. Below she could still hear the hoots and howls of the ravening Returners, along with the occasional scream. Oblivious, or perhaps soaking in the pandemonium he'd sown, Loqrin drifted out over the Hollows, skimming the rooftops, still going lower and lower, until at last he hung over the very abyss of the Sink itself. The Sink was too far away for Kat to see well, and many buildings blocked her view, but she unmistakably saw the silver gleam of moonlight along the zeppelin's back as it descended into the Sink like some monstrous whale vanishing into the deep.

Then her strength gave out. She collapsed. It was all she could do to drag herself back to her rope and drop down into the harem apartment once more.

Chapter 5

With a gasp, she woke up in Loqrin's harem. For a moment she struggled to orient herself, then took a deep breath and cursed. Bodies pressed tight against her, warm and naked. She was on the floor nestled up with the other harem pets, a richly woven blanket thrown over them. In front of her arced a young man's narrow back. The boy breathed in and out, in and out, in what had to be a drugged stupor.

Katya disengaged herself, threw back the blanket and stood. Dizziness overcame her, and she swayed. She needed something to eat.

She was in one of the bedrooms. Various boys and girls lay under the sheets of the bed, sleeping deeply, while others stacked up on the floor, huddling for warmth. It puzzled her that there was no heater, no fireplace. It really was quite cold, and she shivered, wrapping her arms about herself.

Gently she stepped over and around the sleepers. She was freezing, hungry, and needed a bath. As she made her way through the halls, she remembered the zeppelin and wondered what it could mean that Loqrin was descending into the Sink. Was it one of his mad whims, or did it have a purpose? Katya imagined the Below, dark and vast, with the ruins of great Elder buildings lining its cavern walls. She didn't know what the Elders had been, no one did, not where they had come from or where they had gone to, only that they'd left their strange ruins and cities all across the world, sometimes perched along black abysses like the one below Lavorgna. What could Loqrin want down there?

She came upon a utility room to find the honey-blond young woman standing before a great copper pot. The girl lit a burner beneath the pot, nodded to herself, and stepped back. When she saw Katya, she smiled tiredly and said, "Hi."

"Uh. Yeah," Kat said. "What's with the pot?"

The girl blinked at her, as if she hadn't been asked this question in a while and didn't know how to answer it. At last she shrugged and said, "There's no plumbing."

"*What?*"

"Returners bring us buckets of water everyday. That's where this batch came from."

Kat couldn't believe it. "Fuckmunch! This is just great!" She slapped the wall. "But that doesn't make any *sense!* This place is *posh.*" She looked around at the granite walls and gleaming brass corner pieces. Even the utility room was worth a fortune. She could strip it and live high hog for a good while.

"Yeah, well, take it up with Loqrin," the girl said. "He has plumbing. Maybe he'll let you use his."

"But if he has plumbing, and we're *right next door*, we should, too."

"You'd think so."

"So, what, how do you, like, go to the bathroom?"

The girl brightened. "Why don't I show you?" She checked the burner once more to make sure it was heating the water properly, then brushed past Katya and made down the hallway. Irritated, Kat followed. Morning sunlight streamed into the apartment from the sliding glass door of the balcony, making the brass railings and fixtures shine. Expensive wallpaper with floral patterns covered the walls that weren't granite.

"By the way, I'm Heather," said the girl over her shoulder.

"I'm Kat."

"How old are you, Kat?"

"Twenty-two."

"You look sixteen. I'm twenty. Ah, this is it."

She turned into a room that must have been a super-nice lavatory at one point; Katya could tell by the long mirror along one wall with the fancy copper frame depicting beautiful women and fairies lounging and playing. At some point there had probably been a gleaming granite countertop and sink before the mirror—but there had probably been a floor then, too.

"Balls for *breakfast*!" Kat said.

She stared down into the gaping hole where the floor of the restroom had been. Now it was just a straight drop fifty or sixty feet down to the ground into a small mountain of what had to be shit, piss and garbage. Grass grew up its sides. Loqrin must have been making the dolls do this for *years*. Kat was glad she was too high up to be able to smell the stink.

"I don't believe it," she said. "Loqrin turned an aristo bath into an outhouse!"

"He does have his ticks," Heather admitted.

She walked into the bathroom, keeping to the floor that was still there. Teetering on the edge, she grabbed a handful of cables that hung from the ceiling—they must have been bolted there for this purpose—and squatted over the drop-off. Only her feet and her hold on the cables connected her to the bathroom. Her butt hung out over empty air. After mock-demonstrating (thank the gods it was only mock) how it was done, she straightened and pointed to a corner, where a pile of toilet paper rolls promised clean-up. "And if you're finicky . . ." She pointed to another corner where a basin of water stood. Crumbled soap bars crammed the tray.

"Magnar *fucked*," Katya said, staring down at the pile of refuse. Wind blew in, ruffling her hair, and bringing with it the faint hint of what lay below. She quickly pulled back. In horror, she stared at the other young woman.

Heather looked at her sadly. "I'm sorry."

Katya wanted to snap at her, but she held herself back. It wasn't Heather's fault. "Why does Loqrin do this to you?"

Kat twisted a finger through her long auburn hair. "I think he thinks it's funny."

"It's not."

"No," Heather said. "Let's check on the water."

They returned to the utility room. Mops and brooms propped up in the corners, along with an old, dried-up homunculi. Heather saw Kat looking at it and said, "That's Freddy. He's dead."

"Homuncs don't die."

"Well, whatever. He's been that way since I've been here. I think he used to help clean up the place, do the chores for the girls."

"I guess that was back when the old Boss used to rule here."

A strange look entered Heather's eyes. "Yeah . . ."

Kat didn't think much of it at the time. "How long have you been here?"

Heather placed her hands over the water, probably checking to see if it was warm. Not satisfied, she turned up the flame.

"Three years," she said.

"Damn." Katya leaned against the wall. "Three *years.*"

She looked Heather over. She was pretty. She had a round, angelic face, framed by curly auburn hair. She had a small, full mouth, straight, slightly upturned nose that lent her an impish quality, and the hint of freckles on her cheeks. Her eyes were large and hazel, and the lashes were long. She wore only a silken shift colored a pale pink and warm stockings engulfed her legs. They were striped a garish orange-and-green pattern. She had skinny legs, and Kat could see her ribs through her shift. Her complexion was bad. She'd been here for too long.

Heather saw her scrutiny and said, "It's okay. It's almost over."

"How?"

"Because I'm used-up, I guess. I don't know. He keeps saying he's going to kill me. Every week he says it. I think he's let me live this long because I've become the den mother, taking care of the others. But the time is coming, I know it."

"Fuck that."

"You say that a lot. But that's what he does. When he's tired of us or whatever, he'll take one of us out of here . . . and we'll never see that person again. Well . . . almost never."

"Fuck," Kat said again, unable to help herself.

Heather seemed resigned to her fate, even looking forward to it. "It won't be long now," she said, seeming to draw strength from the words.

"Why?"

"Now he's got you. You're fresh and pretty, and since you're new you're sober enough that you can play den mother for awhile. Me, I'm not too sober, but compared with the others . . ."

"I didn't realize—" Katya was horrified. If her playing spy cost Heather her life, Katya didn't think she could live with herself.

"Oh, it's okay," Heather assured her with that same strange blankness. "I want out. There's been many times in the morning when I'm crouched over the poop-hole that I've thought about just letting go."

Kat didn't say anything to that. She didn't think such a suicide would be a very worthy death, but she could sure understand the temptation.

"What does he do to you when, you know, he gets tired of you?"

A dark look crossed Heather's face. "Different things. Some I don't know about. The one really scares me is him turning me into a Returner."

"He does that?"

"Oh, yes. He loves playing with corpses. It's his hobby. Well, I heard him say once that he didn't like his girls and boys to get too old. When they did, he'd stop them aging for good."

"You really think he'd kill you and then bring you *back*?"

For the first time, Heather really looked troubled. "He's done it before. Of course, most of them turn out . . . badly."

Kat remembered the Returners from the arches. "But sometimes he can bring them back okay?"

Heather nodded. Tears built up in her eyes, then trickled down her cheeks. "It's just the odds. Every hundred or so seem to come out all right."

"Hundred . . . gods . . ."

"He brings 'em in sometimes, the girls and boys that've Returned. Some I even knew before. Like Aryn. She was so pretty. But they're not the same after. Even the successful ones. Only Dr. Reynalt can do that. It's bad. Seeing their eyes, how blank they are . . . remembering how they used to be." She took a deep breath. "*That's* what really scares me. That he might do that, bring me back. I'd be trapped in that rotted brain, forced to do what he wants . . . *forever.*"

Kat realized Heather was shaking. Hastily she went around the water pot and wrapped her arms around the girl. Heather trembled against her. A choking breath exploded from her lips, then another. Kat felt tears against her shoulder.

"It's okay, Heather. I won't let him touch you."

"How?" Heather said. Her voice was thick with fear. "You can't stop him! No one can stop him!"

Kat let her cry awhile, and when Heather sank to the ground, Kat sank with her. At last the other girl calmed down, but when she wiped at her eyes, she still looked ashen and miserable.

"Why don't we escape?" Katya said.

"How? And even if we did, he'd just hunt us down." Heather laughed. Such a bitter sound should never come from such a girl, Kat thought. "And he *would* hunt us. Oh, yes. We'd be *interesting* then. And when he found us . . ." Heather winced. "He likes to torture people, Kat. I've heard the screams, even through the wall."

"What if there was some place we could go?"

"There's not. He owns the whole territory."

"Maybe we could go *outside* the territory. The Fifth Ward, maybe. There's someone who could protect us there."

"Who? You're crazy! Loqrin would get us back, and then . . . and then . . ."

Kat stroked her cheek. She felt something well up inside her, and without thinking she said, "I'm a spy."

Heather looked at her. "What?"

Kat hesitated, then said, "I'm here to bring Loqrin down. Ravic sent me. Boss of the Fifth Ward. Loqrin's been hitting him, hitting him hard, and Loqrin's up to some other strange shit, too. Ravic even thinks he could be tied up with the haunts."

Heather looked at her with wide eyes. "No way! You're not a spy!"

"It's the truth."

"If he catches you . . ."

"What, he'll imprison me and make me a sex slave?"

Heather stared off into space, and Kat could see her gather her courage. Her face was white with fear, but hate and determination glimmered in her eyes. "What have I got to lose . . . ?" Suddenly she turned to Kat, and her expression was imploring. "You're not messing with me, are you?"

Kat didn't feel like smiling, but she gave Heather a big smile anyway. Her biggest. She could see it worked. Hope joined hate and determination in Heather's face.

"Fuck's honest truth," Kat said. "Rip out my tongue if I'm a liar."

Heather smiled a trembling, pathetic smile. "Really?"

"I'll take care of you," Katya promised, thinking, *Great. What have I done now?*

Loqrin burst in, surrounded by Returners. Each pushed a silver tray laden with food.

It was late afternoon. The day had passed uneventfully. Katya had asked Heather how the dolls (Katya couldn't stop thinking of them as such) bathed themselves, and Heather had fetched soap and sponges. Later she'd shown Katya to the kitchen. There was no water, but there was an electric ice-box with various leftovers, and they munched on these while the others woke up.

Heather took care of them, feeding and clothing them, making sure they were clean. She even provided some entertainment, directing a group of the inmates to play some musical instruments they'd been given, and they weren't bad, Kat thought. Not great, but not bad. Heather introduced the dolls to Kat, and vice versa, and Kat found that many were personable, though the lot were strung-out, scared and eager to return to their drugs. She could hardly blame them.

Outside it was quiet, the Returners having withdrawn into their Arches for the day. Katya had gone out onto the balcony to smoke and stare at the horizon. While she had, her gaze had drifted to the Arches and she tried not to imagine the thousands of Returners pressed into the stifling, putrid chambers like undead sardines, shuffling and reeking of old rot and fresh blood. Instead she focused on the sunlight shining on the old, leaning buildings and sparkling on laundry lines strung between open windows. Brightly colored clothes billowed and flew on the wind. Pasty, strange men and women made their way to tanneries, merchant shops and the inevitable factories.

But they did not go in, at least some of them. A milling crowd took shape outside one factory, then another, and people chanted things that were too far away for Katya to hear, some holding up wooden placards. They formed a circle and marched in a ring. A few threw rocks at the factory.

"What're they doing?" Katya asked.

Heather smiled. "They're recruits of the Underground Brotherhood. They're striking."

"*Striking?*" Katya had heard whispers about the Brotherhood, had seen the signs, but striking was unknown in Lavorgna, even though she'd heard of it happening elsewhere. "Won't Loqrin just bust them up?"

"Maybe. But remember, it's not his factory, it's the Guild's. They pay him a percentage, but that's it."

"What do the workers want?"

"Better working conditions, I guess. Shorter days. Fewer days. You know they work like twelve hour days or more, and only get a day off every month if they're lucky. And they're always getting ground up in the machines they work with, or poisoned by the chemicals, and who takes care of 'em then? Not the Guild."

Katya nodded. It sounded good, it sounded right. But she didn't think it would work. The Guild wouldn't let them. No one could take on the Guild, especially not these pasty, misshapen men of the Hollows.

"Why do they look so bad?" Kat asked. "You know, the Hollowers? No offense."

Heather was eating an apple injected with brandy. Munching, she'd said, "You're really from Outside, aren't you?"

"Well, the Fifth Ward. I guess it does seem like another planet, doesn't it?"

Heather spat out a bite of the core. It arced down and away. A grackle swept in and gobbled it up, then flew on. "Loqrin doesn't allow in much fresh food, and he keeps people living packed together like rats. Lots of disease, lots of growing up stunted, without the right food."

"Malnourished.".

"Whatever. It all adds up, over generations. Lots of shut-ins."

Katya had raised her eyebrows. "Generations?"

Heather finished the apple, pulled out a syringe and went about tying a tube around her upper arm and sticking herself with the needle. As the waves of the drug washed over her, she smiled blissfully and said, "Yeah."

Then the thick metal doors of the doll house flung open and in poured Loqrin, smiling from ear to ear, a dozen Returners at his heels. All were dressed in tuxedos and wheeled gleaming carts before them.

"I've brought a feast!" he announced, looking even more handsome than usual, dressed in eloquent evening wear, shaven to within an inch of his life. Not close enough, Kat thought.

The harem stirred sluggishly. At the sight of all the food, they roused themselves and shambled over to the carts. Sumptuous smells drifted up, and Kat's stomach rumbled despite herself. She hated Loqrin with every fiber of her being, but for a bite of fresh food she might be willing to make his death throes a little briefer.

"Ta-da!" Loqrin jerked the domed silver cover off one cart.

"Oh, delish!" someone exclaimed. "Frogmouth, my favorite!"

Indeed, revealed on the platter was a huge toad, braised and with its great gaping mouth stuffed with rum-laced cherries. More and more covers sprang from trays, and the dolls stared in anticipation at the feast before them. Kat, who had never seen such a banquet, was suitably impressed.

The inmates lunged on the food. Kat had to spring quick or go hungry. But there was plenty, and it was all rich, all decadent, the food of kings and queens. There was glazed eel stuffed with pâté; mutant lobster from the Qarzatl region of the Atomic Sea (and, like all seafood, carefully processed), injected with an alchemical butter-rum sauce that made every bite burst with flavor; braised giant slug on a bed of rice; raw electric eel fitted with alchemically-produced collars so that each bite delivered a painful but also orgasmic jolt of electricity; big-mouth bass stuffed with live snakes; squidsticks; fried turtle; and more, much more.

The inmates ate like barbarians. Kat had known they weren't aristos, but they acted like they had never even heard of table manners. It was a feeding frenzy of drug addicts, and Kat was obliged to step lively. It wasn't long before she was stuffed and pleasantly reeling, both from the rich food and the alcohol and drugs that laced at least half of the offered items.

Throughout it all, Loqrin stood back, watching them with a small, secret smile. His presence creeped Katya out, but not enough to dissuade her from eating.

"I hope you've enjoyed yourselves," Loqrin said afterward. "I've got to run. Later I'll be back, and then I'll enjoy *myself*."

A few scared murmurs greeted this, and his eyes lingered on Heather as he spoke.

"For now I have things to do," Loqrin said. He left, Returners in tow. The door clanged loudly when he was gone.

Heather sniffed. "This is it," she said. "This is the day he takes me next door, like he did Abby last week. Then you'll never see me again."

"It'll be alright," Katya said. *Somehow.*

Once her fellow inmates were safely ensconced in their stupors, Katya retrieved her sheet-rope from where she'd hidden it in the back of the linen closet. Last night she'd had to pull so hard at the rope to get it down that the heel on the lime-green shoe had cracked; thus she spent some time removing it and knotting the end of the rope about its twin. Done, she stepped out onto the balcony, feeling the cooling wind and relishing it, then hurled her makeshift grapple overhead. This time it only took her two tries to secure it to the roof, and with food giving her strength and her mind afire with hate, she shimmied up the rope with somewhat more ease than last night. *Like a drunken monkey,* she thought.

The wind blew strongly atop the roof. She hunkered low and pressed against it. Her short hair streamed out. Her eyes misted.

Before her the Hollows sprawled out like a vast bowl miles wide, a crater about to collapse in on itself. It made her dizzy, and she swallowed. Hunched against the wind, she fought her way over the strangely rounded roof, the coil of her rope wound about a shoulder.

She moved in the opposite direction from Loqrin's suite.

The sun touched the horizon to the west, descending over the madness of the Atomic Sea. From here Kat could see lightning licking up from its waves. A great gas bubble burst in the middle of the harbor, was lanced by a flash of lightning and exploded furiously, sending fire and the reflection of fire far across the water, then vanishing. By the sun's fading light Kat tried to determine if it would be possible to scramble down the entirety of the Arch and to escape via the roof. The Arch was slightly more rounded than an inverted U, but each side looked very steep just the same. It might be possible to climb down it using the rounded formations as grips—her career as a thief had taught her how this might be done—but the formations were very smooth and offered little purchase, as she found now, with the wind knocking her from side and side and the Arch beneath her slipping under her feet. She was barefoot, but even that didn't help much. The masonry of the Arch chilled her soles, and the wind irritated her eyes.

So, no escape that way. How *could* she get out of here when the time came? And what if she wanted to take the inmates with her?

With a sigh, she abandoned the scouting mission and marched back in the other direction. At least the roof was dry tonight, unlike last night.

After some effort, she reached the section over Loqrin's apartment, pressed herself flat, belly to the roof—cold!—then leaned over the side as far as she could go. Upside down like a bat, she peered into Loqrin's suite. Blood rushed to her head, and her temples pounded. All she saw was darkness and a few dim lamps—alchemical lamps, red and green, set on low. From this angle she couldn't see much. She'd have to go down.

"Damn."

She secured the green shoe around the mounds and lowered herself into the corner of Loqrin's balcony. Sure enough, from here she commanded a much better view of the Boss's apartment. Good. And bad. The setting sun cast a crimson glow over the city, making blood seem to coat the listing buildings. Kat was vulnerable. It was darker inside than outside, and she might be seen. *Damn it.*

She ducked deeper into the corner and cautiously stuck her head around the side. Better, but she still should've waited for nightfall. She just couldn't have idled around the Dolls' House any longer. She'd had to be up and doing something to hurt Loqrin, and now.

Inside Loqrin's suite alchemical lamps throbbed, pulsing like evil little hearts. Their weird, slow light picked out a long table and gleaming instruments on a nearby tray. Dark hands moved, grabbing up a scalpel. The shape the hands belonged to bent over, working on something. The instrument table and the man's bulk blocked Kat's view of what was on the slab, but at last she made out small feet and narrow ankles.

Abby. Heather had said he'd taken a girl into his lair last week. *Shit.* What was he doing to her, anyway?

Loqrin selected a small gear and some piping from the table. It was then that Kat understood. Abby, if that was really her, was dead; Loqrin had killed her, one way or another. But it wasn't over for the poor girl. *Bastard's trying to bring her back.* A clockwork Abby. An Abby that would never grow old. Kat's fists clenched.

Loqrin's work continued at a slow but steady pace, but Kat couldn't bear to watch. The sky grew dark, and the wind blew cold. Looking out at the skyline, she crossed her arms over her chest and rocked back and forth. Some time later she glanced up when the sound of chimes rang throughout the apartment.

Loqrin cursed (Kat could hear it through the glass, only slightly muffled) and moved toward the vault door on the opposite side from the harem door. He passed a cabinet full of books and weird things in jars. Something like a fetus with roots pressed up against a curved glass wall. Another thing that was all eyes and tentacles glowed in the red light, seeming to swell and shrink as the light pulsed.

Loqrin threw the wheel, opening the door.

There stood two of his goons, carrying a man between them, obviously a captive; he was naked and bruised. When she saw the goons, Kat realized that the other half of the Arch must house Loqrin's men and mob operations. One half for business, one half for pleasure, his harem and his clockwork freaks.

"Is it past sunset already?" Loqrin said, shaking tacky blood from his fingers.

"Yeah, Boss," said a goon.

"Strange. Time seems to stop when I'm . . . stopping time." Loqrin eyed the bruised man skeptically. "So you're our next morsel, eh? You'll do, I suppose. But we must make this quick. I'm expecting word on the strike at any moment." To his men, he said, "Show him in."

Morsel? Kat frowned.

Loqrin led the way deeper into his suite, and the goons dragged the limp man after him. The captive was thin, with wiry muscles and curly black hair. Whiskers covered his face. Not bad looking for a Hollower, Kat thought. She hoped nothing bad was going to happen to him, but that seemed unlikely.

Loqrin passed into a dark area of his suite and crouched. An alchemical lamp flared into life, bathing him in a bloody red glow. Like all alchemical lamps, it wasn't lit by flame, but by glowing liquid that occasionally moved inside the orb as if it had a life of its own. For some reason, alchemical lamps had always disturbed Kat. No more so than now.

Loqrin stood before a squat black slab, and beyond it lay some blocky machine with strange antennae curling up from it like stalks.

Loqrin knelt before the slab, pressing his forehead to it, and muttered something Kat couldn't hear. She couldn't see his face, but his body language showed a sense of formality—solemnity, even.

At length he rose and stepped around to the other side of the slab so that he faced his men and their prisoner. He gestured curtly, and the goons forced the man to his knees so that he leaned over the altar . . .

Loqrin opened a panel in the blocky machine.

. . . and the goons shoved the man's head into an aperture. The captive could only protest weakly; he seemed half-conscious at most. Drugged, Kat thought. She felt her breath catch in her chest. *What are they doing to him?*

Loqrin flicked a series of switches, and lights flashed from the machine. Sparks rippled up the antennae. The very air around it seemed to blur.

Kat's eyes widened and a shiver coursed up her back.

Loqrin twirled dials and punched buttons. All at once the interior of the machine exploded with light. Kat had to blink against it. A sound like radio static burst from the thing, and what looked like white electrical sparks surrounded the naked man's head. Over the roar of the static, Loqrin shouted something that Kat didn't understand; it didn't even sound like it was in any language she had ever heard.

As suddenly as it had started, the light and noise faded. Loqrin unstrapped the man, and he slipped backward and thunked to the ground. He was limp as a noodle, but his chest rose and fell. Something about him wasn't right. He looked somehow *less*.

Kat's vision blurred. *Loqrin, that sonofabitch, I'll get him I'll—*

Shame took her. She had stood there and done nothing, just let Loqrin do whatever he had done.

Never again, she thought. *I'm so sorry, whoever you are, I was so scared, it all happened so fast—*

"He's of no more use to me," Loqrin said. "His mind is gone now. I couldn't even make a Returner out of him. Feed him to my children in the Arches."

"No," Kat choked out.

The goons nodded, picked up the body and carted it from the suite. As they did, Kat got a better look at the victim. To her shock, she saw that the man's head *steamed*, just like Fedrik's head after the haunt had attacked him last night.

"Shit," she said.

Loqrin's head jerked sideways. He stared right at the balcony.

Kat leapt back into the corner where she knew she couldn't be seen. The rope dangled above. If Loqrin opened the door she was screwed. *Fuck fuck fuck.* And what had she seen, anyway? What had Loqrin *done*? She was in way over her head. Jack—*traitor!*—had been right.

Footsteps approached the balcony.

Fuck! There was no time to ascend the rope.

Shaking, she rose to her feet and bunched her fists. She still had her rings, damn it. If Loqrin wanted a fight, she'd give him one.

A hand rattled the handle of the terrace. Kat's heart nearly stopped.

A radio squawked inside the suite. She heard Loqrin curse.

The footsteps retreated.

Kat breathed a long sigh of relief and slouched back against the wall. Her legs shook with released tension, and her palms oozed sweat.

"What is it?" Loqrin's voice barked. A radio hissed. "Good," he said. "Bring them up."

By the time Katya heard this last part, she was already halfway up her rope. She hauled herself onto the roof and dragged the rope with her. Just as she pulled up the end of it, she heard the door slide open below. Loqrin stepped out onto the balcony, looked around.

Jaws clamped tight, every nerve on fire, Kat edged back, slowly and silently. The moment seemed to stretch forever. Loqrin looked one way, then another. He began to turn—his eyesight would come into contact with the roof—Kat continued to edge back—Loqrin finished his turn—

She jerked out of view.

Loqrin grunted. Footsteps marched inside, and the door slammed shut. Kat expelled a deep breath. Ragged moths fluttered in her belly, and she wanted to sink to her knees. Damn, but she could use a cigarette.

Dimly, she heard Loqrin speaking on his radio transmitter. Not long after, the vault door clanked open again. Very carefully, Kat lowered herself to the roof and hung over. The vault door wasn't as deep into the suite as Loqrin's Returner lab was and so she could see it, if just barely. Savage-looking men with pistols and repeating rifles entered the room, shoving bound and hooded men before them. The men looked as if they'd been beaten, and their poor patchwork clothes were ripped and bloody.

"Only six?" Loqrin demanded.

One of the goons stepped forward. Quite tall, a great white scar ran down from his hairline, through one eye, down his cheek to his jaw. It deformed that side of his face and caused a slight lisp when he spoke. He was infected by the sea, and a series of jagged fins jutted from one side of his neck like tiered mushrooms; Kat saw redness where the fins connected to the flesh of his neck and knew the mutations must itch.

"The strikers were prepared.," the finned man said. They figured we'd be comin'. We've hit too many before. Fuckin' Brotherhood!"

"We'll have to change our strategies, won't we?" Loqrin said. "Or find a more permanent solution." He'd changed for the event, Kat saw, donning fresh clothes and wiping the blood off his face and hands. Kat was surprised. He didn't seem the type to dress up for his thugs—unless there was some *else* he was dressing up for. "Well, that will keep for another day. For now—ah! I think I hear it."

For a moment Kat wondered what he was talking about, and then she heard the roar of wind and the beating of distant propellers. She turned to see the zeppelin swing up from the south, drifting fast over the rooftops on the far side of the ridge. It must have a hangar somewhere nearby, probably in some warehouse or other. The airship was just a huge dark shape, drawing closer and closer, occasionally blocking out the moons. It occurred to her that the pilot might see her, so she pressed herself into the undulating mounds of the roof.

The huge ship drifted overhead, realigned itself, then sank down to dock with the far side of Loqrin's suite. Gently, so as not to be heard by the men below or to attract the pilot's attention, Katya edged over to that side, feeling the gentle rasp of the roof below her fingertips and along her belly. A lock of hair fell before her eyes and she impatiently brushed it away.

The zeppelin docked. Through the windows of the docking bay, she saw Loqrin march into the zeppelin's gondola, and the rough men shoved their prisoners after him. All vanished within. Various machines sparked through the gondola's windows, and Kat saw that hunched Returners tended to them. Some turned to Loqrin and bowed. Loqrin acknowledged them as a king would his lowly subjects, with head held high and back erect.

The gangsters struck the prisoners with the butts of their guns and forced them to the floor. Kat's heart went out to them. *Strikers*, she thought. She'd known nothing good would happen to them. Lavorgna would chew strikers up and shit them out bloody.

The zeppelin disconnected. Gently, it lowered itself slightly, pointing its bow toward the Sink. What would happen to the men who'd rebelled against the factory— what did Loqrin *want* with them? Perhaps the same thing he wanted with the men he abducted from the Fifth Ward, Kat thought. She'd imagined him sacrificing them all on his stupid altar and electrocuting their heads, but no. It seemed he had other designs.

And what was producing the haunts, anyway? If Loqrin had any part in it, she had yet to see it.

The zeppelin slowed in its turn, almost finished aligning itself. It hung like a great dark cloud, just a couple of feet from the docking bay.

Kat needed to know what Loqrin was up to.

But come *on*. She wasn't mad. Not *that* mad. There was no way she could . . .

No. Fucking. Way.

"Oh, to hell with it," she said. It was either this or stay in the harem another day.

She descended to the roof of the docking bay, carefully. Her feet touched the metal, and the wind whipped her hair and stung her eyes. Balancing precariously, she stepped along the top of the tube toward the great ship that blotted out the sky right in front of her. The wind softened against her, blocked by the ship. She heard the creak of fabric, the whup-whup of propellers. As she went, she turned her jagged rings so that they faced inward, not outward. She didn't need them for punching now.

The zeppelin began to drift away.

"No you don't," she said.

She ran the last few steps and flung herself out into space, toward the side of the ship. *This had better work!*

Chapter 6

She seemed to hang suspended in air for an eternal moment. She was weightless, a dandelion puff on the wind. She could see everything clearly, every detail of the zeppelin and the city below.

Then she struck, hard, and the impact rattled her teeth and bones. Worse, she couldn't find a handhold. She slid, helpless, and panic welled up inside her like a live thing. The fabric of the zeppelin burned her cheek, rucked up her blouse and skinned her belly. The ground waited sixty or more feet below, eager for her to fall. The emptiness seemed to suck at her like a void.

She slapped her hands down, sinking her jagged rings into the fabric that stretched tightly over the metal alloy frame of the ship. Her slide slowed. She hit one of the struts that ran underneath the skin. If she'd been going any faster the strut would have bounced her off and flung her into space. As it was, she clung to it for dear life, digging her fingers through the fabric. The zeppelin swung through the skies, and dark tenements sulked below. Panting, Kat thought she smelled the stench of boiling onion in some family's soup, but it was probably her imagination.

The propeller's roar filled her ears. It sprouted from the hull just twenty feet from where Kat clung, and beyond it jutted the side fin—the rudder?

A plume of factory smoke enveloped her. She coughed wretchedly, her eyes burning. The zeppelin passed through it, drifted lower, while tenements scrolled below.

The great gaping maw of the Sink loomed ahead. Blackness waited. Nothing but blackness, going down and down.

The tenements ended, and the zeppelin swung over the pit. Kat stared into it, down into all that darkness. It seemed cold and alien, and the last thing she wanted was to go into it. *Too late, kiddo.*

The zeppelin's propeller, the one she could see, stopped spinning, then angled upward so that the blades faced the sky. She heard the ticks of machinery and enjoyed the moment of quiet. With the propeller still, she could hear the wind, then some tinny music coming from a tenement near the lip, maybe someone's birthday. Katya remembered her birthdays with her mother, back before her mother had started hooking. She'd always baked Katya a cake, every year. Of course she'd used the cheapest possible ingredients, and the frosting was slapped on a bit too thickly, but somehow the result always satisfied.

Don't think about her, Kat! Think about the living.

The propeller burst into new life, and the zeppelin shuddered. The propellers forced it down toward the Sink. Katya felt the hairs on her arm prickle as the lip of the pit approached her, passed her . . . then was overhead. She could literally feel the change in temperature as shadow rolled over her. *This is it*, she thought. *We're really doing it.* I'm really doing it. *What have I gotten myself into?*

The zeppelin plunged into the depths. The maw of the pit became a circle of light above, then dwindled until at last it was just a tiny dot.

Suddenly massive floodlights blazed from the zeppelin forefront. Great beams cut the darkness, their reflections hurting Kat's eyes. She saw the beams scroll along rough walls, searching, searching. Then—ah!—a huge yawning cavern revealed itself. It must be hundreds of feet wide, a huge mouth in the side of the pit, and from what Kat could see it ran perpendicular to the pit tube. She couldn't see its bottom. Maybe, like the pit, it had none, one abyss leading into another. The propeller Kat could see stopped spinning, adjusted itself so that it faced the rear, then cranked back into life. Without hesitating, the zeppelin passed through the grand archway and into the cavern. Although . . .

Kat strained her eyes into the darkness, scanning the walls that were just barely revealed, more like hinted at, by the reflection of the floodlights that continued to light the way forward.

By their illumination, she thought she saw ordered lines, signs of architecture, not random curves and rough protrusions. This wasn't a natural cavern at all. Her mind reeled. *The Below*, she thought. She was in the Below!

Sweet fuck, Magnar save me. She was in the godsdamned Below!

The walls were black and far apart, maybe half a mile or more, but she saw undeniable crenulations and vertical grooves that were almost organic, like the ribbing of the throat, proud terraces and massive bulwarks that might be buildings, just dimly guessed at by the refracted light, more intuited than actually seen. *The Elders built this.* What had they been, anyway? No Elder bodies had ever been found, at least as far as Kat knew. The Elders were ancient and unknowable, mighty beyond human ken. The mystery behind their disappearance had fascinated historians and thinkers since the discovery of their ruins long ago.

Kat found herself breathing fast and hard. Sweat soaked her hair, dripped into her eyes. She blinked it away. Her arms ached as she clung to the strut, and she didn't know how much longer she could hang on.

To her relief, the zeppelin drifted toward one side of the great chasm, adjusting its angle as it went. Kat saw the lip of a precipice and what might have been a road, though not a human one. Alchemical lamps burned on the ground, winking, perhaps signaling to the zeppelin. The ship neared the precipice, then drifted over it. Firm ground below. Kat let out a deep breath. *Just a little bit more.*

It was quite bright below, actually. Many lamps blazed, set on high. Who had lit them?

And, more importantly, could they see her?

She climbed sideways, shimmying along the strut, making for the propeller. The engine that powered it had shut off, and the blades whirred slowly to a stop. Whup. Whup. Whup. The fading wind stirred her hair. By the time she reached the propeller, it had stopped completely, and she hid behind it while Loqrin, his men, and the people below secured the zeppelin to the ground. A rope was thrown from the gondola to the ground, and the zeppelin was reeled in by dim figures that might have been homunculi. Another rope was thrown about the tail section, stabilizing the ship.

The gondola touched ground, and the zeppelin shuddered, nearly throwing Katya. She clung desperately to the propeller shaft, eyes wide. She noted that even though the airship had come to rest, it did not entirely stop moving. It creaked and drifted a bit. The rope about the tail was drawn tight, and it grew more stable. A breeze blew up from the abyss, curiously warm.

Loqrin marched from the zeppelin's interior onto solid ground, his servants and prisoners in tow. Kat cursed him silently from her hiding place.

Half a dozen men bearing alchemical lamps met him in the open. Bizarrely, the men wore suits and hats, and not the gaudy ones favored by gangsters, but expensive, tailored suits designed to be as bland as possible.

Guildsmen, Katya realized. It was for them that Loqrin had dressed up, not his goons. Katya should have known. But what would members of the Guild of Alchemists be doing down here? For that matter, what would Loqrin?

One or two of the Guildsmen touched their hats in a gesture of respect to Loqrin, and others nodded their heads, just slightly. He inclined his head, too, but only just. Peers acknowledging each other, nothing more. No one admitting inferiority.

They exchanged a few words that Katya couldn't hear, then turned about and strolled down the lamp-lit pathway. In the distance, set into the rock of the chasm wall, loomed a great dark structure of some sort. Katya was too far away to see any of its details, and there was too little light to see it by in any case. It was the only building on this shelf of rock, the only one in the area for that matter, which struck her as odd. She thought the zeppelin had passed numerous other buildings, maybe even a city of the Elders, but if so then this building had been isolated, remote from the city. Why would the Elders have set it apart?

Loqrin and the others vanished inside, Returners, homunculi and prisoners bringing up the rear.

Eerily warm wind gusted up from the abyss. Katya clung to the propeller, wondering what she should do. She was all alone, weaponless. Surely she didn't dare follow them. But if she didn't then why had she come?

"Damn it all," she whispered.

With great care, mindful of her aching arms, she crawled over to the fin assembly and found one of the ropes that moored the tail section to the ground. Very slowly, hand over hand and leg over leg, she shimmied down it, and, when she at last alighted on the ground, she collapsed. Quivered. Her arms shook, her hands spasmed, and her back muscles bunched and writhed. She bit back cries of pain. *Fuck fuck fuck!*

When at last the agony diminished, she just wanted to lay there and rest, but she knew she couldn't. She hauled herself up, stretching her shoulders as she did so. *Ravic better appreciate all this.*

She picked her way toward the building, along the line of lamps. Another line led into a tunnel in the chasm wall, off to the side. The Guildsmen hadn't flown here as Loqrin had, then. Maybe their homunculi had carried them on little litters, like kings, down through corridors in the rock.

As she went, Kat twisted her rings so that the jagged edges faced outward. She was ready.

She neared the great building, feeling tiny hairs stick up on the back of her neck. Green lamplight lit the structure's bulging lower surface, and she saw what resembled a massive protruding belly, studded with odd projections and architectural flourishes that were alien to her. Above the belly stretched a large, thick tower that vanished into darkness. At the very edge of the light above, she thought she saw protrusions like spikes jutting out from the building, high, high above. Things that might have been large bats wheeled about the points.

She faced the opening, a large archway of inhuman dimensions right in the middle of the bulging belly, something that was almost obscene. The Guildsmen's lights were vanishing up the tunnel, and she knew that if she didn't hurry she'd lose them.

"Rat piss," she whispered, and started after them.

Organic lines arched over her, similar to the ones she'd seen in the chasm chamber, like the ribbing of someone's throat. *I'm walking into a gullet*, she thought. Organic-looking archways opened right and left, but the light of the procession of alchemists and mobsters continued straight ahead. She followed, light on her feet, back hunched like a feline, ready to spring into the shadows at the least provocation.

The procession wound up a spiral rampway that must be what the Elders used instead of stairs. *No feet, maybe.* Whatever, the procession continued up the ramp two floors, then took a hallway to the right. Kat followed, breathless and sweaty. At last, finally, the procession reached their destination: a strangely cavernous room, its walls lined with what looked like black grills and a huge apparatus toward the center rear. Kat hung back, watching from around the corner of the doorway.

Machines that looked like they were man-made littered the room, and cables snaked from them, across the floors, vanishing into the black grills. As Kat watched, the alchemists toyed with the machines, which began to hum, click and pulse with lights. Loqrin Mars watched on, face impassive. The captured strikers were still hooded, so they couldn't see where they were, but they must have felt something unnatural, or perhaps they merely knew something unpleasant was going to happen to them—it wouldn't have taken much effort—because they suddenly began shaking and struggling against the ropes that bound their wrists. One wet his pants; the urine puddling on the floor. Another tried to bolt, blindly, but was struck in the face with the butt of a rifle and knocked off his feet. Kat said a prayer under her breath. She wished there was some way she could help them. But if she revealed herself, she'd only wind up next to them, hooded and bound.

The alchemists finished with the machines, and the huge apparatus began to make an odd thrumming noise. The Guildsmen must have found some way to hot-wire the machine, to awaken Elder technology using human devices. How long had they been working at this? Katya couldn't imagine it had been easy.

"Let the first one go," announced a Guildsman. He was not the tallest, but he was the broadest and he carried himself with a certain air of authority, more so than the others. He had a short black mustache and a square, balding head. Intelligent eyes peered out from gold-rimmed frames. "Do you agree?" he asked Loqrin.

"I do," said Loqrin. He motioned to the man with the scarred face, who oversaw the other goons. At the man's command, they dragged one of the prisoners toward the huge machine.

The Guildsmen pressed buttons, and the machine . . . *opened*. Kat gasped. Made of the same weird black material as the walls, it was shaped something like two great, monstrous bells, one pointing up and one pointing down, joined like clamshells, and now the upper bell rose, revealing a cavity inside, huge, maybe fifty feet high. More man-made machines stood here. Obviously the apparatus had not been meant for people, but the alchemists weren't letting that stop them.

The mob men forced the prisoner up a shallow ramp to the lip of the upward-facing bell, which was slightly submerged, so that the bottom of its bowl was visible. The goons chained the hooded striker to a narrow wall the Guildsmen had installed, and then the mobsters yanked the hood off. The man was pasty and jowled, with an open, honest face and bugged-out eyes. He blinked against the sudden light, then, obviously perceiving that he was in no place he'd ever imagined, he opened his mouth and screamed—and screamed.

Katya jumped at the sound and drew back behind the wall. *What are they going to DO to him? He's probably got a wife at home, kids. Fuck. He didn't do anything to them.*

She peeked out again. The man had screamed himself out and stood there, ragged and panting. Tears coursed down his whiskered cheeks. His legs trembled and had given out, but the chains held him upright.

Completely oblivious to his terror, the Guildsmen stood over their machines, punching and tapping at buttons, spinning dials. Intent expressions twisted their faces.

"Well?" Loqrin demanded.

The black-mustached man glared at him. "Just a moment more, Minister."

Minister? Kat thought. *But that doesn't make any sense!* She knew the Guild was run by a cabal of Ministers, the chief one being Archminister Barnes. But Loqrin was a Boss, not a Guildsman.

"As you will," Loqrin said, then added, "Minister."

Kat frowned. They were *both* Ministers?

The black-mustached Minister went back to his work, until at last he straightened. "There. We've reached the next frequency on our list. Everything is on schedule." He said this shortly, as if insulted by Loqrin's doubt.

"Excellent," Loqrin returned, as if he were humoring the man.

The Guildsman narrowed his eyes behind his gold-rimmed glasses. Rather than reply, he directed his attention at a subordinate.

"Begin," he said.

The subordinate began a procedure, tapping buttons into a console. The huge overhead bell-shaped dome that had lifted before, revealing the cavity, slammed closed, locking the striker inside and sealing him off from view.

"Beginning translation," the subordinate said.

The humming noise the bell-shaped apparatus emitted grew in intensity. The room began to shake. Loqrin and the Guildsmen were prepared, donning ear-muffs. The sound washed over Kat, shaking her, making her bones ache, her ears pop. She stuck fingers in them and ground her jaw.

At the same time, light flashed out of the machine, seeping through the minute crack that joined upper and lower portions, and out of light-vents at its top. The illumination, to Kat's shock, was *purple*. The air seemed to ripple around the machine, and Kat smelled strange scents, things she had never smelled before. She had no names for them.

Above the high-pitched, chalkboard-scraping hum she heard another sound: the striker screaming.

Fuck fuck fuck.

The screaming went on and on. Gradually, the light and noise, including the screaming, died away. When it had tapered off, Kat removed the fingers from her ears but still heard a ringing. Purple spots danced before her eyes.

"Well?" the black-mustached man demanded. "Did it work?"

The subordinate scanned a crude monitor. "Indeterminate, sir. He definitely made contact with Plane 249K-F. And his mind has altered."

"Wonderful. Take him out and open up his frontal lobe. Then we'll know for sure." He pointed to the line of homunculi that stood silently along one wall. Each held a strange-looking object, a sort of metal spear, except that the tip was not sharp but looked like some bizarre light bulb ringed by metal bars. "You lot stand ready, just in case."

The homunculi made no sign of acknowledgement.

The Minister turned back to the apparatus. "Open it," he ordered.

More punching and tapping, and the upper half of the Elders' machine lifted up. Purplish gas flooded outward, and sparks danced inside it. The bell-shaped top half rose, at last gliding to a stop. Dimly through the smoke, Katya thought she could see a dark figure, but she couldn't make out any details.

"Fetch him," the black-mustached Minister ordered.

Loqrin, instead of looking eager like the others, seemed cagey. He stepped back and nodded significantly to the scarred man, who returned the nod. The goons also stepped back, raising their weapons.

Kat held her breath.

The Guildsmen moved forward, cautiously. The Minister stood back, jaw set, eyes hard.

The purple gas flooded out, then began to thin. The dark shape started to take form. Backs hunched in unconscious defense, the Guildsmen reached the short ramp leading up to the cavity of the apparatus. The dark shape *moved*.

It flowed outward. It did not step, it did not spring. It *flowed*. Even as it moved, it seemed to enlarge, and Kat saw a strange, unnatural outline, an outline that moved and changed with every moment—like water, she thought, though it was anything but.

Gelatinous and horrible, the shape flowed toward the Guildsmen. At the last second, they dove away. Too late. A cord-like appendage whipped out from the thing and penetrated the head of one of the Guildsmen. Instantly he jerked, twitched. Saliva ran down from one corner of his mouth. His eyes popped.

The cord withdrew. Skull steaming, the man slumped to the ground.

The thing rolled forward, hovering above the floor, and more cords whipped out, striking into more Guildsmen skulls. Screams echoed off the weird black walls.

It was chaos then, purple smoke drifting everywhere, the thing flowing here and there, appearing and then vanishing through the walls of smoke. The black-mustached Minister fled behind his line of homunculi, and the surviving Guildsmen tried to follow. Loqrin's goons fired their guns. Kat jumped at the noise.

Loqrin, however, stood firm. When the thing materialized out of a roil of smoke right before him, he made a strange sign in the air, and the being moved off. Kat stared, speechless. Her own legs shook, and a deep, dark, cold terror awoke somewhere in her guts and at the base of her spine. She felt like a rat might have felt in primal times, huddling beneath the ground as some massive saurian thing rocked the earth above it. Helpless and tiny and, as Jack would say, over her head.

The black-mustached Minister barked an order to the homunculi, and they sprang forward. The tips of their black spears burst into life, crackling and distorting the air around them. When the haunt, for that it most surely was, flowed toward the shrinking Guildsmen, the homunculi thrust their electric lances at it. The tips exploded, and the haunt shrank away. A high-pitched, inhuman scream made Kat gasp.

The haunt apparently decided it was time to go.

It flowed up out of the room, toward the exit. Toward Kat.

She stumbled back. Gunshots rang out, as Loqrin's goons continued to fire at the creature, but if they made any impact it gave no sign. Kat turned and started to run, the gunshots covering her footfalls.

From the coldness behind her and the prickling on the nape of her neck, she felt the haunt draw closer, closer. It was going to feed on her brain!

Oh shit oh shit oh shit oh—

At last it was on her.

She wheeled. Threw herself to the floor. Stared up at the being as it descended on her. She saw its strange, gelatinous mass, oddly-shaped wings extended, more like the wings of a manta ray, she thought, than a bat, really, cords rippling around it like the tentacles of a jellyfish. As it moved closer to her, she saw something at its core, like a bright blue fire, revealed now as if shadows parted from its depths, and inside that blue fire was the striker, the man the Guildsmen had imprisoned within the apparatus, the man they had used as a guinea pig. He did not seem alive, or in any way aware. He hung slackly, eyes open but flat and dull, mouth agape, suspended like a puppet with its strings cut in the midst of the blue flame, which did not seem to consume him. Then the shadows changed, concealed the man and his enveloping flame once more, and the haunt fell on her.

Her mind spun, frantic. Almost without thinking she raised her hands and made the sign Loqrin had. Before her face, she traced a sort of spiral with the index finger of her left hand. With her right hand, she made a fist and placed it over her heart.

She felt coldness wash over her, and the shape eclipsed her sight. The haunt was gone.

Gasping, shivering, she turned around, but the thing was nowhere to be seen.

Chapter 7

Inside the chamber of the apparatus, the Guildsmen arranged their dead—four fallen, all with steaming skulls. They seemed more concerned by their equipment, however, which was in disarray. Loqrin and the Minister exchanged heated words in a corner while the others cleaned up. Katya, still shaking, listened in:

"It's taking too damned long!" Loqrin said. "Delay after delay!"

"Why, that's nonsense," said the black-mustached Minister.

"Is it, Tully? This is the second time in as many attempts that we've produced a haunt. Tell me, is that your goal? Is that what I've spent so much effort facilitating?"

Minister Tully, if that was his name, looked both angry and abashed. His face was red and sweaty. "You know good and well that's not true. Two nights ago we achieved a good measure of success—eliminated three frequencies—"

"And on the fourth—" Loqrin drew a line across his throat, by which Katya took to mean a haunt had been produced. "*Three out of four.* Are those really acceptable odds to you?"

Tully glared. "A few losses are acceptable . . ."

Loqrin started to say something, but held himself back. *Katya* knew why, even if Tully didn't. Loqrin *wanted* to produce haunts. That much was obvious. She didn't know why, she didn't know how, but clearly Loqrin and the haunts were in league, involved in some unholy bargain— yet Minister Tully and the other Guildsmen had no idea.

Katya had half a mind to stand up and tell them, but, like Loqrin, she held herself back.

The Guildsmen doctored their equipment for a time, then debated on whether or not to continue the experiments.

"If only we knew why the equipment was acting faulty," one of the subordinates said. "According to our readings, it should have translated successfully."

"Then I'm paying you too much!" Tully snapped. He shook his head, agitated. "Well, we're not quitting now. We've got too much invested, and too much at stake. Do you realize what it could *mean* if we're successful?"

The subordinate nodded eagerly, but looked fearful. "Of course, sir. Great things. Marvelous things. But . . . dangerous."

Tully shoved his face close to the other's, and the subordinate swallowed and glanced away. "Ready the equipment for another try, damn you. We still have five more test subjects to go through."

At this, the five prisoners, still hooded, screamed and cursed and wept, and Loqrin's goons beat them until they subsided. Katya closed her eyes and counted to ten, then opened them.

The next two hours passed slowly and horribly. Once the equipment was readied to the Guildsmen's satisfaction, they chained one more bloody factory worker up inside the apparatus, closed it, fired it up, then opened it up again, this time sending in the homunculi first. The homuncs came back out dragging a limp body with a steaming head, and the Guildsmen excitedly gathered around it like a pack of hungry vultures. Katya watched in disgust as they, with scientific patience and precision, hoisted the man on a steel lab table and sawed open his skull. Gouts of steam issued forth. Careful of the heat, they studied various portions of the brain, cutting some pieces away for study later, making notes on clipboards all the while. From time to time they would take out strange-looking cameras that looked overly bulky to Katya and flashed pictures; the bulbs flashed various colors, from red to green to purple and more. Not white.

Then they moved on to the next poor, doomed factory worker, and the next, until at last all were dead and their skulls cut open. Katya couldn't watch the dissections after the first one, and she felt nauseous and weak throughout the whole ordeal. She just wanted to jump up and scream at the alchemists, to grab up one of their scalpels or bone saws and hack away at them. Instead she wept quietly in the corner, shaking and holding herself. *One day*, she thought. *One day they'll get theirs, the fuckers. I'll make sure of it.*

The worst thing about it all was how calmly the alchemists went about their grisly business. Not for one second did they evince the slightest concern for any of their test subjects, not once did they offer them any words of comfort or even a glass of water. The least they could've done was tranquilize the poor bastards, Kat thought. Whatever happened in the translation chamber—a phrase she overheard the Guildsmen using—was evidently very painful. Every time it was fired up, the victim screamed and screamed, until they could scream no more.

There were no more haunt visitations, or creations, and the Guildsmen were plainly quite relieved at this. Loqrin paced back and forth, silent for the most part, holding his own counsel. What was his game? Whatever it was, Katya vowed that she would find it out and shove it up his ass.

At last the moment came when the Guildsmen completed their experiments and prepared to leave. They were tired and sweaty from stress, but they were clearly enthusiastic about their results. They talked heatedly among themselves as they walked toward the chamber's exit, and Katya wished she had time to eavesdrop—not that she could understand their techno-babble anyway. In any case, she ran ahead of them, back down the hallways and ramps, retracing her steps, once getting lost—she nearly died of fright when that happened—until at last she left the building of the Elders behind and returned to the zeppelin. Climbing up that rope was much more difficult than shimmying down it, but she managed it. The old aches in her hands, arms and back started to flare again, but they'd had a few hours to relax and were more manageable. She hid herself behind the propeller as Loqrin and his goons entered the gondola, then crawled upwards. She had gone to the narrow tail end, and it was easy to scamper up to the top. This way she would be better concealed and also able to rest a little.

One of the goons untied the rope wrapped around the tail assembly and joined his master in the gondola. The ropes connecting the gondola were reeled up.

Below, the alchemists spoke passionately to each other as they filed toward the passageway Kat had seen earlier and vanished down it, homunculi surrounding them, guarding them—from what?

Whatever, as Heather would say. The important thing was that they hadn't even glanced Katya's way. She was safe. Idly she supposed that there must be easy access to the surface from the direction they were going, and that they had swift and comfortable vehicular travel waiting for them.

The zeppelin's propellers roared to life, and the zeppelin was off. Relief washed through her as she saw the strange building of the Elders, with its horrible translation chamber, diminish—slowly, too slowly—into the shadows.

After some time, the zeppelin ascended the vertical shaft and Kat had to blink her eyes against the sudden brightness of stars and moons above. It was a welcome pain, though, and she savored the sight of the night sky as the airship passed above the lip of the Sink and rose over the sleeping tenements below. She nearly let herself drowse, but the constant whipping of the wind wouldn't let her.

Time to leave. Time to leave Loqrin, and the Hollows. She had learned just about everything she could. She still didn't know what it was about, not exactly, but she thought she knew enough. She would tell Ravic to send some of his men into the Below and wait till the next time Loqrin went down there. Ravic could take him by surprise, then get the rest of the answers out of the mad bastard the hard way. Katya would gladly pitch in.

Her gaze drifted to the west and, after some searching, picked out the broad buildings of the Fifth Ward. *Home.* It seemed very far away. Somewhere over there Ravic was waiting for her.

Ravic . . .

He's just a father figure. Gods, girl. Give it up.

The zeppelin docked with the Arch, and the impact nearly knocked Kat off. In any case, she was jarred back to herself. She heard the noises of Loqrin and company exiting the gondola below. When they seemed safely away, she descended the face of the blimp, clawing her way down with her jagged rings like a cat descending from a tree, but slowly, very slowly.

When she was most of the way down, her eyes picked out a tiny flame in the docking bay—a cigarette! Her heart nearly stopped. She couldn't see the smoker's details, not exactly, it was too dark, but by his tall frame and noble profile she knew it could be no one but Loqrin. He must have lingered to have a smoke and watch the zeppelin drift off.

Her sliding, scrabbling movement seemed to have drawn his attention. His shadow-cloaked head snapped up toward her. His shoulders tensed. The cigarette paused halfway to his lips.

"Fuck," she said.

Suddenly, the pilot of the zeppelin fired up the engines. The shudder jolted Kat out of her paralysis.

Frantic, she slid down the rest of the way. Nearly missed the docking bay altogether. She leapt. Landed on her belly. Struck her chin, bit her tongue. Cursing and spitting blood, she shot to her feet. Not a moment too soon. Gunfire erupted. A bullet punched through the ceiling of the docking bay right where she had lain.

With a yelp, she jumped forward, over the bullet hole

Another crash cut the night. Another. Bullets whined about her head.

"Fuckfuckfuckfuck."

She threw herself off the docking bay and onto the ceiling of the Arch. The roof here was thicker; she doubted a bullet could pass through it. Still, no reason to linger. Sweat beaded her brow, stuck her blouse to the small of her back. Her legs shook.

What could she do? Loqrin probably hadn't been able to tell who she was, just as she hadn't been able to tell who he was, not really. He would have just seen a woman-shaped shadow sliding down the zeppelin. That meant that all he had to do was return to the harem and find which girl was missing.

She had to beat him to it.

Picking herself up, she found the sheet-rope where she'd left it, stuck between two of the decorative mounds, and ran as fast as she could back to the roof over the harem. The wind blasted her and the mounds slipped under her feet. She fell twice, but she popped right back up. Her heart smashed against her ribs like a bulldog trying to break its chain.

Quickly, she placed her shoe-anchor—it looked like it would only last one more time—and lowered herself to the harem balcony.

Her fingers trembled so badly she could barely open the sliding glass door, but somehow she managed it, slamming it shut behind her. Inside the Dolls' Club the inmates lounged drunkenly, pretty much in the same places she'd left them. Heather, long black cigarette in her lips, walked around emptying ash trays into a trashcan she carried in one hand. Vaguely phosphorescent smoke drifted up from her cigarette.

Her eyes lit up when she saw Kat. She dropped the trashcan and started to run over. Frantically Kat shook her head, warning her off.

"No time—" she started to say.

The heavy vault door made a ticking sound, indicating the wheel on the other side had just begun to spin.

Heather gasped.

Hells, Katya thought. Her clothes were in disarray and stained with the grime that coated the zeppelin. In one quick motion, she tore off her blouse, stepped out of her skirt, and flung them both in the corner.

Before they even landed, the door flew open, and Loqrin stood in the doorway.

Heather took a step back. Some of the dolls stirred, shrank back, or even cried out. One fled from the room, weeping. Katya did the only thing she could think of. She gyrated her hips and shook her arms over her head and said, "And that's how you do the Bolustin." Panting and standing in her mismatched underwear, she turned to Loqrin and smiled, perhaps too widely. "Hi," she said.

He narrowed his eyes. She cursed herself. Dancing had been the only thing she could think of that would explain her sweat and position. She was all too aware of her skinned cheek, but she hoped the strike Loqrin had dealt her earlier would explain that.

He glared at her, then swept the rest of the room. Heather stood staring at him, a deer caught in the headlights. She looked even more frightened than Katya felt. Perhaps too much. Loqrin seemed to focus on her.

"What's going on here?" he said.

Heather opened her mouth but no words came out.

Loqrin glanced to the balcony. "Ah-ha!" In four strides, he had torn the balcony door open and was outside, jerking at something.

Shit. Katya hadn't had time to discard the sheet-rope. Now Loqrin yanked it down and returned inside, holding it up triumphantly.

"What's *this?*" He shook it in Kat's face because she was closest, and she made a show of swallowing and widening her eyes.

"I-I don't know," she said.

Her apparent fear seemed to irritate him. He struck her. She reeled backward, stumbled over the prone body of the black-haired boy and fell on her backside.

"Whose is this?" Loqrin roared, shaking the sheet-rope.

Silence greeted him. Wind hissed in through the open terrace door.

"Fine," he snarled, "then I guess I'll have to *extract* the information." Savage pleasure lit his eyes.

No no, Kat thought. *I can't let him torture the dolls.* She started to open her mouth to confess, knowing as she did that she was damning Lavorgna to whatever madness Loqrin had gotten under way.

Heather overcame her shock first. Though still trembling, she stepped forward. "I believe that's mine," she said.

It was Katya's turn to stare. *Heather, what are you doing?*

"You!" Loqrin bellowed. He marched forward and belted Heather, hard, across the face. She flew backward, hit the rear of the couch, toppled over it and went sliding across several drugged-up dolls. One of them swatted at her feebly. Another shrieked, tried to stand, and fell over. Some of the more lucid ones, however, had already risen and were backing up into the corners of the room.

Loqrin leaned over the couch, grabbed Heather by the throat and hurled her to the ground before him. "Why?" he demanded. As he strode toward her, he raised the sheet-rope in his arm. Like a whip, he cracked it, and the broken green shoe smashed Heather's upper right arm. She screamed. "Not such a fun toy *now*, is it?"

Kat had seen enough. "No," she said. Shakily, she stood to her feet. "Don't—"

Loqrin started to turn his attention to her, but Heather spoke up suddenly: "Because I *hate* you!" she said.

He returned his attention her. Her words seemed to amuse him. "Well, that's too bad for you, girl. But, you know, I can't help but think that's not the only reason. There's something funny going on here, and I mean to find out what."

"No, really—" Kat started, stopping only when Heather shot her a furious glare that said, *Don't waste this!* The look contained such venom that Kat closed her mouth.

Loqrin hadn't seemed to notice. After coiling the sheet-rope in one hand, he crossed over to Heather, grabbed a fistful of her pretty auburn hair, and dragged her across the floor and into his lair, slamming the vault door shut behind them. Just before the door shut, Heather's gaze met Katya's, and Kat saw a single tear under Heather's right eye. Then BANG! Katya jumped at the stark, metallic sound. And she knew, right then, that she could not let Heather do this. Katya could fight her own godsdamned battles. She wouldn't let someone else sacrifice themselves, especially not someone like Heather, who deserved so much better.

Furious, Katya turned to the glazed-eyed dolls. "Well," she demanded, "are you just gonna lie there, or are you gonna *do* something?"

They stared back at her as though she were an alien. Well, most of them. A few of the more sober ones looked fearful and worried. They had looked on Heather like a mother. One or two even looked ashamed.

"What can we do?" asked Brennon. He sat on a sky blue couch holding a clay pipe in his hands.

"Well, for a starter," Kat said, "you can put down that fucking pipe."

He blinked down at the pipe. "The pipe?" It was as if she was speaking a different language.

"Yeah." She snorted. "Like this." She marched up to him and snatched the pipe away. He tried to swat it out of her hand, but it was a weak effort. Angrily, she grabbed up another pipe, and then a pouch full of Az. Complaints rose about her, but in the face of Heather's disappearance the complaints were muted. "Like *this*!" she said.

Heatedly, she ran down a hallway toward the bathroom. Perhaps sensing what she was about to do, more cries and shouts rose behind her. She flung the drugs down the hole onto the immense mound of shit below, and laughed. Gratified, she marched back into the main room and snatched up more drugs and drug paraphernalia.

"You can't do that!" one girl said. She slapped Kat across the face.

Kat slapped her back. "I just did!"

Again she ventured to the shit-hole and flung the drugs into the fecal mound below. "This is where it belongs!" she shouted. Another trip, and another. "See?" she demanded. "Right fucking down there!" A couple of the dolls, the ones who had looked ashamed, were actually helping her, earning them sharp glances and punches on the arms from their confederates. "She's right," said her helpers. "We should've done this a long time ago!" "Fuck you!" came the response. A few fights broke out.

When Katya had at last disposed of most of the available dope, she returned to the living room to find many of the dolls on their feet, cursing her and shouting angrily. The few that had helped her shoved them back, clearing a way for her.

"You oughta be ashamed!" Kat said. "Ashamed! How could you let him do this to you? Look at yourselves!"

The girl she had slapped earlier stepped forward. "What would you have us do, bitch?"

Kat lifted her lip in a snarl. "There's almost *thirty* of you! There's *one* of him! Next time he comes to you, rip him to fucking shreds!"

Most of them just gazed at her with those same watery, fearful eyes.

"Well, then, if you can't help me," Kat said, "then get the fuck out of my way!"

As if her angry words had invoked some wrathful spirit, just then screams of pain drifted into the room. The dolls started. Eyes swiveled to the vault door. The screams didn't come through the door, Katya realized—what could?—but they came through the glass of the terrace door. And they came from—there could be no doubt—Heather. As the dolls stared in horror at the door, she screamed again.

Chills coursed down Kat's spine. "We have to *do* something!"

"But what?" said the girl she'd slapped. Kat thought her name was Magan.

"You're going to help?" Katya said.

Magan stared at the people about her, then nodded, as if daring them to argue.

Kat felt a sudden swell of pride. "Well, for starters, I'm going to need some more sheets. And a shoe."

Three minutes later saw her scrambling, desperate, over the roof of the arch. Wind knocked at her, nearly spilling her off. A storm swept in from the Atomic Sea to the east. Thunder rolled in the distance. Winter weather, she knew. She thought she felt a touch of winter chill as she scrambled along. Below and before her, in Loqrin's suite, Heather screamed in pain, and Katya ground her teeth. *I'm gonna get that bastard,* she thought. *I'm gonna make him wish he was never born!* Lightning stabbed down, lighting the sky to the west, over the Fifth Ward. Kat longed to return there.

At last she reached the roof over Loqrin's suite. Carefully, she placed her sheet-rope and lowered herself to Loqrin's terrace. Just as her bare feet touched down, another scream pealed through the night. Katya winced.

The apartment was dark, as before, with just a few alchemical lamps providing alternately green and red illumination. They hinted at expensive paintings, mirrors, a chandelier, but they were only hints, the sparkle off glass, the reflection in brass.

Heather was all too visible. Katya felt something sick trickle through her as she saw what Loqrin had done to her.

Completely naked, Heather hung by her wrists from the ceiling, her back to the terrace.

Loqrin paced back and forth behind her, tiger-like. He had discarded the rope-whip for a true whip, made of rawhide. Fury twisted his handsome features.

"Who set you up to this?" he roared, raising his arm.

"No one—" Heather started.

That was all she got out, as Loqrin brought his arm down, with all his strength, and the lash struck Heather's narrow back with the force of a hurricane. She screamed so loudly her lungs should have burst. The lash peeled away a long strip of skin, and blood wept down from the wound. Her back was criss-crossed with long, similar gashes. *Dear fuck,* Katya thought. *What has he DONE?*

The impact of the whip rocked Heather forward, then back. Blood trickled down her legs, finally dripping from her toes to form a puddle on the floor.

Katya could take no more. She'd had a full day to think about how she might have saved the man from yesterday, and now she knew what she could have done. She swiveled the glittering, silver rings on her pointer finger so that they faced inward, then scratched a line in the glass around the door's locking mechanism. Taking a deep breath, she stuck out her tongue and pressed it to the cut-out section of glass, then, very gingerly, pulled her head back. Presto! The piece of glass fell into her hand.

Even more gingerly, she snaked her hand through the opening and unlocked the terrace door. A soft scrape, and the door glided open.

"What's this?" Loqrin said.

Every hair on the back of Kat's neck stood up. Her heart trembled.

"Gone into a faint, have you? Well, that won't do."

Kat's heart started again.

In his torture area, Loqrin pulled a lever, and Heather's limp form unwound from the ceiling. He untied her hands and carried her over to what looked like a surgical bed. It's where he had been playing with Abby's body earlier. There was no sign of Abby now, but Katya saw leather straps where wrists and ankles should be. Loqrin laid Heather down—*back down, the fucker!*—on the bed, and began to strap her down. A table of gleaming instruments lay on his right, some of them sharp, some of them dull, some of them shapes Katya had never seen before and that she could not imagine the purposes of. She did not want to.

"Well, my dear," Loqrin said, though Heather still seemed to be out, "it has been a long journey we have taken together, you and I. Perhaps, if you cooperate, it will not end here. I have ways, techniques. I could extend your service to me . . . indefinitely." He stroked one of Heather's legs as he said this, and Kat shook.

Loqrin was utterly absorbed. He did not notice Katya sneaking up behind him. As light as a feather, she made her way through that dark, spooky lair, until she was almost breathing down his neck.

"But," Loqrin said, a trace of sadness—but also, strangely glee—in his voice, "if you do *not* cooperate, I'm afraid, I'm very much afraid, that your mind will be a meal for the Leviathan."

Kat reached him. Then, without thinking very much about it, she picked up the sharpest-looking scalpel she could find on the instrument table—and stabbed him as hard as she could in the back. The blade penetrated under his left shoulder-blade, and she *pushed down*.

He screamed and spun. Almost as reflex action, he hit her, hard, sending her flying backward. Kat struck the floor and slid.

Meanwhile, Loqrin's scream and the pain of being placed on her back seemed to have half-roused Heather, who began to sit up.

Ignoring her, Loqrin raised his head to let out a howl: "GET HER!"

Katya, feeling a ringing in her skull, felt a vague premonition. Then, before she had time to rise, clicking and scuffling sounded in the edges of the room. Dark, shadowy shapes lurched toward her.

Her blood ran cold.

They were dolls. Every one of them, and there were probably half a dozen. Young men and women. All naked, and all . . . mechanized. Clockwork gears spun inside visible skulls, or gears ticking in ribcages, or handles jutting from sides. Lifeless yet moving in odd jerks and twitches, the wretched things advanced on Katya. Tick. Tick. Tick. A long blade gleamed where a boy's arm should be. A coo-coo clock thrust past one girl's lips, then retracted, then popped back out again, but instead of a bird there was a corkscrew on the end of it. Scissor-like appendages snapped in place of one girl's hands.

It was the young woman called Abby, Katya was sure of it. "No . . ."

Abby stepped forward, scissors snapping, eyes blank.

The wretched things had been still until called, but now they moved with surprising speed. Katya had a plan, but she had not expected this. Anything but this. Feeling as if she was about to vomit, she sprang up and leapt at the vault door that connected Loqrin's suite to the harem, which stood at the base of a short flight of dark granite steps. This side, of course, was not locked. She grabbed the wheel in both hands, wrenched it to the right. Metal squealed. Clicked. She pulled—*pulled*—

Footsteps right behind her. Tick. Tick.

She *pulled*.

The clack-clack of scissors. The whish of blades.

Kat ducked, spun aide.

The door drifted open. Light flooded up from the harem chamber. Katya jumped at Abby, sweeping under her lethal arms and tackling her to the stairs. One of the arms fell off. Loqrin hadn't quite finished with her, and the stitching was crude. Kat sat on Abby's chest, thinking, *Poor girl.* Abby's skull was still intact, and Kat wondered how much of the girl's brains still survived. Was she present? Was she staring up at Kat out of that gray, pretty face? If so, she must long for death.

Half hating herself, Kat obliged. She grabbed up Abby's fallen arm, raised it overhead so that the blades pointed down, and stabbed, right into the smooth white forehead. There was a crunch, the sound of a spring snapping, and the girl sagged.

And *still* she moved, her clock-work parts still working. A leg kicked. The scissors on her one arm still snapped. But she did not rise.

Gasping, Kat stood up and stumbled back. To her right, Loqrin was swearing and cursing at one of his dead dolls as it tried to yank the scalpel from his back. Blood drenched his clothes. Behind him, Heather sat up, shaking her head. She looked weak.

Three dark figures lurched toward Kat. Tick tick tick. She staggered backward. She felt the warmth of light on her back, heard the sounds of the boys and girls in the harem. They had seen her fight Abby. Some were impressed. Some were afraid. Which way would they go?

Angrily, she turned to them, at the same time pointing a finger toward the direction of the approaching clock-work dolls.

"You want your damned drugs!" she said. "Go and get them! Loqrin has stores of them in his lair! Come on, you pussies, get off your asses and help me out, if only to get your motherfucking drugs back!"

A full dozen of them stepped through the doorway and moved around Kat. The young woman Kat had slapped earlier squeezed her shoulder. "Are you all right?" Genuine concern touched her voice.

Surprised, Kat nodded. "Better hurry, Magan. The others'll get to the dope first."

"I just came for the fight."

She grinned a hard grin, and Kat returned it.

The living dolls came upon the dead ones, and numbers were on their side. The dead ones cracked and splintered, breaking apart on the floor, as the living ones struck them with jars filled with specimens and unopened champagne bottles. Loqrin, watching from his lab, sputtered in rage. "No!" he shouted. *"No!"*

Wild-eyed, he disengaged himself from the single remaining clock-work doll, the one who had been ineffectually helping him, and vanished deeper into the apartment. While some of the harem girls and boys scoured the rooms for drugs and others for weapons, Kat approached Heather and helped her to her feet. Heather winced with every movement. Blood caked her back and the table where she had lain.

"Damn," Katya whispered. Then: "Thank you."

Heather offered a small, pain-filled smile. "Thank *you*."

"Come on."

"GET THEM!" thundered Loqrin, appearing from nowhere.

Behind him stood a huge Returner, dead flesh peeling off his wide face. Worms wriggled through it. A foul reek rose from him, making Katya gag. He must have been sealed up somewhere, an early model, a last resort. He was certainly no doll.

The monster lurched toward Kat and Heather, heavy and huge but slow.

Satisfied, Loqrin slipped away. A scalpel gleamed from his hand, and as his former playthings tried to fall on him, he slashed and wheeled, and they fell back, clutching at themselves. At last he reached the far door and spun the wheel. On the other side, Katya knew, were the quarters where Loqrin's goons lived. She figured it must be a great humiliation for him to ask them for aid against his harem subjects, and she relished it, even as she helped Heather stagger to the harem door.

The creature stalked after them, one heavy footfall after another. He moved slowly, but inexorably, an approaching storm.

"Run!" Kat shouted to the dolls. "Get out of here now! Loqrin's goons are coming! And watch *this* bloody bastard!"

Heather couldn't bear having an arm go around her back, so instead both of her hands gripped Katya's left arm tightly, so tightly it felt as it the blood had stopped flowing in that limb. Not caring, Katya helped her through the door. Half-naked young men and women flooded past them, screaming. The monster stalked right behind.

Katya turned her head to see several of the dolls try to slam the vault door in its face. Too late. The creature knocked them away, ducked its head to avoid the ceiling, and stepped through.

"Shit," Kat said. "What have I *done*? It'll kill us all!"

"This way," Heather hissed, pain making her voice ragged.

She guided Kat down a hallway.

"What do we do?" a boy yelled.

"Follow us!" she said.

The creature stomped after them, trailing blood. It must have stepped in someone's body, Kat thought. A length of intestine coiled around its ankle. One of the dolls, probably, a victim of Loqrin's scalpel.

Kat and Heather stumbled into the bathroom. The shit hole gaped. A breeze gusted up, bringing with it a nasty stench. Katya thought she realized what Heather wanted. Maybe she could improve on the plan. Thinking fast, she pressed herself against the wall. With a squeal of pain, Heather did likewise. Several of the boys and girls followed them in, chased by the creature. Others must have scattered throughout the apartment, because Kat could hear their screams. Loqrin's goons might have already appeared. She hoped not.

The creature stomped in, a groan on its lips.

"Now!" Katya said.

She jumped on its back, keeping one hand on Heather's wrist as she did so, forcing Heather to jump with her. The monster teetered on the edge of the shit hole. Katya wrapped her arms around its thick neck, rocked her body to tip the Returner. She felt Heather wrap her own arms around Katya's middle.

The monster teetered . . . teetered . . .

. . .*fell* . . .

Katya knew it was coming, but when it did she screamed anyway. Wind tore through her hair. She pressed her face against the monster's neck. They fell, and fell, and her stomach churned. Heather screamed in her ear.

This better work. If the shit mound didn't soften their landing—

Splat! They struck. Kat knocked her forehead against the creature's skull—

Blackness.

Then, "Come on, come on."

Rain pattered down on her. Heather stood above her, framed against the light of a gaslamp. Katya blinked, her mind catching up. Slowly. Groaning, she felt about her. They were on a great soft mound, with grass growing up its sides. Then the smell hit her, and she wanted to retch.

"No time," Heather said, tugging on her arm.

Kat groaned, allowing Heather to pull her up.

Sudden terror swept her. "The others!" she gasped. "Oh, shit, we've fucked them all!"

She looked up. A small flicker of light revealed the outlines of the shit-hole in the Arch fifty feet overhead. Small faces ringed the hole, staring down at them. Katya could imagine their fear. Behind them, somewhere in the suite, gunshots rang.

Then, to her horror, she saw one of the shapes detach itself from the others—

And jump.

"No!" Katya cried.

It was too late.

The shape fell and fell, resolving into a boy, she thought it might be the one with the black hair but couldn't be sure. He fell, fifty feet at least. Katya couldn't bear to watch. She turned away right before he struck the mound of shit and piss and grass and mud, all wet now because of the rain, softened further by the creature's impact. *Thunk.*

A long silence stretched. Rain pattered on the mound, trickled over folds and bulwarks of fecal matter.

"Well?" she demanded.

Heather just stood there, pale and stiff.

Katya realized she'd have to look. Trembling, she forced her head to turn. At first all she could see was the mound, ten feet high, glistening and awful, the reek filling her nose. Somewhere in that mound was the Returner, possibly still alive—or whatever. Hopefully it was sinking to the bottom.

Just as she thought this, something stirred inside the mound. She began to scream, then saw that it was not the Returner but the boy. Not the black-haired one, but the boy with the birthmark on his arm.

Panting and laughing, he pumped his fists over his head and whooped in delight. A ragged cheer drifted down from the dolls above.

Happiness ran through Katya so quickly and so fiercely that she wrapped her arms about Heather, forgetting the other girl's injury for a moment, and hugged her tight. And so happy was Heather that she hugged her back, at least for a second. Then a pained gasp in Katya's ear reminded her. Abashed, she drew back her arms.

"We have to get out of here," Kat said.

Heather nodded tightly. "You're taking me with you?"

Kat combed a strand of hair over Heather's ear. "You need to see a doctor, H. You've lost a lot of fucking blood."

Heather smiled tiredly. She really did look pale. "There's that word again."

Kat gripped Heather's hand. "Come on. No, wait!"

She'd spotted something sticking out of the mound of feces. She ducked down, snatched it up, and handed it to Heather. "This should help with the pain."

Gratitude filled Heather's eyes as she saw the syringe, half filled with amber fluid. Hurriedly, but only after cleaning the needle in the rain, Kat helped shoot her up. Heather's face shone with relief almost instantly. That done, Kat tossed away the syringe and took up Heather's hand once more.

As they turned away, another shape leapt from the opening above. Shortly another ragged cheer signaled success. But overhead thunder boomed, and somewhere nearby Loqrin would be livid.

Chapter 8

Loqrin's auto garage sat near the base of the nearest leg of the Arch. Katya had barely noticed it when she arrived, but she led Heather there now. Heather limped, and with every step hissed in pain. Her hisses grew less sharp with every step, though, as the drug took effect. Kat knew they didn't have much time. Whatever goons guarded the garage would receive the alert soon, if they hadn't already. As she drew closer, Kat saw that the garage was a rusty building fashioned of sagging aluminum sheeting. It looked like it would fall down at any moment. Strange to see such a wreck half-leaning against the proud Arch. The rain tap-tap-tapped on it fiercely.

Kat could smell nothing but feces and urine. A layer of the stuff coated her, clogged her nostrils, pasted her mouth. She spat as she went along, pining for a cigarette to mask the taste, then gratefully stepped out from under the Arch.

The rain fell full upon her. She raised her arms and basked in it. The cleansing water pounded down on her, washing away the filth, and she opened her mouth and let it fill up, gargling with the rainwater, then spitting and refilling. She let the rain wash her as much as it could, her hands helping as it did its wonderful work.

Heather joined in. It was obvious that the water cascading over her back pained her even with the drug, but she gritted her teeth and took it. She looked a sight, Kat thought: naked, bloody, mutilated, covered in nastiness. Kat's heart went out to her, but she tried not to look too pitying.

At last Kat got herself as clean as she was going to get. Hopefully it was enough for what she had to do. The storm and the tap-tapping of rain on aluminum were so loud she had to shout to be heard: "You stay here!" she told Heather, who frowned at her. "I'll be right back."

Katya strode toward the open overhead doors of the garage, combing her hair back with her fingers as she went. A half dozen gleaming cars sat under the roof. A single man kept guard. He looked like he was enjoying himself, Katya saw. In shirtsleeves and fedora, he casually leaned against a polished car and smoked a cigarette, staring out at the rain. He wore a pistol on a holster slung beneath his left arm. On the wall behind him dangled his jacket and several sets of keys.

He was young, with stiff black hair and whiskers. He bore the common pasty look of the Hollows, but he was not unhandsome. Too bad he worked for Loqrin.

His eyes widened as Katya sauntered into the garage, and a slow smile slipped across his lean, wolfish face. Kat knew she must look good. Dripping wet, wearing only soaked underwear and bra that was now pretty much see-through, her dark eyes shining with adrenaline. She played it up, shaking her slender hips one way, then the other. The man's eyes followed them like a dog's gaze would follow a treat.

"Well, hello," he said, with the accent she was coming to associate with the Hollows. It sounded somehow old-fashioned, as if people here hadn't had much contact with the outside world for a while.

"Hello," Kat purred. It was good to be out of the rain. It smelled of car wax and grease in the garage. She liked it.

He shoved himself off from the auto and stood up straight. Still smoking, he angled his fedora down low over his brow. "A bit wet for a stroll, ain't it?"

She gave what she hoped was a taunting smile. "I guess you'll have to find out."

He threw back his head and laughed, his hat going askew. "A little hussy with fire! I like it! Who are you, anyway? One of Reddin's girls? Gotta be. I know all of the Boss's. But you *know* I can't nibble Reddin's wares—sad a state as that may be."

She sauntered closer. She could smell his cigarette now. It smelled cheap, but strong. Her limbs felt on fire. She loved the lust in his eyes, and the rain trickling down her made her feel alive.

"Forbidden fruit's the sweetest," she said.

Somewhere thunder crashed. The man jumped, then chuckled at himself. "Yeah," he said, "I guess."

She was near him now. "My rates are reasonable."

"Shit, Reddin must be gettin' bold to send his girlies this way. But—shit—a man can only take so much." He flung down his cigarette, stepped forward and wrapped his arms around her waist. He had narrow hands, with long hairy fingers. They felt warm against her skin.

He bent down to kiss her. She let him. His mouth tasted of nicotine.

At last he drew back. "Oh, girl . . ."

"Mmm," she murmured, running her hands over his chest. With one, she cupped his manhood and began massaging it.

"Yeah," he said. "Yeah . . ." Suddenly his nose wrinkled. He sniffed. "What's that sme—?"

Kat squeezed his balls as tight as she could with her left hand. He lifted his head and screamed. Before he could strike her or pull his gun, she hit him with all the strength she had with her right, smack in the jaw. Her jagged rings bit deep. Blood sprayed from his face, and she instantly felt guilty.

Howling, he collapsed to the side of the car, still moving, trying to get up.

"You bitch!" he said, trying to climb to his feet.

Kat stepped forward, wondering if maybe she could kick him. What would she do if he got up?

Suddenly there came the ringing of metal, and he slumped to the ground. Heather stood behind him, a tire iron gripped in her hands. Behind her flapped the rear door of the garage, banging against the sides.

"Last time I tell you to stay put," Kat said, breathing heavily.

"Darn right," Heather said.

Then, as if she'd used up all her strength in wielding the tire iron, she fell against the car. Kat leapt to her side and caught her.

After several deep breaths, Heather nodded. "I'll be all right."

Kat doubted that. Heather needed serious help, and soon. She patted Heather's arm and went to the rear wall. There she grabbed all the keys from their pegs and returned to the auto Heather leaned against. She ripped open the door, slid inside, not caring about ruining the leather seats. She tried one key after another. Finally the engine roared to life. Heather cheered.

Smiling in satisfaction, Katya threw the rest of the keys in the mud, then popped open the passenger door for Heather. When Heather seemed to be having problems, Kat jumped out and helped her around the side of the car and into her seat. Heather trembled and Katya realized she must be going into shock; she was white as a ghost.

Damn, Katya thought, but tried not to show her worry. She had to put on a brave face for Heather.

"Hang on," Katya said. She ran to the wall, grabbed the goon's jacket and dashed back. With shaking fingers of her own, she helped Heather wrap it about her front like a blanket. It smelled of smoke and grease.

"Thanks," Heather said, snuggling in.

"Yeah," Kat said. Then, in a fit of motherliness, she leaned forward and kissed Heather on the forehead. Drowsily, Heather smiled.

Thunder crashed. Somewhere gunfire sounded. Katya knew she had no time to lose, so she raced around to the other side of the car and kicked the goon away. He was an ass for working for Loqrin, but she didn't actually want to run him over. Before she left, she unbuckled the holster under his armpit and flung the heavy revolver on the car floor beneath Heather's feet.

Katya was just about to go when a last burst of inspiration hit her. She rifled through the goon's pockets. With a cry of delight, she found his pack of cigarettes and lighter, then sprang behind the wheel of the auto.

"We're off!" she said, sticking a cigarette in her mouth and sparking the flame. Light flared, tobacco burned, and she inhaled a deep lung-full of wonderful smoke. "Fuckin' aye," she said, as she kicked the car in gear and rolled out, into the night.

"Do you know how to drive?" Heather asked.

Katya smiled. "We'll *see*, won't we?"

Heather did not look reassured.

Gunshots sounded nearby. Katya jerked her head to see a door burst outward on the far side of the Arch and a tide of angry goons storm out, guns glinting in the rain. Like ants whose nest had been kicked, they swarmed over the grounds. Almost immediately they noted the auto rolling out of the garage and made for it. Kat saw the escaping dolls either scatter or hunker low to the mound of waste. They needn't have bothered. The goons couldn't see them in the dark, and besides they had found their quarry.

"Don't let them escape!" Loqrin bellowed from somewhere.

A gun cracked, and one of the rear windows of the auto exploded. A piece of glass cut Katya's shoulder. Heather screamed.

"Shit!" Kat said.

She punched the gas. The engine roared, and the car lurched forward haltingly. Swearing, she stomped on the clutch, wrestled with the stick. At last it popped into gear, and she drove off. Guns barked and spat behind her, but with the darkness and the distance most missed. A few bullets smashed taillights or punched holes in metal. Another explosion of glass. Spiderweb cracks veined half of the rear window.

"Get down!" Kat said. She leaned over and shoved Heather down.

"Watch where you're going!" Heather screamed.

Kat looked straight ahead, saw a dark blur that may have been another auto. An angry car horn trailed away into the night.

Kat hunched behind the wheel. She could only see part of the road. Either she was too short, or the seat was too low, or the dash too high. Whatever, the bottom half of the front view was obscured. More guns split the night behind her. Then, a terrible sound: engines groaning to life. "Fuck!" she said. "They found the keys!"

"We should have taken them with us," Heather said.

"Now you tell me."

Kat turned down a street, narrowly avoiding a horse-drawn carriage. The driver cursed her, and one of the horses neighed and half-reared. Kat drove on, still wrestling with clutch and gearstick. This was harder than it looked in picture shows.

Her rearview mirror flooded with light. She craned her head to see two autos barreling down on her.

She swerved down a cross-street, nearly hit a pimply man in a threadbare jacket, who shot her an obscene gesture. Then his eyes widened as the goons' cars made the turn, and he bolted.

Rain smashed down on the windshield, pattered on the roof. It wasn't loud enough to mask the clack-clack of a gun, though.

Kat cut the wheel sharply, stomped on the gas. They barreled down another cross street. The car bounced over a pothole, and Kat's teeth clacked together.

"Hey!" Heather said.

"Sorry."

A bullet smashed the driver's side view mirror. It erupted in a shower of glass, and Kat screamed, instinctively pulling the wheel. The car scraped against a building wall, bounced aside. They flew down an alley. Dark walls leaned over them, listing toward the Sink. Laundry lines flapped above. Housewives were reeling their clothes in to save them from the rain.

"Use the gun!" Kat said.

"What?" Heather said. She sounded dazed: shocked and drugged. Great.

"The gun!" Kat repeated. She took a hand off the wheel just long enough to point at the pistol between Heather's feet.

A moment passed. "Oh."

"Oh! Use it!"

Somewhat dreamily, Heather swept up the gun. "I've never fired a gun before."

"Well, now's the time to learn."

Kat swerved the wheel again, and the car lurched down another alley, the passenger side squealing as it ground against the walls. Sparks sprayed. The goons came on. Kat saw their headlights as they made the turn behind her.

"Now!" Kat said. "Now now now!"

Unsteady, Heather rose to her knees, turned about in the seat and raised the pistol. It wavered. "Okay," she said. "Here goes."

She trembled. Pulled the trigger.

Click.

"The safety!" Kat said. "Hit the safety."

"The what?"

"That thing!" Kat pointed.

"Oh." Heather's voice sounded far away. Nevertheless, she clicked off the safety and lifted the gun again, aiming out the rear window.

They hit a pothole. The gun erupted, paining Kat's ears. The cabin stank of gun smoke. More gunfire from the pursuing auto. Glass exploded. Heather screamed. Fired again, this time on purpose. Kat thought the round went wild.

Kat saw an opening to the left, mashed the brake, jerked the wheel, and took off down the next alley. A fat, pasty man was rutting with a skinny, pasty woman with her back against the wall. As the headlights swept them, they screamed and ran, the woman hollering for the man to pay up as they vanished down a cross-alley.

Kat fled. The goons pursued. Gunfire tore through the night. Metal screamed as bullets punched it. A puff of leather as a bullet grazed a seat. A round smashed through the front window, and cracks webbed out from it.

"Shoot! Shoot!" Kat screamed.

Heather, wobbly on her knees, rocked back and forth. Out of the corner of her eye, Kat saw Heather set her mouth, narrow her right eye, and squeeze. The explosion rocked the cabin, but Kat was prepared. In the overhead rearview mirror she saw a hole appear in the goons' windshield.

"Good!" Kat shouted. "Again!"

Heather fired. And again. The goons' auto swung aside, smashed into a wall and lodged there, smoke pouring from the engine. The car behind it slammed into it, and a section of the wall fell down, raining bricks onto both cars.

Katya laughed.

Heather, smiling strangely, sat down and dropped the gun to the floor. Smoke trailed up from it. "I did it." She said this slowly, almost philosophically.

"You *did* it!" Kat corrected. Excitedly, she slapped Heather's knee.

She knew there would be more cars out looking for them, though. She had to get to a main road and make tracks. With that in mind, she swung the wheel, and the auto lurched down an alley in what she thought was the direction of the main road. It was an old alley, and they were nearer the Sink now. Both sides of the car scraped against the leaning walls. Kat cursed, gunned the engine. The car sprang forward. Metal screamed. The doors buckled inwards. The windshield burst. Kat covered her eyes, but no glass hit her, at least not hard enough to break the skin.

She stomped on the gas, again and again. No use.

"Fuckballs," she said.

She glanced at Heather. The younger woman smiled strangely, and her dilated eyes gazed all around. The drugs had definitely taken effect. "We're stuck," Heather said, and somehow she sounded happy about it.

Rain slammed down, and thunder rolled.

Katya had no shoes on, so she picked up the fallen gun, made sure it was empty, and used it to smash out the rest of the already cracked windshield. Much of it already glittered on the hood, twinkling by the illumination of lightning. Rain swept in, raising further gooseflesh on her arms. She scraped the edges of the windshield, then cautiously climbed out, careful not to cut her feet. She slipped once on the hood and had to catch herself on the coach top.

"Come on," she said to Heather, holding out a hand.

Heather eyed the hand spacily, then looked up into Kat's face. "Hey, Katya."

Kat sighed. "Hi, Heather. Now *come on!*"

"Do I *have* to? I'm so *comfortable.*"

"Yes, you have to. Now!"

"Oh, *all* right."

Heather took the hand, and with much groaning and grunting on Kat's part Heather emerged into the night. To her horror, Kat saw the seat back Heather had lain against was absolutely coated in red. Katya's stomach dropped.

"Oh, it's so *pretty*," Heather said, staring up at the storm that roiled overhead. Kat looked. Somewhere deep inside the cloud formation lightning struck, revealing the different levels of clouds and making them seem to glow for a moment from within, as if the storm was powered by some great electric heart.

"Here," Kat said. Gently she removed Heather's coat and swept some of the glass away from the hood, then she helped Heather down from the auto and gave her the jacket back. Heather smiled as she accepted it, holding it to her chest fondly. She began stroking it and cooing to it. Rain trickled down her auburn hair, matting it.

The road was cold on Kat's feet, and she was miserable in the rain, but she grabbed Heather's hand and led her down one alley, then another. In the distance she heard goons calling to each other. *Fuckworms.*

Her stomach growled in hunger, and she realized it had been hours since she'd eaten. If only she could find some nook for her and Heather to hole up in, some place with some canned food—

Piercing alarms cut the night.

A chill started at the crown of Katya's head and shuddered down her body like a wave. In the distance, alarms continued to blare. People in the tenements all around screamed. Kat saw a gang of filthy children run into a doorway and slam a thick metal door behind them, then heard them lock it shut.

"No," she said. "No no no."

Loqrin wasn't taking any chances. He wanted them dead. *He knows what I found out is dangerous to him*, Kat thought. *Good.*

And, obviously, bad.

Heather stared blankly about them, as if trying to locate the source of the alarms. Kat realized she must've given Heather too much of whatever was in that syringe.

Well, there was nothing for it. Kat gripped Heather's hand in hers and ran, bare feet slapping on cracked, hole-ridden asphalt. Dirty rainwater splashed in potholes. She took one alley, then another, looking for an open door. She passed a bar, saw through the thick glass windows a row of hunched, pale figures crouching along the bar. They nursed crusty mugs of beer while homely women tried to entice them. Kat banged on the doors, but the doorman showed her his shotgun. "Get lost!" he said.

"Please!" she said.

Alarms sounded louder.

Various emotions crossed the man's face, and at last he sighed and began unbolting the door. First one bolt, then another, then a chain . . .

"Hurry!" Kat said, slapping at the door.

Another bolt, then . . .

Suddenly she heard the first scrape and shuffle. With dread, she turned to see a line of ragged figures slouch around the nearest corner, moaning and gibbering. Even in the rain, the stink of rotting flesh rolled before them. Lightning flickered above, and Kat was afforded a brief glimpse of the approaching creatures and felt the blood drain from her face. She saw an enormous fat woman whose belly was splitting open like an over-ripe pumpkin, a man with worms wriggling from eye socket and nose, a muscular fellow whose face had been *skinned*. It was raw, red and glistening in the rain, but its teeth shone pearly white.

There were many, many others, flesh rotting on their bones, some with clockwork gears visible through holes in their bodies.

"No," Kat said. "No . . ."

Even Heather seemed to sober. "Damn," she said. It was the first time Kat had heard her curse.

Kat turned to the doorman, who looked miserable, but he just shrugged his shoulders and began re-locking the door.

"I hope you get eaten!" Kat said. Turning to Heather, she said, "Come on."

She tugged Heather's arm and ran up the alley. Heather's breathing became more labored, and she swayed on her feet as she ran. She couldn't make it much more, Kat knew. She'd simply lost too much blood.

A stream of Returners appeared around the corner of the alley she was fleeing up, blocking her off.

"Shit," she said.

She wheeled to face the other way, dragging Heather with her. When she reached the intersection, she saw a tide of Returners coming up toward her from one alley and heard sounds of more coming from a third direction. That left her one choice, and she took it. Heather stumbled along behind her. Panic and fear overcame Katya, and she just wanted to sink to her knees and cry. It all seemed so hopeless. Loqrin feared what she knew, and he wouldn't let her leave. There was no way out. Why even try?

She shoved the thoughts away. She remembered her mother, and Ravic, and knew she had to fight. Nothing was ever given to anybody in this world.

Heather collapsed to the ground.

Kat's heart sank. She knelt over the girl, slapped her cheeks. She couldn't see Heather's face in the dark, but she could see the glitter of water in her eyes. "Heather! *Heather!* Wake up!"

Returners shambled up the alley, hooting and groaning. Kat saw large, misshapen forms, but among them smaller, more petite shapes. Whatever they had been in life, though, they were no more. Their minds were broken, damaged things, filled with hate and anger. Some Returners were manageable, but Loqrin had seen to it that these were not. *Sick bastard.*

Katya slapped Heather's cheek. The Returners drew closer.

"Come on, H!"

No reaction. It occurred to Kat that she could leave Heather and maybe escape, save herself. *Fuck that.* Heather had nearly killed herself—maybe *had* killed herself—to save Katya. Katya would do anything for her.

"Sorry about this," she said. She reached around, slung one of Heather's arms over her shoulder and hefted Heather up with one of her own hands on Heather's waist. She had to reach around Heather's back to do it, and put some pressure on the whip-cuts, but it was the only way. Grunting under the weight, she pulled Heather upright and staggered, a step at a time, up the alley.

Thunder crashed. The Returners scraped and shuffled behind. Closer. Their smell thickened.

At last Heather moved her feet, just a little. Then a bit more. A harsh breath escaped her lips.

"Thank the gods," Kat gasped. "I thought I'd lost you there for a sec."

Heather didn't answer, just sucked in a pained breath.

A set of steps ahead, leading to a door just slightly ajar. Kat all but ran to it. Half hopping, half stumbling, she helped Heather up the steps and kicked it open. A dim hallway stretched inward. A strange-looking woman knelt on the floor before what looked like a heavy metal door, burglar's tools arranged on a cloth beside her.

And a gun.

Evidently startled, she picked up the gun and aimed it at Kat and Heather. Kat's bladder nearly released in fright as the muzzle of the gun swallowed the world.

"Who are you?" the woman demanded. She had a thick accent, and she spoke so fast the words sort of blurred together so that they sounded more like *Whoareyou?*

Kat opened her mouth to answer—

"Nevermind," the woman said. "Just close the fucking door!" Half to herself, she mumbled, "I thought I might have time to get in and out, but—*just close it!*"

"Can we come in first?" Katya said.

"Ifyoumust."

Kat pulled Heather inside and propped her against the wall. Heather slouched down, hissing in pain. Frantically Kat turned back to the doorway. The tide of Returners had reached the steps. Several shamble-stumbled up them, rotted hands reaching for Kat. She slammed the door in their faces. It was a large, heavy door, made to resist Returners, and it slammed with a satisfying thud. Returners scratched at it and howled on the other side, but for the moment, Kat and Heather were safe. Overhead, thunder shook the tenement.

"Fuck," the burglar woman said, throwing down her pick. "Jim's gotten better at keeping me out."

Kat's heart beat fast and hard under her ribs. Blood coursed like fire through her veins. Water dripped from her eyebrows into her eyes, and from her hair down her shoulders and back. Her soaked bra sent rivulets down her stomach, some to pool in her navel. She was thoroughly drenched, and she felt her shoulders shake in cold and fear. Just a few inches behind her, Returners scratched at the door.

Partly to get her mind off it, partly to ingratiate herself with this woman, she said, "Who's Jim?"

The woman snorted. "Jim McKray. You've hearda him. Ona Loqrin's pimps."

"Ah." Kat remembered the bar she'd passed, remembered the homely prostitutes there. If this was McKray's area, those were probably his girls, and he was likely at the bar even now, trapped by the tide of Returners. He may even have been the man that locked her out. No wonder the burglar woman was so bold. She'd probably been waiting for the alarms to sound just so she could sneak here and start picking. "So you're one of his girls?"

The woman snorted again, trying a different pick. "Do I *look* like one of his girls?"

In truth, she didn't look like anything Kat had ever seen before. For one thing, she was completely black. Kat had known some dark-complexioned people before, of course. Most of the ones in Lavorgna hailed from Mdbai, a vast jungle-y place on a different continent. Ancient stone towers hundreds of feet high rose from those jungles, and an ancient order of alchemists and occult practitioners ruled there, oppressing the Mdbains with iron fists. Little wonder many escaped, some foolishly fleeing to the vastly corrupt yet somewhat freer cities in the Confederation, of which Lavorgna ranked high. Mostly they kept to their own quarters of town, but a few tried to blend in.

This woman did not. For one thing, she was covered from head to toe in glowing, green tattoos that swirled like thorny vines up and down her ebony arms, legs, over her throat, her cheeks and forehead. Kat had seen alchemical tattoos before, but never any so intricate or all-encompassing. The woman even had them on her eyelids and—shit!—on her *tongue*. The tattoos actually glowed in the darkness, an eerie pulsing green. The glow seemed to ebb and flow, just a bit, probably in time to her heartbeat.

Kat stared at her, mesmerized. She realized the woman must be in her late twenties, was very athletic, and was stone cold beautiful. It took a while to see that, though, since the tattoos sort of distracted the eye.

"Don't stare," the woman snapped.

"Sorry," Katya said.

"Tree of Hell!" the woman said, flinging down her current pick. "Jim musta hired someone to Aqa-proof this bastard."

"Aqa? That your name?"

"Yeah, what's it to ya? Fuck!" She slapped the door. With a sigh, she gathered up her tools, wrapped them in the cloth and shoved them into a pouch that stuck out from her belt. She wore dark, soft clothes that hugged her body. Kat could mainly see the clothes as an absence of tattoos.

"You steal from Jim a lot?" Kat said.

"Him and the other fuckwads Loqrin runs. I try not to rip off the honest Hollow-men."

"That's good of you."

"Yeah, well."

"That's a mean set of picks you have there."

Aqa's eyebrows rose. "You in the business?"

"Yep, and I'd kill for a set like that." Katya ran the words through her head again and corrected herself: "Well, maybe not *kill*."

Smiling a little, Aqa's dark gaze drifted to Heather, who slumped unconscious against the wall. "What's with yer friend?"

Kat crouched by Heather, swept some hair from her face. "She's hurt. Bad. She needs a doctor." She pulled Heather away from the wall so Aqa could see her back.

"Holy Tree of Life and Death!" Aqa said. "What have you done to her?"

Kat met her eyes. "It was Loqrin." She tilted Heather's face up so Aqa could see the mutilations.

"FUCKER!" Aqa picked up her gun from the ground and stuffed it angrily into the holster on her hip. "Some day . . . So, wait, you two're some of his little playmates? Don't tell me you've escaped?"

Kat nodded. "Yeah, we—"

The door exploded inward. Rain washed in, and Returners surged after it. Teeth gnashed, and ragged hands groped.

Kat screamed.

Aqa yanked out her gun and fired. One of the Returners stumbled backward, brains flying. Another came. Aqa fired again. It fell. Another. Again. Another. The tight hallway filled with the stench of gun smoke and torn corpses. Kat gathered Heather up and forced her to stand. "Just a little more, H," she promised.

"Why didn't you lock the fuckin' door!" Aqa roared as she reloaded.

Kat gulped. "I didn't think they could *use* doors!"

"Fool! Well, come on!" Aqa turned and started to walk away, snapping the pistol's cylinder back into place as she went.

With Returners after her, Kat carried-walked Heather after Aqa, who found a stairwell and bound up it. Groaning and tired, Kat followed.

"THERE'S BEEN A BREACH!" Aqa shouted, slamming her palm on the walls on the hallway on the next level. "BARRICADE YOUR DOORS! GET YOUR GUNS!"

A fat man stepped out of his hovel wearing a stained shirt and carrying a shotgun. He was hairy and pale. "Who let a breach?" he demanded.

Katya, pulling Heather along behind, tensed.

Aqa said, "Never mind. Just do what I say!"

He spat, slamming his door. Katya heard furniture being dragged on the other side. "See what you did?" Aqa said, glaring at Katya.

"S-sorry."

"Yeah, well. Come on!"

Aqa continued marching up the stairs, level by level. Katya saw that as the walls listed, some had cracked and been patched up over time. Some hadn't. Wind gusted in, and with it rain. The hallways stank of mold and cigar smoke. Only some of the floors were electrified. Katya shivered in the cold breeze. Her legs ached in weariness. Sometimes Heather roused herself and was able to help, sometimes not. Aqa kept yelling for people to fortify their doors, and the groan of Returners continued rising from below. Katya felt like she was in a labyrinth that was being flooded.

At last they reached the top, and Aqa kicked open the final door. Rain swept in.

The black woman moved onto the rooftop, gravel crunching under her feet. Gasping for breath, wishing Aqa had volunteered to carry Heather, Kat followed, wincing at the cold drops of rain. Behind her, the howls of the Returners drew close.

Unheeding, Aqa strolled over to the edge of the roof, turned and beckoned Kat over. Every step was an effort. At last Katya stood beside Aqa, staring down into an alley. The buildings listed terribly, and the roof was actually far outstretched over the alley. If Katya fell, she'd fall right in the center of it, maybe even toward the far side. Great. Good thing there were Returners down there to break her fall.

A rickety board spanned the gap from this sagging rooftop to the next.

"That's where we're goin'," Aqa said.

"Fuck," Katya said.

"Think of it as an adventure."

"What about her?" Kat indicated Heather.

Heather wilted at her side, half conscious if that. There was no way Heather could cross over that board on her own and no way Kat could carry her.

"Oh, fuck it," Aqa said. She bent over, flung Heather across her shoulder, and stood straight with a grunt. "Heavier than she looks. Come!" She turned and nimbly bounded across the board, which made popping noises under her weight. At last she reached the other side and indicated for Kat to follow.

Kat hesitated. Thief or no thief, she hated heights. The Returner-filled ground below her seemed to sway, sometimes shrinking away, sometimes jumping up at her.

Scraping noises behind her. Kat spun to see the doorway filled with Returners. Moaning, gnashing their teeth, they flooded out onto the roof. Rain gleamed on their rotting flesh. A worm wriggled through one man's cheek. A skinny woman glared at Katya out of half-dissolved eyes. Rain beat down on the cloven skull of another, a river of water cascading over the naked brain.

Katya risked a step onto the board. It bent beneath her. The world swayed. *Shit.* Her heart hammered in her temples. She took another step, then another. She teetered, sticking out her arms to catch herself.

"Come on, girl!" Aqa said. With Heather slung over her shoulder, she raised her gun and aimed at something behind Katya. Fired.

Kat felt the heat of a bullet pass her cheek, a thunk, then something wet and nasty spraying her back. Grinding her teeth, she took another step. Another. The board shifted. Maybe it was her weight, maybe the rain, but she felt it. It sent a shudder up through her toes to the top of her head. She froze.

Aqa fired again.

"You can do it!" she said.

Katya could smell the rot of Returners behind her. She had to cross before they could try to follow her, or, worse, dislodge the board.

"Fuck fuck fuck," she said—but she took a step with every word, and at last jumped off the board.

A gaggle of Returners had reached the board on the other roof. One tried to cross. Aqa fired again. Its skull exploded. Brains spattered the creatures behind it.

Aqa stooped, set Heather down, and dropped her gun. She grabbed the board with both hands and *pulled*. Sweat beaded her brow, and her jaw muscles bunched as she did it. The board was heavy, Kat saw, and water-logged. She crouched down by Aqa, grabbed the board, and added her meager muscles to the effort. At last they dragged the huge board across.

Panting, they both sat on the rooftop and watched as the Returners howled and raged on the opposite side.

"Thank you," Aqa said.

Kat laughed. "Thank *you*. Nice shooting." Her gaze strayed to Heather, who lay still. For a moment Kat thought she'd stopped breathing, and something cold gathered inside her. But then she saw Heather's chest rise, then fall, and she relaxed. "We have to get my friend a doctor."

"All the docs in the Hollows report to Loqrin, kid. They'd recognize your friend for one of his playthings right off." Before Kat could despair, Aqa grinned and patted her on the shoulder. "But I know someone who might help you."

Aqa placed Heather over her shoulder again, shoved her gun back in its holster, and set off. Katya followed. Aqa led from rooftop to rooftop, and Katya realized there was a whole network of aerial transportation. *A highway in the skyway*, Aqa told her. Katya trembled the first few boards she had to cross, but after a time she grew better at it. She knew she'd never be as nimble as Aqa, but at least she wouldn't shiver herself off the damned board. Rain flung down on them, and lightning lit the skies. Below, Returners raged and howled, and the sounds of screams and braking glass drifted up.

"How can he do this to his own people?" Kat panted once as they sheltered against a pigeon coop.

Aqa looked at her levelly. "Because he's a fuckin' madder, that's why."

"Yeah. He is." But there was more to him than that, Katya knew. Loqrin Mars was up to something, something horrible, and she had to tell Ravic what she knew. Maybe with her pieces of the puzzle added to his they could begin to see the full picture.

After a rest, Aqa continued on, and Katya ached in weariness. Finally she heard music and laughter. What was this?

Aqa led her over a final board, around a bend, and to— well, it looked, to Katya's surprise, like some sort of *celebration*, of all things. Jury-rigged tents of various colors held a host of people, some dancing, some drinking. Most were Hollowers, but some seemed to come from Outside, as Heather had put it. A few were infected by the Atomic Sea, and Katya saw some odd mutations—one man's arms sprouted what looked like stingray wings--but most were healthy. Swarthy musicians played on a makeshift stage, and before it whirled shopkeepers and factory workers and more.

The women among them were housewives and spinsters and prostitutes. The latter did not try to hide what they were but strolled among the dancers, grabbing crotches or offering a glimpse of a heavy breast. From time to time one of the men would accept, and the two would leave the open dancing tent and disappear into one of the smaller, closed tents—but not before handing money to a hard-looking man of maybe forty, shortish but strong, with a grizzled, shaven head and hard jaw. A tattoo of an eye stared out from his forehead, between and above his real eyes, which lit up at seeing Aqa. After Aqa set Heather down, the two embraced—and kissed. It was not a quick kiss, either.

Kat cleared her throat.

"Oh, yeah," said Aqa, "I met these strays on the job—a bust, by the way."

The man that must be Reddin lifted an eyebrow. "Yeah, me love, an' why's that?"

"Locks've gotten good." She said it without a hint of shame.

"They must have, to keep you out. Better luck next time, then. Well, now, what's this?" He stared from Katya to Heather. His eyes widened when he saw Heather's back. Instantly he crouched over her. "Magnar reamed!"

"She needs help," Katya said. "Aqa said there was a doctor."

Reddin frowned. Nodded. With a glance to Aqa, he said, "Send Dana to fetch our fair wee sawbones, would you, lass?"

Aqa nodded, and without sparing a glance at Katya disappeared into the throng of dancers. They danced on, despite the storm that raged all about them, not having seen

Heather. Alchemical lamps blazed brightly, throwing a warm if eerie light on the scene. Some of them had been draped around a defunct steam-man that stood, more statue than anything else, on the rooftop, covered in pigeon crap and scrawled with graffiti. Kat supposed this gathering was probably illegal, at least according to Loqrin. The booze they were drinking was probably from Outside, and the girls were Reddin's, not Loqrin's.

"Shit, lass, what've ye been doin'?" Reddin said, looking up from Heather to Kat.

Feeling suddenly unsteady, Katya grabbed her knees and took deep breaths. "Running, mostly. We—"

"Zeppelin!"

Katya didn't see who had shouted the alarm, but the results were instant.

"Shit!" Reddin stood. Raising his voice, he said, "Douse the lights! Get inside!"

The partiers followed his orders, and in moments darkness draped the rooftop, and the dancers huddled inside the main tent, staring out at the night fearfully. Katya pressed in amongst them, relishing their warmth. Thunder rocked the heavens, and lightning struck down from the roiling clouds. Briefly she caught sight of a huge, torpedo-shaped form drifting slowly over the tenements to the north.

But he just got back. It puzzled her that Loqrin would have called the airship back and gone out again so soon. But then again his suite and his harem were in shambles. There was little reason for him to stay, and he had, apparently, things to do. *Like what?*

"Does he often go out like this?" she asked Reddin, the next time he bustled past, carrying an armload of beer.

"Oh, aye, ever' night mostly." He paused. "Dana's gone to fetch our doc. He'll be 'ere shortly, an' if anything can be done for your lass he's the man to do it." By his tone it was clear he didn't think Heather would make it.

Kat walked over to go keep Heather company, but just then someone shouted, "Look at *that*! What are those?"

The people began to murmur.

Katya stared out in the direction the revelers were pointing. When the next flash of lightning struck, she saw the zeppelin, going west—not toward the Sink, but somewhere else. She also saw dark shapes drifting up from the shadows of the streets, one at first, then another, both joining a group of several more that circled behind the tail of the airship, as if drawn on by it. Sparks flashed in the gondola, and Kat could imagine the tall figure there, striding back and forth among his Returners, barking orders as his strange machines belched smoke and fire.

The zeppelin cruised north, and shadows that Katya knew too well floated after it. At the realization, she felt a shiver that had nothing to do with wind or rain. *Loqrin is gathering haunts.*

Chapter 9

Doc Harris arrived, drunk and tired, not half an hour after Dana went to fetch him. An infected fellow with brilliant purple fish scales on his face, he sobered up quickly enough when he saw Heather and immediately set to work, dressing her wounds and feeding her pills—"They're alchemical," he said. Kat didn't need to be told they were stolen. "Designed to boost blood manufacture," he added, then burped and went back to work, sewing up Heather's cuts. Kat stayed by her friend's side, helping the doctor however she could. She watched how to sew and dress a wound and tried to memorize the names for various ointments and instruments.

The party died before dawn, and Reddin ordered the tents broken up and moved. Doc Harris put Heather on a stretcher face-down and two of Reddin's men carried her as the company went on the move.

"We try an' keep mobile," Reddin explained to Kat. "Loqrin's boys're always out lookin', and we havta keep a sharp eye out. Hence—" He tapped the tattoo on his forehead. An alchemical tattoo, it glowed red, and Kat assumed this had something to do with his name.

"Right," she said. *As mad as Loqrin.*

Reddin slapped an arm around her shoulders, and she jumped. They were descending a stairway inside the tenement, bound for some undisclosed location. "You're a good lookin' lass," he said. "A bit skinny, but pretty enough to tip you over the edge. If you're lookin' for work, I'm more'n happy to consider an arrangement."

Kat figured half the reason he was helping her and Heather was because he wanted to hire Kat on, so she was quick not to dissuade him. "Yeah, maybe," she said. "I'll think it over." She said it brightly, and he smiled wider.

"Good, lass, ye do that." He patted her rump, laughed, and marched down the stairs ahead of her.

Katya sighed. At least they'd given her food. A day old hamburger, but it tasted like heaven. Lots of mustard, just the way she liked it. When she smacked her lips, she could still taste the grease.

Reddin led the crew down into the sewers, some of which were still functional—and smelled like it. He brought them along the sewer for a ways, then into a section of the underground that must have been carved out of ancient ruins. There were a lot of those, Kat knew. Lavorgna was an *old* city. It had been thriving when the Qaran Empire collapsed a thousand years ago, and it had been doing pretty darned well two thousand years before that when the Qaran Empire crossed what was then called the Twilight Sea to conquer Xara. Lavorgna, already a hub of commerce, had betrayed its masters and opened its arms (and legs, it was said) to the Qarans. Thus it had been spared much of the destruction the rest of Xara suffered. Still, the Qarans had remade it over time, and Loqrin's Arches were proof that some of their buildings still stood.

The upshot was that there was a lot *of* Lavorgna, and of Lavorgnas, both above ground and under. The Qarans had worshipped the Elders and their nobles had built vast dwellings underground to be close to them; it was into one of these areas that Reddin led. Kat saw high ceilings studded with mirrors and arcs of brass that led up into fabulous domes, domes that may once have admitted sunlight through windows above. The windows were gone, and the areas where they had been were mortared over. Niches where inset jewels had gleamed (and been looted long ago) lined the walls. A mosaic covered the granite floors, which was heaped with dirt and rubble, and scratched with graffiti.

"Set up shop," Reddin told his people, and they complied, erecting tents and stringing lights.

Kat saw that Reddin's folk were more like carnies than traditional mobsters. They bore tattoos, or rings in their noses—or lips or ears or eyebrows or nipples, for that matter—or strangely colored hair, or all three together. There was a big woman with a tattoo of an open, fanged-lined mouth on her bald, square dome. There was a short, weasely-looking fellow who had tattooed dark circles around his eyes like those of a raccoon, and he moved in quick furtive bursts. A rough man with spiked red hair and a chain running from one nipple ring to another constantly stared at Katya.

They stayed underground all that day, and Kat took the opportunity to rest and eat while Heather healed. Reddin gave Katya some clothes to wear, thank the gods. Of course, the dress was tawdry, and there wasn't enough of it, but it was better than nothing.

Around dusk she woke up to find the crew breaking down tents and packing up to leave again. She discovered that Reddin had sent out scouts during the day to find a new location, which they had. He tried to move at least twice a day, Aqa told her. Thus they relocated from the Qaran ruins to a more modern ruin, also underground. Here the walls were lined with gray stone and the ceiling was much lower. Still, the few fixtures that remained were posh, as were the elaborate bas-reliefs in the walls. Aqa told her that this had been a siege shelter for some ancient king. His castle had stood above. Of course, it was long gone, but the siege shelter remained, unbeknownst to the people above. Ravic would love it, Katya thought.

There was a whole subterranean world beneath Lavorgna, Aqa told her, much of it connected, sometimes by sewer tunnels, sometimes by old smuggling routes, sometimes even areas of the Below. Kat had seen all of the Below she wanted.

Through runners and drop-spots, Reddin sent word out to his customers, and they arrived, first in trickles, then in streams. Apparently Reddin threw parties almost daily in order to sell his beer and advertise his prostitutes, both men and women. There were over a dozen of these, Kat discovered, and though few were very attractive, they seemed content enough with their lot. All were willing, not slaves like Loqrin's whores were said to be, and they were free to come and go. The tents hopped with noise and music, and people danced and fucked. The old king's lair echoed with laughter and grunting, and Reddin smiled as he counted his money.

Katya stayed with Reddin for three days waiting for Heather to heal, and every day was the same. They would rest somewhere during the day, move and do business at night, sometimes underground, sometimes on a rooftop (where they would marvel at the far-off harbor and the lighting that licked up from the Atomic Sea), always somewhere on the fringes, in the cracks of the Hollows. Occasionally there would be a Loqrin-scare, and they would hastily break and scatter, then reconvene at some prearranged place.

Several times Kat asked about the dolls, wondering how many had escaped. Word had it that almost all had gotten free; Loqrin's men had been too busy hunting Katya. Part of her rejoiced. The other part vowed to end Loqrin so that the few dolls that remained in his so-called harem would be saved, too.

Katya's favorite times during those three days were the ones she spent with Aqa. Aqa, though usually busy stealing or alone with Reddin, nevertheless set aside some time every day to spend with Kat. She showed Kat some self-defense moves, told her Mdbain history, how to hold a gun, and, best of all, how to pick aristo locks. Katya had never had any formal training in her trade, and so she was confined to stealing from people with crappy protection, though she'd always dreamed of taking from the wealthy, especially those who contributed to oppressing so many people. She simply had never been able to figure out how. Now Aqa taught her. The older woman even took a pin out of her own hair and put it in Katya's so that she would always have a pick to use. Next they worked on cracking safes.

Reddin seemed disappointed in all this education. He wanted Katya for one of his workers, not a thief. At least he took it well. She didn't think he was a bad man, not like Loqrin. He was just a man, with his good points and his not so good. He had two main virtues that Katya especially appreciated: his undeniable love for Aqa—although he would screw any other woman any chance he got—and his undeniable hatred for Loqrin.

Katya did find a way to pay for her keep. She served beer, passed out peanuts, cleaned up puke, learned how to break down tents and was even put to work carrying duffel bags.

On the fourth night, just as the party wound down for the evening, she noticed a strange stirring among Reddin and his crew. A new sort of energy buzzed among them. It crackled through the air, even lighting the faces of some of their patrons. To Kat's surprise, they all prepared to go off somewhere together, patrons and patroned alike.

"Where are we going?" Katya asked Aqa, who had just returned from burgling something valuable ("Tomorrow I'll take you," she had said, which had delighted Katya) and was cleaning her gun.

Aqa eyed her with amusement. "*Some* of us are going to set up shop for the day," she said. It was clear from her tone which group she placed Kat in.

"Yeah," Kat demanded. "And the others?"

Aqa's voice lowered. "Some of us are going to a meeting of the Brotherhood."

"Really? The *Underground* Brotherhood? The ones've been doing all the striking?"

Aqa went back to cleaning her gun. "The very same."

Kat made her voice firm. "Then *I'm* coming with you."

"Oh? An' why is that, girlie?"

Kat didn't tell her that it was because the Brotherhood was a city-wide phenomenon and might be able to help her back to the Fifth Ward. She had to get back, as soon as possible, to warn Ravic about what Loqrin was up to, and also to warn him that Death's Head Jack was in league with Loqrin.

"Cause I wanna," was all she said. When that didn't seem to be enough, she added truthfully, "Cause I hate the Guild and wanna be part of, you know, fighting it."

Aqa shrugged, snapping the cylinder back in place. "Fine with me, girlie."

Behind her a shape moved, and Aqa spun to face it, lifting her gun.

Heather smiled weakly. "Hi."

Aqa breathed out and lowered her piece.

"Heather!" Kat sprang to her feet and hugged the girl tightly—carefully, but tightly. Heather hugged her in return. She seemed much stronger now.

"I'm coming, too," she said.

Smoke drifted up to the ceiling, and the noise of all the people hurt Kat's ears. It stank of beer and sweat. They were underground, in the huge old boiler room of one of the collapsed tenements in the Domino, the series of fallen buildings that led down to the Sink. People—strikers mostly—pressed thick about them, talking loudly. They stank of chemicals, oil and sweat. Not to miss an opportunity, Reddin's gang sold the strikers various and sundry while they waited.

"Want some hot fresh peanuts?" Kat called, shoving her way through the thick crowd, carrying a tray laden with paper bags stuffed with less-than-fresh peanuts.

"I'll take a hot fresh *somethin'!*" a man called, groping her rear. She stomped on the arch of his foot, and he gasped and fell back.

"Nice," Heather said.

"A little move Aqa taught me."

"She's something, isn't she?" Kat couldn't tell by Heather's voice if this was a good thing or a bad thing.

"Fuck yeah!" Katya said. "I'm gonna be just like her!"

Heather smiled. "You're going to become tall, black and tattooed? Good choice. And don't curse so much. It's not ladylike."

"Fuck that." Someone snatched a bag of peanuts and stuffed a dollar down Katya's bra. She elbowed him away, and not gently. She kept the dollar.

They moved through the crowd, Katya selling peanuts, Heather selling beer. At other places Reddin's prostitutes strutted, tickling chins and pressing themselves against grizzly factory workers. Most of the workers were too interested in the coming speech to leave, but the girls and boys of the tribe were trying to make impressions for afterward. Apparently Reddin made good money off servicing the gatherings, but there was more to it than that. As an enemy of Loqrin, he helped finance them and organize them. However, there was some Outside power that ran them city-wide. Reddin wouldn't say who.

"Well, maybe not the tats and stuff," Katya said. "But maybe the burglary."

"You're going to be a *thief?*" Heather said.

"I already am, H. But I'm going to be a *good* thief."

"Whatever."

"She's just such a badass. I've never met a woman like her." Katya thought even her mom would have been impressed by Aqa.

"Me either. You could use her as a flashlight."

Kat shot Heather a dark look, then sighed. Heather considered anyone not born in the Hollows an Outsider. Someone born in Mbdai must be almost like an alien to her. And Aqa wasn't typical, even for someone born there.

"Anyway," Kat said, "I think she's great."

A man (infected, with octopus suckers across half his face) bought a beer from Heather, then spilled his drink on someone. A scuffle ensued.

"It's like a riot," Heather said. She spoke in her usual flat voice, but there was a hint of elation just under it.

"Fuckin' aye," Kat said.

The men and women of the factory yelled and laughed all around, and she could feel the anticipation on the air. These people, their parents and their parents' parents had slaved away for the Guild of Alchemists, working like dogs and being cast aside when sick, injured or old, and now finally, after all this time, someone was standing up to the Guildsmen. That person, or one of their representatives, was about to give a speech on the makeshift stage that stood against the rear wall, and these men were eager to soak up every anti-Guild word. They risked death just being here. A feeling almost of revolution flooded the boiler room, and Kat felt heady with it.

Heather seemed to feel it, too, perhaps even more keenly. After all, they were in the Hollows, her home, and these meetings were like spitting in the face of Loqrin, the man who'd raped her for years. Guards were posted all over outside, perching in the ruins of the Domino above, watching out for a possible raid launched by the Boss.

"You think they can really do it?" Heather asked breathlessly. "You think they can really bring down the Guild?"

"I don't know about bringing it down," Katya said. "But building up some protection from it, putting checks on it, that's the main thing. In other countries they have workers' unions. If we could just get those, the Guild would have to back off. They couldn't exploit people any more."

Heather' face fell. "But who would do that? Who could stand up to the Guild?"

"I guess we'll find out."

A few minutes later the lights dimmed, and instantly the crowd quieted. "This is it," Kat whispered. She squeezed Heather's hand, and Heather squeezed back. Just then, the stage flooded with light and all eyes went to the doorway that emptied out on to it.

Movement. The crowd murmured.

Several thuggish men and women in rough suits stepped out of the doorway, onto the stage. Bulges showed under their armpits. The crowd murmured louder. These must be the speaker's guards, Kat thought. That meant he would be coming any second!

"Are you ready?" shouted one of the men. The crowd responded enthusiastically. "Well, then here he is, the man himself!"

The crowd roared out their love, and even Kat couldn't help issue a whistle.

A figure appeared in the doorway and paused, still in the shadow. The crowd hushed. Katya felt a surge of adrenaline. Now she thought she knew what the democratic revolutionaries must have felt when they gathered in secret to plot the overthrow of the King hundreds of years ago.

She wasn't sure exactly what she expected, but the man that stepped out stole her breath. He was tall and lean, dressed in an immaculate suit with a garish pink tie, fedora cocked rakishly. His face was long and not unhandsome. However, it was, without question, the face of a corpse.

He grinned and strode to the edge of the stage. The crowd cheered. Some of them muttered in confusion, but most seemed to have expected this. Evidently he had given similar speeches before. He lifted his hands, his very normal, living hands, basking in the adulation, then made cutting motions, and the crowd quieted.

Kat opened her mouth to say something. Nothing came out.

"Thank you all for gathering," said Death's Head Jack. "I know it's difficult to do so in these times, and in this place. I know Loqrin watches you like a hawk, and that he's always sweeping the skies, ready to pounce. *But we are not mice!*" The crowd roared, some stomping their feet, some banging their beer bottles. *"We are men!"* More cheering. Kat felt sick. "We will *show* that bastard, we will *show* the Guild! We are *men*, and we *deserve* the *respect* of men!" More cheering, louder yet. He was whipping them up into a fine frenzy. "I know it's tempting to succumb. I know you have families to feed, roofs to pay for. But do not give in. Do not go back to work. *This strike can succeed!*" He made a fist and shook it, and the crowd cheered, shaking their fists as well.

"No no," Kat said, but she said it in a murmur, and only Heather heard her. "This is all wrong."

Heather looked at her worriedly. "You mean because he's a deader? Well, it ain't like you've never seen one."

Kat shook her head, at first cautiously, then violently. All at once she shoved her way forward, elbowing her way through the crowd. Workers protested, pushed at her. She pushed back, slipping through them. Heather called something after her, but she didn't catch the words. Up above Jack spoke on, and around Kat the crowd ate it up. Hope lit their eyes. Fools!

She reached the stage and, without another thought, climbed up onto it.

One of Jack's thugs moved to stop her. She stomped on the arch of his foot, hard, just like Aqa had taught her. When he doubled over, she punched him in the jaw with her jagged rings. Blood spurted, and he stumbled back. Two more goons moved toward her, but she leapt toward Jack.

Upon seeing her, his eyes widened. A strange look came over him—almost like relief, as if he had worried about her and was glad to see her safe—and he shouted to them, "No! Don't! Leave her be!"

The crowd had quieted somewhat, but Jack's momentum had been broken.

Unconcerned, he stared at Katya as if seeing a ghost. "Kat!" he said. "What . . . what are you *doing*? And . . . can't it wait?"

Angrily, she pointed a finger at him and turned to the crowd. "Don't listen to him! He's a liar!"

They booed her angrily.

"A liar!" she shouted at the top of her voice. "He's a *spy*! He *works* for *Loqrin*!"

Most of them stopped booing. Confusion swept them.

"Kat, have you gone mad?" Jack said. "What in the world do you think you're doing?"

She ignored him. "He's a spy! I was a doll of Loqrin's and I heard him conspiring with Loqrin with my own ears!"

Confusion and anger rippled through the crowd. "Get off the stage!" someone shouted. A beer bottle exploded at her feet.

Not all were angry at her. "A spy!" some shouted. "He's a fuckin' spy!"

More beer bottles hurled through the air. One hit Jack on the shoulder. Another exploded on the wall behind him. A third whizzed by Kat's ear. A whole wave of strikers surged toward the stage, fists waving, some of them angry at Kat, some angry at Jack.

"He's a spy!" Kat yelled again. She helped Heather onto the stage and, with Heather's permission, pulled the back of her blouse up to reveal her mutilated back. "Look! We really were Loqrin's prisoners! That *thing* you've been listening to is a spy!"

The crowd surged closer.

Jack's thugs trained their guns on the crowd. The factory workers slowed, but they did not stop. Angry and wary, they advanced, step by step. Not all of them had turned against Jack, but more than enough had to overwhelm him and his guards.

"Get him!" Kat said.

Murder in their eyes, the ones that opposed Jack stepped forward.

"Shit!" he said. To his people, he said, "Grab her! We're going!"

One of the guard women moved toward Kat. She bunched her fists to fight. A lean ball of fury jumped on the woman's back, pulling at her hair. Heather.

Kat felt an arm around her waist. She twisted, punched. The thug grunted. A large hand seized one of her wrists, then the other. Carrying her like a toy, the man bounded down the hallway beyond the door. Jack ran ahead. Cursing, Kat craned her head to see the other goon running up the hall, Heather still beating at her head and pulling on her hair, perched on her back like a monkey.

Jack led down hallway after hallway, at last emerging into the cold night air. A limo guarded by chained homunculi idled on the street, steam rising from its engine. The driver reclined against the side, gun in hand.

Breathing heavily, Jack turned, saw that his guards had brought two girls instead of one. Taking it in stride, he shouted, "Put them in!"

They tossed Kat and Heather in the back. Hissing and spitting, the young women tried to climb out, but Jack shoved them back in. Another man followed him, Kat supposed to keep her and Heather in line. Doors slammed. The engine revved, and the limo shot off into the night. A last beer bottle smashed against the rear window.

"You bastard!" Kat yelled at Jack. "Let us go!"

Jack, still breathing hard, glanced from her, to Heather, to his man. Then, to Kat's surprise, he sat back in his seat—and laughed.

"What's so funny?" Kat demanded.

He didn't answer directly. Still chuckling, he said, "Well, this isn't how I pictured it going, but, as they say, if fate wills, it is done."

"Robunis Nobur," Heather said. "From *The Philosophy of Herqil.*"

"Well quoted," he said. "And you would be . . . ?"

She smiled, and Kat was impressed. "Heather. Heather Elizika Lakosta."

"Jack. Jack DuMond—at least, that's the name I go by now. A pleasure."

"Likewise."

Kat stared at Heather as if she were mad. "Are you *mad?* He's a spy!"

"You have to remember, I've been a guest of Loqrin for three years," Heather said. "Anyone else is an improvement."

Jack chuckled again. With shaky hands, he opened a panel and poured himself a drink. "Would you?" he said to Heather.

A wide smile lit her face, and Kat remembered she'd been days without any drugs save the medicinal kind.

"I'd be delighted."

While they drank, Kat stared. Part of her was surprised that Jack hadn't killed them yet. He was a traitor, wasn't he?

But he made no move against them. She supposed she'd have to wait for answers. At any rate, it didn't look as though she were going free anytime soon.

"Make mine a double," she said.

After she'd had her first sip and the car seemed safely away, Jack said, "Kat, do you honestly believe I'm a spy?"

"I *know* you're a spy."

"Yes, well. A spy for Loqrin."

"I *know* you're a spy for Loqrin. I *heard* you."

He frowned, evidently thinking, then slowly nodded. "Yes, when you were in his auto after he took you in, you must have overheard some things—"

"Some *things?* Yeah, just you plotting to fuck over Ravic."

Jack smiled, a strained, patient smile. "Kat, do you honestly believe I would do that to my own brother?"

Chapter 10

Kat stared. "Your *brother*? Ravic is your *brother*?"

Jack sipped his whiskey. "Indeed he his."

Heather had finished her drink some time ago. "May I?" She leaned over and refilled her glass. No one stopped her. Gravel spattered the underside of the car, and the tires squealed.

In the distance, Kat heard sirens. Long, peeling sirens that sent shivers up her spine. "Shit," she said. "Loqrin must be sending out Returners."

Jack grimaced. "Yes, a most lamentable hobby of his."

Heather nodded and in a placid voice said, "Several of my friends are Returners." She sipped her drink, smiled. "*I* was almost one."

Jack eyed her skeptically, then faced Kat again. "Would you like to hear the story?"

"That depends."

"On?"

"Do you have a cigarette?"

Jack looked irritated, but he politely pulled out a pack of expensive smokes and lit one for her. She puffed away contentedly. On her second inhalation, she saw something outside and coughed.

"What is it?" Jack said.

Then he saw it too.

A stream of Returners poured from around the side of a cracked, listing building. Katya saw a man whose patchwork face was coming apart at the seams, showing the bone and gristle underneath. Behind him marched a woman with worms for hair. Beside her crept a young boy with no lower jaw but razor-sharp, steel-plated fingernails.

They converged on the limo faster than Kat would have expected. A rotting hand beat at the windows, leaving trails of ooze. More and more gathered around the vehicle, which started to slow. One of the thugs in the front compartment opened his window and started shooting. Then one on the other side. *Rat-rat-rat.* Returners fell back. Gore splashed the windows. The limo's pace increased.

"Shit," Kat said.

"It will be all right," Jack said.

"And why should I believe anything *you* say? Including this bullshit brother story?"

He stared at her steadily. "Listen and decide."

Returners howled outside, but they were far enough away now not to be an immediate threat. Still, Kat shivered. Even Heather seemed subdued. If nothing else, Kat thought, Jack's little story might take their mind off things. *As if Heather needs any help.*

"Alright," Kat said. "Speak up, already."

"Well," he said, sipping intermittently, "there once were two brothers. I won't bore you with their family situation, but it was not a normal one. One of the boys was a tough lad, brawny and bold, the other was quieter, more bookish."

"I see where this is going, and the quiet bookish one became a pimp."

Jack rolled his shoulders. "We all must do what we must."

Kat jumped as more gunshots issued from the front. Heather leaned into her and Kat squeezed her hand.

"Don't let them take me," Heather whispered. She was not playful now.

"I won't." Katya patted Heather's hand. "Jack, you were saying."

"Well, the one brother became a mobster and rose fast in their ranks, while the other brother studied, preparing to become an attorney. The tough brother became Boss in due time, and he needed someone at his back that he could trust. Perceiving that he could make a greater impact as a Boss's second than as an attorney in our failed judicial system, the second brother abandoned the law firm that had taken him in and joined up with his tougher, more streetwise brother. The two quickly made a name for themselves, earning respect amongst the other Bosses and the people of the Ward. With the tough brother's charisma and muscle, and with the other brother's book smarts and managerial skills, they were unbeatable. But then *she* came."

"Who, Vivia?"

Jack looked grim. "Not quite. Sonya. Her name was Sonya." He said the name like a curse.

Heather nodded solemnly. "Sonya is a dangerous name."

"Anyway," Kat said.

The limo banked sharply, and when it turned Kat saw a whole wall of Returners blocking off the street. Groaning, they shambled toward the limo. The auto roared and shot off down a side street. It hit a pothole. Kat's drink sloshed. A droplet hit her knee.

"Sonya was a great beauty, and a master manipulator," Jack said, ignoring it all. "She started out as a whore but quickly caught Ravic's eye—"

"Finally!" Kat said, rubbing her knee. "We're using *names* now."

Jack's mouth hooked down. "He took her on as one of his women, and she rose to the top in due course, assuming title as First Concubine and essentially ruler of the roost. Ravic thought she loved him, fiercely. He loved her, just as much. But I knew her feelings weren't as strong as she pretended. You see, in secret she would shoot me glances, would whisper things in my ear."

"Don't tell me you banged Ravic's *girl*."

Jack looked chagrined. "If only it were so simple. You see, Sonya wasn't satisfied with being First Concubine to Ravic. She wanted to bump him off and for me to take his place, then for her to be the shadow ruler pulling my strings. She didn't want the responsibility of ruling herself, she said, only the power. She said Ravic was a barbarian, a monster, he was a blight on the Fifth Ward, a corrupter. Only I could save it. It was the *noble* thing to do. The *right* thing."

Kat set down her glass. "Shit. Don't tell me . . ."

Jack glanced away. "I let her fill my head with dreams of renewing the Ward, of making it a paradise. Somewhere inside I knew she was lying, that she would have me murdered at the first opportunity, once she was able to consolidate power for herself, and she would have been far worse than Ravic, who after all has only tried to do his best. But I let myself believe. I'm still not sure if I would have gone through with it, but I did go some distance. We made plans, revised them, began to put them into motion. I'd like to think that I wouldn't have done it, but who can say? I'll never know. Somehow our plans were betrayed. Ravic found out. Sonya escaped, but I was rounded up and imprisoned in the Factory. Ravic's men demanded my death. He was reluctant, me being his brother and all. But, at last, knowing he had to make an example of me or suffer similar conspiracies later, and surely hurt by what I had almost done, he decided to punish me." He paused. "He wielded the axe himself."

"Magnar!" said Katya. Heather gripped her knee tightly. A gunshot popped, but Kat hardly noticed.

Jack nodded. "He cut off my head in the Pit in front of thousands of people and had my body thrown in the furnace, where so many have gone before. In secret, he had my brain preserved, but for show he had my head mounted over his fireplace. Hence its regrettably withered appearance. Some days after the 'execution', my head conveniently vanished from his mantle and reappeared at Dr. Reynalt's laboratory, along with my brain."

"The Doc!" Katya smiled. She'd heard many stories about the legendary Doctor Reynalt, and always loved a new one. "Awesome!"

"Yes. Well, Ravic offered him a handsome sum to bring me back—discreetly, so as not to alert the Guild or anyone else that might care—and he did. He always has bodies lying around that he purchases from grave robbers and such for just this purpose, and he was able to put my brain back inside my skull, then stick my head on a new body, a fresh one. It wasn't as simple as all that, of course, and it took several days, and more than one body was involved, but at last it was done. Afterwards I asked Ravic why he couldn't have given me a new head as well as a new body, but he replied that I should suffer for what I'd done, that I should bear the mark. And so I do."

"Damn."

Jack drained his glass, then stared at her frankly. "Ravic gave me my life back, Kat. Even took me back in, gave me a position in his ranks. Not as high as before, no—and under a different name—but not too low, either. And he still listens to my counsel. He still *trusts* me. Do you honestly think I would betray him?"

"But what I heard that night . . ."

Jack waved the thought away. "That bit of treachery was meant for Loqrin, not Ravic. Believe me, I would not betray my brother, not again. I owe him my life, and my deepest gratitude."

Kat eyed him warily. It occurred to her that if Jack could screw Ravic once, he could do it again. And now he had a new bone to pick with Ravic, a little matter of an axe. But she didn't press the point. She was in Jack's power for the moment. Maybe later she could act on her suspicions, but that would have to wait.

"Fine," she said. "I guess I believe you."

Jack let out a breath. "Good. Good." He refilled his glass, took a drink. His gaze drifted outside. Almost instantly he said, "Shit."

Katya tensed. "What?"

"*Look.*" He pressed a button. "Driver, stop."

The auto jerked to a halt, engine idling, the driver clearly eager to be gone. And no wonder, Katya marveled, as she leaned forward to stare out the window.

In fleeing the Returners, the limo seemed to have made a large circle around the Domino, and now they sat on the opposite side of the rubble from the one they'd exited on. A bunch of Loqrin's autos—Kat recognized them—half-encircled an opening in the ruined tenement. In front of the broken doorway milled a large crowd of factory workers. Kat recognized them, too. Some had been pinching her ass not thirty minutes ago.

They must have been trying to escape the boiler room meeting, but Loqrin had found them. Kat saw what looked like fighting going on inside the rubble, and the factory workers there were smashing unseen opponents with bricks and crowbars. *Returners,* she thought. They had flooded in from the other side and forced the factory workers out into the open, where Loqrin's men had found them. On the other side of the half-circle of autos a horde of Returners shuffled listlessly, groaning and clenching their fists—but not advancing. The reason for this was obvious. Blue and purple light-bulbs flashed from radar-shaped devices some of Loqrin's goons carried and emitted odd beeps and whistles; evidently these machines controlled the creatures, hypnotically perhaps, or maybe they worked on the transmitters implanted in their skulls. Whatever, it seemed to work. The creatures stayed back.

Katya heard gunshots. Movement drew her attention. A tall, dark figure veined in glowing green tattoos slipped down an alleyway, firing a gun as she went. Katya grinned tightly. *Go Aqa!* Goons chased her into the alleyway. More gunshots. Kat felt her belly contract in fear. *Please, Aqa, be all right. And Reddin, too.*

Trapped between the goons and the Returners, the doomed factory workers fought with every weapon they had available, but the goons did not give them a chance to win. Heavily-weighted nets arced out, enmeshing the factory workers—first a dozen, then two, then all of them. The Returners underground tried to climb out and rip them apart or devour them, but Loqrin's men trained their lights and sounds on the creatures, and they backed off, covering their ears and growling.

"Loqrin's men want the strikers alive," Jack whispered. "What in the world for?"

As if you don't know. "Lab rats," Katya said. "Or—" Suddenly a horrible notion swept her, and she felt cold. Very cold.

"What is it?" Heather asked.

Katya could only shake her head. She tried to block out what she had thought, to imagine it couldn't be so. And yet how could it not? The Guild, to her way of thinking, would never have authorized Loqrin to round up so many lab rats at once. They wouldn't want the publicity. A few a night, sure, but dozens all from the same place at the same time?

Which could only mean Loqrin was doing it on his own, and *that* meant . . .

"We need to get back," she said. "We need to get back to the Ward." She had to tell Ravic. Something had to be done before it was too late.

Jack hit the button again. "Driver, go. Fast."

Surely relieved, the driver obeyed, and the limo shot off down a side street. Over the noise of the distant sirens and the groaning of the Returners, Loqrin's goons didn't seem to hear. Besides, they were occupied with binding and subduing the factory workers for transport.

Most of the streets were clear, Katya saw. The Returners had been drawn to the Domino, lured by the violence and noise. She wondered if Loqrin had used them to flush out the strikers intentionally. He was not as mad as he seemed.

It took forever, but at last the scenery around the limo began to change. The crumbling, listing tenements gave way to taller, straighter buildings.

"The Hollows are behind us," Jack said.

They were entering the Fifth Ward once more. The buildings here were poor, but proud. The people that walked the streets did so straighter, too, and they looked *right* somehow.

Heather gripped Kat's hand tightly. "The Outside," she said. "We're going Outside."

"Don't worry," Kat said. "I'll protect you." She refilled Heather's glass. "Have a drink."

Heather drank.

Katya saw brightly-lit bars, a topless club called ZeZe's, and soon the familiar corner of Navvers and Trilston where Aggie stood with her associates. Aggie was laughing and popping chewing gum, leaning into the passenger seat of an auto, chatting it up with a prospective john. Kat tried waving at her, but it was useless with Aggie's distraction and the dark windows. Nevertheless, Kat felt her spirits rise, seeing the activity, hearing music playing. They passed a nightclub, and smoky, brassy tunes issued forth. Kat had a sudden longing to go there, to drink something sweet and strong and just lose herself in the music. Later, she promised herself. She wondered if Heather had ever been to a show.

They cruised down one street and then another, the driver taking his time now, maybe relishing being back in the Fifth. Then, suddenly, they passed an intersection and saw a group of police autos grouped up the street, parked, lights flashing, red-white, red-white. Gunshots sounded.

"Fuck," Katya said, and Heather didn't protest.

"Driver, take us there," Jack said, depressing the button.

Once they reached the scene of activity, Jack and Kat climbed out. Heather followed more reluctantly. The breeze was cool, almost bitterly so, and somewhere a woman screamed. Katya ran forward to see a plump woman kneeling, weeping over the corpse of a portly man with a gray beard. *A gray beard and a steaming skull.* All over the road bodies lay strewn and twisted, skulls smoking.

"A haunt!" Kat said.

The policemen saw something up above and fired at it, as they must have before. The gelatinous dark mass rippled through the night, tendrils extended, sweeping down on the policeman as if to feed from them. They screamed. Most kept firing. One fled. An otherworldly terror seized Katya, and she felt ten times colder than she had just a minute before. Still, from somewhere she dredged an ounce of foolhardiness, and she sprang forward, before the policemen, putting herself between them and the descending haunt.

"No!" Jack screamed.

"What are you *doing?*" Heather cried.

Kat felt the girl's fingers on her shoulder, trying to drag her away. Not even the haunt could scare her off.

The thing came closer, and Kat smelled ammonia and sulfur and other, stranger things. She could just barely see, as the shadows inside it parted, a pale blue fire, and inside it, a figure . . .

It was upon her.

Quickly she made the sign she had before, the one she'd witnessed Loqrin making. She fashioned her right hand into a fist and placed it over her heart, while with her left pointer finger she made a spiral before her face.

Gunshots roared. Someone screamed.

Kat felt a whoosh, a stirring of air, a reek of ammonia, and when she looked up the haunt was flying away, blotting out the stars, then seeming to disappear into them.

Heather was shaking her and shouting something into her ear, but Kat barely heard it. Her heart hammered so fast and hard she thought her ribs would break, and every limb trembled. She tried to stand, but couldn't. Then she was aware of Jack coming around, taking her under the arms and hefting her up. He smelled of incense and spices. A strange look was in his eyes, a look of questioning. She couldn't speak to answer his questions, even if she'd wanted to.

A policeman approached—a sergeant, Katya saw by his stripes. He had short-cropped black hair and beard and wore the usual blue-gray of Lavorgna. He recognized Jack—Jack *was* fairly distinctive—and nodded. The sergeant eyed Katya respectfully, but fearfully. He likely wasn't sure if his bullets had scared the haunt off or if she had, but it was clear which direction he was leaning.

"Thank you," he said. "I think."

She nodded shakily. Jack gave her to Heather, who held her and said, "That was amazing."

"It truly was," Jack said. To the cop, he said, "How many did it get?"

The cop grunted. "*This* one got eight. But it ain't alone. Three more've been seen tonight. I'm afraid the total dead'll be more'n forty, and that's if we don't get another before morning."

"More every night," Jack said, and swore.

"What beats me is why they only attack the Fifth lately. All the *other* districts're safe. Could there be somethin' here?"

"Like moths to a flame," Jack nodded.

"Some fucking moths," the sergeant said. "And what flame?" His eyes strayed to Kat again. "What did you do to it, girl?"

She couldn't explain even if she wanted to. Who would believe her? "N-nothing."

"Nothing! We've been shooting at it for five minutes, and all a sudden you show up and—poof!"

She stared up into the stars, searching for haunts, searching for . . . there! She pointed, and heads turned. It was gone before anyone else could see it, though, slipping between constellations, but she was sure of what she had seen: a vast, torpedo-shaped silhouette, drifting over the Fifth. Perhaps *he* was the flame, she thought. But why the Fifth? She thought she knew the answer to that, too.

It wasn't soon enough that Heather and Jack escorted her back to the limo, and she didn't stop shivering until long after they had quit the scene of the attack. Only the familiar sights of the Fifth cheered her, and she had to pinch herself to keep from imagining she was back in the Hollows.

And then, at last, the great trio of belching chimneys loomed ahead, pouring uselessly colored smoke into the night sky. The Factory stood proud, defiant, surrounded on all sides by bombed-out buildings, like foothills surrounding a mountain. Kat saw the red light washing out from the huge hangar doors, and it was as if she felt warmer already. A strange thought crossed her mind, but she did not dismiss it: *Home.*

Heather murmured excitedly as they crossed the huge open area of the Pit Room. Down below a fight was going on. A pair of armored gladiators—paid and willing, Jack assured her—fought half a dozen Returners with iron maces and flails. The crowd cheered, bets flew through the air faster than blood, and the furnace filled the room with heat and light. Girls strutted throughout the room, hawking beer, peanuts, cigarettes, themselves, you-name-it. Kat and Heather split a fried eel wheel, and Heather loved it.

The elevator ride up was long, and the ticks of the machine made Kat wince. It was Ravic's elevator, she saw, somewhat surprised that the Boss let his wayward brother use it. Maybe all the lieutenants had access to it. The ground grew further and further away. Heather and Kat held hands. At last the cage stopped, and Jack led the girls through the homunculi hallway. Heather was surprisingly calm when passing through it, but it still gave Kat the creeps.

Almost there, she thought. *Almost to . . . oh, grow up, Kat.*

Then they were there.

The suddenness of it shocked her. They stepped over and around the immense fireplace and there he was. Katya squeezed Heather's hand.

Big as life, Ravic sat on his throne, sipping a goblet of wine, watching a young woman dressed in scanty swatches of silk perform a dance before him, swaying this way and that, the fire at her back blazing brightly. She was very pretty, Kat thought, and a jewel twinkled from her navel.

But Kat's eyes were for Ravic. When his gaze fell on her, it was as though lightning struck her. She held herself back.

"Stop!" Ravic called to the dancing girl. He looked so big and strong, and his dark mane, just showing the first streaks of silver, made him look like an aging lion. He shoved his drink into the hands of a serving girl and stepped down from the throne.

First he and Jack shook hands. "Back sooner than I thought you would be," Ravic said.

Jack grunted, ironic. "Me, too." He flicked his gaze at Kat. "This one turned the crowd against me."

"What?"

"Yes, it'll be some time before I can get those men back on our team—well, what few are left of them." In answer to

Ravic's unspoken question, he added, "Loqrin raided us, caught a bunch of them."

"Gods damn it!" Ravic pounded a fist into a meaty palm. "Food for his Returners, no doubt." He shook his grizzled head, disgusted.

"Maybe not," Katya said, stepping forward. Again his gaze turned to her, and again she felt warmed all over. *Just the fire*, she told herself. He was a paternal figure, nothing more. "I think Loqrin has something much fuckier in mind."

Ravic raised his hairy eyebrows. "And what would that be?"

Katya glanced around nervously. There were many ears around, serving girls and goons. From the corner Vivia eyed her cattily. "I'd rather tell you in private."

Ravic grinned. "Well then, all right."

She swallowed nervously, exchanged a glance with Heather. Heather's face was very pale, but she winked. *What does she know?*

Chapter 11

Ravic's bedroom fireplace blazed with light and heat, and Kat stood over it, rubbing her hands. She was all too aware that she was still in the short, tawdry outfit Reddin had dressed her in. The fire felt good, and sweat beaded her pores. Flushed, she turned to Ravic, who stood at the bar pouring drinks. Ice clinked.

He took an experimental sip, added a dash of whiskey to his glass, then strode over and handed the other glass to her. Nervously, she sipped. Stared up at him. There was just so much *of* him. She took a stronger sip. It burned.

He brushed hair back away from her face, and as he did his fingertips just lightly brushed her forehead. They were rough, but warm.

"I've never seen someone tremble so much standing in front of a fire," he said.

"I aim to amaze," she said, and mentally rolled her eyes.

Hastily, she stepped away, downing another sip of her drink. With her back to him, she said, "I don't trust Jack."

A sigh. "The few that know who he is typically don't."

"Is it true he's your brother, and that you beheaded him?"

"He is, and I'd do it again."

As she walked away from the fire, she grew colder, but the further she got from Ravic, the less she trembled. *What's up, Kat?* she asked herself. *Get a hold of yourself!* Another, more mischievous part of her said, *Let HIM get a hold of you!*

Clearing her throat, she turned around to face him. He still stood before the fire, half leaning on the mantel, a lion at rest. She wondered if that's where Jack's head had hung, but doubted it. Ravic would have put it on the mantle in his throne room, where it would be seen by his visiting lieutenants and so on.

"I still don't trust him," she said.

Ravic's face made no expression. "You're smart."

Her heart sped up. He had complimented her! *Magnar, I'm pathetic.* She took a steadying sip. "Loqrin's making haunts."

Still his expression didn't change. What was he, made of stone? But when he spoke, his voice was coarser, harsher. "Haunts? Are you sure?"

She nodded emphatically. "The Guild of Alchemists, they've made some sort of deal with him. He's provided them with lab rats, and they're giving him . . . what, I don't know. Money, alchemical shit, who knows? But it's not what they're giving him that he cares about."

"No?"

"He's using them. Using the Guildsmen, their machines, their labor, to make the haunts."

He moved toward her, and for a moment she didn't know whether to stay or flee. She fled, moving closer to the bed. Too close! She edged away from it. He hadn't been going toward her, though, but to the bar. He refilled his drink and turned to her.

"Want more?"

She swallowed, nodded. He came toward her, and she could smell him, all smoke and sweat. He poured her two fingers of whiskey, and the glug-glug sound of liquor leaving bottle seemed very loud. He stoppered the bottle with a squeal of cork, then returned to the bar and sat it down.

"They go to the underground city," she said. "The Elders' city, the one they found. Some building there. That's where they do it."

He eyed her fiercely. "Why?"

A sip of whiskey stung her throat, but it warmed her too, and unlike the fire it helped sooth her shudders. "The Guildsmen, they're doing some sort of experiment, I don't know what, something about frequencies or translation. Loqrin doesn't care about that. It's the machine he's interested in. They have the tools to use it, he doesn't, so he tolerates them, does their bidding. Brings them lab rats, strikers and whoever. But he's found ways to tinker with the machine."

"Has he now? A machine of the Elders?"

"Well, using the Guildsmen's gizmos. They've kinda hot-wired it. I think he's found a way to tap into it, use it when they're not looking."

"Why?"

"I don't know, exactly. But I saw him going into the Below—he uses a zeppelin—the night before he and the Guildsmen met down there. He was doing something to the machine *when they weren't around*. That's what I think. And the next time—wham!—one of the Guildsmen's victims went into the machine and came out a haunt."

Ravic sipped his drink, his gaze straying to the fire.

She relaxed. "And he's got some box in his suite, a machine. Near an altar. He puts people in there and it makes their heads steam, just like the haunts. So does the Elders' machine. I think his box is sorta a homemade version of the thing in the city."

Ravic frowned, still staring at the fire. "An altar? Perhaps a god . . . a god of the Elders?" He took another drink. He could drink a lot, Katya thought. He sighed. More of a groan, really. Slowly, his gaze returned to her, and she had to resist the urge to smooth her hair. "This may be too much for me, girl. I can't fight gods."

She forced herself to take a deep breath. "I don't know about gods, but if there is . . .*some*thing . . . out there . . . then *some*one has to fight it. And tonight, Loqrin rounded up a bunch of strikers. Men that went to the rally. *Dozens* of them."

"I know. Jack told me." He rubbed the side of his face. "Magnar . . ."

She nodded. "I don't think he means to give them to the Guild. I think he's going down there again tonight, right now, to the Below. I think . . . I think he's going to make dozens of haunts!"

He looked momentarily ashen. "Dozens?"

"Yeah. Some major shit's goin' down, maybe *the* major shit, and I think it's all because of me. After I escaped, he knew he'd better hurry or else I'd tell what I knew and you'd have time to stop him. So he's sped up his plans, whatever they are, and that's why he took those workers to make haunts out of tonight. I still can't figure out why, though."

Logs popped in the fireplace, and sparks flew up. At length Ravic remembered his drink, took a sip. "The bastard can't do this, not to my boys."

"Your boys?"

"My strikers."

With a start, she remembered something that should have been obvious all along. "It's you! *You're* the one organizing the strike!"

He grinned humorlessly. "Like you say, someone has to."

"*That's* why Jack was giving the speech . . ." Floored, she stepped back. Idly, half noticing, she sat down on the bed. Gently, like a lion moving through the jungle toward prey, Ravic moved across the hide-covered floors and stood over her.

"But why?" she said. She realized a different kind of fear now. The fear that Ravic was mortal. "Don't you know what they'll do to you? The Guild? They've got black cells beneath their main office downtown, no one gets out of there alive, and the rumors of what they do there . . ." She shuddered. "The Guild won't tolerate what you've done. And if they have a say in what Bosses do . . ."

"They have a say, all right. They control the damned *country* girl. Even the mob. Oh, we run ourselves pretty well, I guess, but if they say jump, we'd better be prepared to flex our fucking legs. That's why I use lieutenants, let them give the speeches in different parts of the city, places they're not likely to be recognized. And when we can, we filter it through local crews, crews that don't bow to the Guild . . ."

"Like Reddin."

He nodded absently. "Yes, like him. There are others, many others, a wide network I've built over the years."

She looked at Ravic and suddenly he didn't seem like a mountain, he seemed like a man, frail and mortal. The Guild was so much bigger than he was. They were the mountain, and he was a lone man standing before it, shaking his fist at it. *He's going to die!* She felt tears burn her eyes.

"I think they know," she said. "They must. *That's* why Loqrin's been targeting you. I thought it was just to mask his stealing Fifth Warders—to make haunts out of—and that's probably part of it too, but I think . . . I think maybe the Guild directed him, sicced him on you."

"I hope not. If that's true and they know what I've done, then I'm dead. Or worse. Maybe he's doing it on his own. I know he has spies here. I find new ones all the time, turn them up like moles." He grunted. "If he has, then that's another reason I have to take him out. I suppose that's unavoidable now."

"But I still don't understand! Why take the risk? Why try to form a union? What place is it of yours?"

His voice hardened. "It should be everyone's place." She felt rough fingers pull her chin up, and she stared up into his stern face. "Everyone's."

She swallowed.

"And I'll have you know it's my place especially," he said. "Why you, I don't know. I haven't told many. I think you can take it."

"I can take it," she vowed. "Whatever it is."

He indicated the wall behind his large low bed, where hung the oil painting of the ancient king, mounted on his horse before his castle. "That's Salus Gianna, King of what was then called Crostervich some five hundred years ago. Lavorgna, it was still Lavorgna back then, was Crostervich's capitol. That castle stood about ten miles from here. I wish I could say it was in the Fifth, but it's not. Close enough, though. That man is—was—my ancestor."

Kat looked at Ravic in shock. "You're shitting me."

There was no amusement in his face. "I have the records to prove it. After the kingdom fell and the democrats began rising and bungling our glorious Confederation of Wallach, my family went on the run, hiding, never staying in one place too long. And they were hunted, oh yes. The democrats lynched them every chance they got. It was a large family, though, and they spread out, underground." He grinned. "Like moles."

With a sigh, he sat down beside her, and his weight bounced her up and down. She was all too aware of his warmth. His arm pressed up against her, but he hardly seemed to notice. She did. It made her shiver, but she didn't draw away.

"According to the existing records," he continued, "I am the oldest male of the particular line that was dominant during the last kingship. Different branches of the family dominated at different times during the royal days, so that makes a difference."

With wide eyes, she looked up at him. Sweat beaded her forehead. "Don't tell me . . . you're . . ."

He nodded. Shrugged. "There are no kings anymore, not here. But if there were, the records indicate that if the family dynamics . . ." He sort of smiled. It was a small smile. "Yes."

"Wow." She hardly noticed putting her hand on his. His skin was very warm. And covered in hair. Strangely, she liked that. A Crostervichan prince! Or king! It was too incredible to believe. And yet, for some inexplicable reason, she did. If nothing else, it explained Ravic's obsession with medieval shit.

She realized she was staring up into his face, his proud, leonine face, and she forced herself to look away. "Listen," she said, and her voice came out as a choke. "I really think we should talk more about Loqrin." She took a breath. "And the haunts."

"No. No more about him. I'll take care of him, have no worries on that. Before the night is done, he will be a memory." He said it with such hate and conviction that she believed him.

"What will you do?"

He smiled enigmatically. "Leave that to me."

"I want to be a part of it."

"I want you here."

He cupped her face in his hands. He had such large hands. She felt his rough warm fingers on her cheeks. Her breaths came quick and shallow. She shifted her legs.

He traced her cheeks, her lips. "Katya," he said, "I am very impressed with you. I want to show you how grateful I am."

She allowed herself to run a hand up his hairy, naked chest. She could feel his heart beating beneath his ribs, slow and heavy, like some great jungle drum. Its rate seemed to increase slightly the longer she touched him. His smell of sweat and musk surrounded her.

He tilted her chin up, and she parted her lips.

Yes, she thought. *Oh yes . . .*

He bent down to kiss her, and his lips just brushed hers—

She shot up and stepped away. She saw that she'd unknowingly sat down her drink on the floor. Hastily, she retrieved it, took a sip. Too big! It stung. "I'm sorry," she said, her voice raw. "I . . . I can't . . ."

Pained, he stared at her. "Why?"

She opened and closed her mouth, but no words came out. She didn't know what to say. Then it came to her. "Because you have *all the power.*"

"What?"

She spread her hands out, indicating the room, the fire, the painting. "I'm just this thief, this woman, and you're . . . hellfuck, a *king.*" She shook her head. "Don't you get it?"

He tried to smile his slow, handsome grin. It didn't come out quite as cocky as he wanted it, though. "I know you want it with me, girl."

"It doesn't matter! It doesn't fucking *matter!* You still have all the power, and I don't have any."

He eyed her hungrily. "You have power enough."

"Yeah, the only power I have—the power to cross my fucking legs, and that's what I'm doing." Defiantly, she sat down her glass and crossed her arms over her chest.

He looked haggard. "I just wanted to . . ."

"I know," she said sadly. "And I *want* to. But not . . . not like this. Not before your stupid fire, before your stupid picture. And if you think I'm stupid enough to believe you've never tried that king line on another girl . . ."

He looked at her innocently. "I've never needed to."

She waved it away. "Bullshit!" She took a breath. She knew she was flushed, sweaty, drunk and probably not making much sense. She stared at him and saw him eyeing her somewhat sadly, like a little boy whose puppy had run away. *Well too bad. He's got plenty of puppies.* "Anyway, I want you to do something about Loqrin. You say you have a plan. Well, do it. Whatever it is, I want to be part of it. I want to see that fucker burn!"

With that, she turned and stormed out of the bedroom, leaving Ravic staring after her. A log popped in the fireplace.

Fuming, though Katya wasn't sure who at, she marched down the hall, nearly knocking over Vivia on her way.

Vivia bristled. "He's mine, girl. Back off."

"I'll do what I please," Katya said. How long had Vivia been there? What had she heard?

Whatever. Katya stalked away, feeling the electricity in the air behind her as if Vivia's glare gave off a charge of its own. *Screw her.* To either side stood the closed doors of Ravic's guards, like Gunnerson and Syd. Kat pushed past the crimson and gold tapestry at the end of the hall, entering the throne room. The fire flickered, the flames low, the embers white. Serving girls lounged on pallets waiting for instruction, and Katya was reminded uncomfortably of Loqrin's harem. But *these* girls were happy and all too healthy, and they were free to go at any time. That made all the difference. Soft music played. *Like another world*, Katya thought. Could she ever think of this as home? She realized in some way she already did.

Branching off the throne room to either side of the fireplace were the two other wings, each opening hidden by a tapestry. Guests stayed in the rooms there, but also concubines and lieutenants. Jack apparently lived up here. *The viper and the breast.*

Where to now? For a moment Katya fidgeted, unsure where to go. Should she grab a pallet by one of the wait staff?

"Come with me," a young woman said, approaching. "I'm to show you to the room you'll be staying in while you're here." She took her to a small room down one of the wings and left her. Heather lay passed out on the only bed under a wooly orange blanket, a bottle of something greenish curled up beside her. The light was off, but soft moonslight flooded in through the small window.

Kat brushed her teeth, scrubbed her face, slipped into a nightgown (Ravic's serving wenches had plenty, and they were happy to share, though few were small enough to fit her) then stared at the bed. It wasn't a big bed. Sighing, she moved Heather close against the wall and squeezed in beside her. To her surprise, Heather rolled over and smiled. She did it so suddenly that she gave Kat a start. Moonslight bathed Heather's face, but it pooled her eye sockets in shadow, so deep they didn't seem to have a bottom.

"So!" Heather said. "How did it go? Couldn't have gone *too* well, I don't think you were gone for very long. Were you? I was kinda taking a nap."

Katya still reeled from drink. "Nothing happened."

Heather patted her on the arm. "Sorry. Maybe he'll grow to like you."

"It was *me* that didn't want it."

"Of course it was."

"Really!"

Heather gave an indulgent sigh. "I believe you. Besides . . ." (she made an icky face, which was very unsettling) ". . . isn't he, you know, a bit *old*?"

"Maybe I'm a bit young."

"Yeah, that too." She put the bottle to her lips and upended it. Chugchugchug. Then burped right in Kat's face. Kat waved the smell away. "Sorry. By the way . . ." Heather looked sheepish. "Did you happen, you know, to talk about me at all?"

Kat gave her an encouraging smile. "Yeah, before we got into it all. I told him you have years of experience playing mother hen to a harem, and guess who's got a harem, whether he calls it that or not?"

"I understand he has two or three official concubines. Is that right? I could be one, then someday First Concubine, then seduce someone younger and take over. Jack's story was very inspiring."

"Heather!"

Heather laughed. "Just kidding." Another drink. Her next words came out quite slurred. "Thanks for speaking up for me."

"No problem."

Heather chuckled. "You really like him, don't you?"

"Do *not*."

"Don't *tell* me you love him!" In a singsong voice, she said, "Katya loves Boss-man/kissin' in the shade/first comes tongue-in'/then he's diddlin' the maid." She giggled.

Katya rolled her eyes. "Fuck off."

"As if." A hint of sadness entered Heather's voice. "No one will want me now, Kat, not after what Loqrin did to me. No one."

"Someone's had too much booze."

"No. Really." She laid her head against Katya's shoulder.

Katya stroked her hair. "We'll find somebody for you, H. Don't worry."

Heather took another swig of her drink, then screwed the cap back on. In moments she was snoring. Kat shifted in the bed, getting comfortable. She hoped Ravic gave her a bigger room, or else gave Heather one of her own. This bed wasn't made for two. It was barely made for one. Ravic . . .

I'm being stupid. H is right. He's way too old. She told herself she was just mixing up father figure and lover. She'd never known a dad.

She made herself think of Jack. Not erotically, but just of him. Maybe she'd been wrong about him. Ravic trusted him enough to allow him a room on this floor. Maybe Katya should give him a second chance.

Slowly, sleep overcame her. It wasn't restful, however. Loqrin loomed up before her, holding a bloody knife, the same one she'd stabbed into his back. He cradled Abby in his arms. Blood covered the young woman, and scissors stuck up where her forearms should be. Loqrin was smiling down at her. Then he dissolved into Death's Head Jack, and she imagined him on his hands and knees, head on the chopping block in the arena. Ravic towered over him, teeth bared in a snarl, blade flashing down—

Katya woke up with a gasp. Sweat beaded her brow. Shaking, she climbed from the bed and splashed water on her face. When that didn't work, she stared at herself in the mirror. Dark eyes looked back at her out of a pale, high-cheekboned face. Small, straight nose, small chin, black bangs falling just over her eyes, the rest of her hair framing her face and ending at her jaw.

Acid roiled in her belly. She didn't feel well. Something was wrong, horribly wrong. She didn't know what it was, what it meant. The world was just subtly *off*.

In any case, she couldn't sleep. Not now. Maybe a stroll around her new home would help blow out the cobwebs. Her old sneaking reflexes needed a workout.

Leaving Heather curled up with her beer bottle, Katya slunk from the room. The hallway was cold and dark, only lit by a few torches. She crept down the hall, emerging into the throne room. Glanced around. Nothing going on. She stepped over sleeping forms. A woman sighed, touched her leg, then turned over and went back to sleep. Kat moved on, veering around the fireplace. Little lamps covered with swaths of colored fabric lit the room in soft, leaping light. A few scented candles gave off hints of cinnamon and nutmeg. Only a few white embers glowed in the fireplace.

She wondered if it ever went out entirely. For some reason, she hoped not.

She made it to the other side, ducked beneath the tapestry and tip-toed down the hall of the wing opposite hers. From one room she heard women laughing and heard tiles moving. Some sort of late-night board game. She knocked and stuck her head in, but they told her they didn't have any openings. Maybe next time. She moved on, trying the occasional door, just for fun. Not looking to steal anything, really, just getting her kicks. At one point a broom fell out at her from a broom closet and she just barely put it back before it woke up half the hall.

She was just about to give up on this wing, too, when, toward the end of the corridor, she heard whispered voices behind a door. She couldn't tell what they were saying, but she recognized one of the speakers.

Vivia.

Katya, unable to help the lifetime habits of a professional thief, placed her eye to the keyhole. At first all she saw was darkness. Then, vaguely, moonslight pouring through thick drapes. The drapes muffled the light, making the room dim and strange.

" . . . is so exciting," she heard Vivia say. "The time is here! At last, can you believe it?"

A weird voice answered, "It is glorious." The voice was garbled somehow. It sounded both watery and electronic. It gave Kat chills.

Squinting, she saw the tall form of Vivia pace back and forth in the dim room. She was just a vague silhouette against the corpse-light spilling in through the drapes. Voluptuous, with high-piled hair.

"But we must be careful," Vivia said, stopping suddenly in her pacing. "This is the critical point. One misstep and we're done. I don't think your brother will be as forgiving as last time."

Brother? Could that be Jack speaking? It didn't *sound* like him.

But then the speaker said something that stole Kat's breath away.

"No, Sonya, I don't think he will."

Kat thought she'd misheard at first. *Sonya?* It couldn't be. There was no way Vivia could be Sonya, the woman who had seduced Jack and betrayed Ravic. *Surely.* How was that even possible?

"It won't matter soon," said Vivia, or whoever she was. "Just stick to the plan. I can't believe it's all going down now. For so long, all the waiting, and now tonight . . . ."

"I know."

"And you're sure you've told me everything?"

"Yes, damn it. Ravic and I just spent an hour talking it over. The plan is simple. He means to hit Loqrin now with everything he's got, before Loqrin's project can be completed. I still wish you would tell me more about what he's up to, with the haunts and all. But keep your secrets if you must. Anyway, I'm not going over Ravic's plan again."

Vivia hissed. "Now isn't the time for your theatrics, Jack."

So it *was* Jack. For some reason the thought saddened Katya. She'd hoped she had misjudged him. Suddenly she realized she was barefoot and the floor was cold stone. The chill crept up through the soles of her feet to her legs, then spread throughout her body. Her back hurt from hunching over to peer through the keyhole.

Vivia stopped before a squat table in the middle of the room. Something stood there, Kat couldn't see what. "If you've left anything out . . ."

"I haven't." Jack's garbled, watery voice came from the object on the table. Frowning, Kat made out a wide bed against the wall. A form rested there. Various machines hooked up to it, and she heard pumping noises, and some sort of chugging. It was only after staring at the form for several seconds that she realized that the body on the bed had no head. Shocked, she nearly gasped. At the last second she clapped a hand over her mouth.

The thing on the table . . .

"Sonya, for you, I would do anything," Jack said. "I think I've already proven that. I've told you all I know."

"Very well," Vivia said. "Then I guess I have a call to make." She crossed to one corner of the room and lifted two small objects from their cradles. One must be an earpiece and the other a mouthpiece. Cradling the former against her shoulder and holding the latter with one hand, she began to spin the dial. Click. Click.

No! Katya thought. She couldn't let Vivia do this. There was only one person she could be calling. Loqrin. Jack and Vivia meant to betray Ravic, feed Ravic's plan to Loqrin so Loqrin could set a trap for him. *I have to stop them.*

But with what? She had no time to summon help. Vivia was making the call right then!

Cursing herself, knowing she was acting rashly, she hurried back to the broom closet. Mop in hand, she returned to Jack's bedroom door. Pulling out the pin Aqa had given her from her hair, she quickly, and as silently as possible, picked the lock, exactly as Aqa had taught her; Ravic's locks were not cheap. Fear lent her focus, and the lock clicked open.

She wrapped her hand around the doorknob. *This is it*, she thought. *Last chance to turn back.*

Gritting her teeth, she jerked the door open, stepped in, and slammed the door shut behind her.

Chapter 12

"Get your hands off that phone, you bitch!"

Shocked, Vivia dropped the earpiece and mouthpiece, then turned to stare at Katya. "What? Who—"

Katya didn't waste time. She lunged forward, bringing the head of the mop down at Vivia's head. Vivia ducked, stumbling back. Kat thrust. The mop hit Vivia's cheek a glancing blow.

With alarming quickness, Vivia overcame her shock. One of her hands went to a thigh, yanked out something sharp and glittering from a sheath. In the darkness, Kat hadn't even seen the knife.

She struck at Vivia again, but the taller woman, with practiced deftness, hacked with her knife, her arms moving with hard muscle almost like a man's. *Crack*! Wood splintered, and half the mop fell to the floor.

"Shit," Kat said.

Vivia kicked the section of mop away and advanced on Kat, blade raised so that it caught the light. Its tip pointed down, right at Kat's breast. Kat coiled her legs, waited for Vivia to get close—

Kat sprang.

Vivia struck.

Kat's half-staff hit the knife, knocked it from Vivia's fist.

Vivia slapped Kat, hard. Shocked, Kat reeled backward.

Vivia stared at the floor, turning her head this way and that, scanning for the knife. Katya couldn't give her time. She lunged forward again, thrust the jagged end of the broken mop at Vivia's midsection.

Vivia was prepared. Her hands found the mop handle—jerked. Kat was flung off balance.

Vivia pulled up violently, ripping the mop handle from Kat's fingers. Kat nearly collided with her as she stumbled forward.

An elbow struck Kat's cheek. She spun around. Crack! Elbow between the shoulder blades. Kat's breath exploded from her lips. Something, maybe the mop handle, struck her head. She fell to her knees. Another hit near her ear, and she crumpled to the floor.

"No!" Jack was saying. "That's Katya! Don't!"

Vivia evidently wasn't listening, or didn't care. Katya felt hands seize her hair, jerk her up from the floor, slam her face back down. Pain flared. She tried to move, but she felt weak. Stunned. Her vision wheeled.

Vivia yanked her up. Katya saw the floor roll beneath her. Dazed, she swatted at Vivia, but Vivia ignored her. The woman dragged her to the squat low table where the strange object stood. Kat saw what looked like a box-shaped aquarium, with all sorts of tubes feeding into it. The water churned and bubbled, stinking of rot and chemicals.

Dimly Kat realized what Vivia meant to do. "No," she said, though the word came out so weakly she wasn't sure if Vivia even heard it. "No . . ."

"Yes, you little strumpet, this is what I do with ones like you."

They reached the table. Kat gazed down into the bubbling water. It was too dark to see what was in there, but an electronic, water-muffled voice issued from it: "No, Vivia, don't! We can talk through this!"

Vivia laughed. "No more talk, Jack."

She plunged Katya's head under the surface. Water, or something thicker than water, engulfed Katya. She tasted nasty, bitter chemicals, and the taint of rotted flesh. Her eyes stung. Her cheek bumped something, and she shuddered—Jack's head, she knew, receiving its nightly regenerative bath. That's how he managed to stay so well-preserved despite his withered state, and why he had looked so refreshed the night of the haunt attack.

But these were just vague, distant thoughts. She tried to hold her breath. She fought and thrashed. Kicked her legs, trying to break Vivia's shins or knees. Vivia was no novice to violence, though. She very efficiently elbowed Kat's spine, sharp and hard, stunning her whenever she grew too unruly. Katya's mouth filled with the nasty stuff soaking Jack's head. Her lungs ached. She wanted nothing more than to take a breath, a breath of anything, it didn't matter. Stars danced about her vision. Darkness gathered. Strangely, the stars grew brighter. Black spots danced before her, too. Her lungs caught fire.

At last, unable to resist, she breathed in. The black, vile stuff filling Jack's head-box entered her mouth, her throat, her lungs. It burned her, seared her. She vomited even as she breathed in. Distantly she felt her limbs thrash and flail. On and on.

At last they relaxed.

. . . blackness . . .

. . . blackness . . .

Then. Something. Shuddering, sputtering. Fluid leaving her. Running from her nose, her mouth.

" . . . *alive* . . ." she heard. Vivia's voice.

"Still time . . ." Jack.

A snort. "She's dead, she just doesn't know . . ." Blackness again. Then Vivia's voice. " . . .'at to do with the body . . . Well, there's always . . ."

Some time later Kat felt herself bumping along. Impacts coursed through her. Footsteps. She was on someone's shoulder, being carried. Each footfall jarred her. In the distance, she heard Jack calling for a servant. Perfume filled her nose. A tapestry sailed over her head.

The lights of the throne room blinded her. She blinked. Gunk dripped from her hair and nose. She groaned. What was happening?

Blackness.

Then: sleeping faces, the faces of serving men and women, the staff that kept Ravic's people comfortable. Vivia stepped on one's ankle, there was a grunt. Eyes fluttered opened. Stared, horrified, upward. Katya stared back, pleading.

"Say anything, bitch, and you're dead," Vivia said.

The serving woman paled.

Blackness.

Then: a hall.

A hall . . .

In the back of her mind, a fear grew in Kat. It began to awaken her. Fire coursed through her limbs, shaking off the paralysis. *No*, she thought. *Not this. Not . . .*

Too late.

Vivia marched into the homunculi hallway, careless. She had no reason to fear the homunculi sentinel that guarded Ravic's lair, as Ravic had branded the memory of her into the homunc hallway. He hadn't had time to do that with Kat.

No no no .

"This oughtta do it," Vivia said. "What's left of you will be absorbed." Satisfaction filled her voice. "And there won't be much left."

Kat was slung, moved, dropped. Another impact jarred the breath from her. Her fingers scraped the ground. Muddy stuff slid under her fingernails.

Vivia wasted no time. No parting remarks, nothing. As if she had just dropped off a load of garbage, she walked away, a victorious swagger in her hips.

Katya sputtered, and black gunk came up. She choked, retching. More gunk.

Vivia was gone.

Almost instantly, the hallway responded. Katya was not an authorized visitor, and she was not accompanied by one.

The hallway rippled. A hand snatched at Katya's shoulder. She rolled away, but weakly. Stars and black spots still skipped about in her vision. Dark fluid still gunked up her lungs and trickled down her nostrils and over her lips. It tasted foul, making her cough some more.

A black hand grabbed her ankle. She kicked it away.

More limbs stirred to life. They began groping for her.

Gotta get up, Kat, she told herself. *Gotta move. Up!*

She tried. She climbed to her hands and knees, kicked and slapped at a few more homunculi hands, then a coughing fit seized her and she doubled over.

Fight, Kat!

She crawled forward, punching out with her ringed fists. Jagged rings tore into soft, muddy homunculi flesh. Mud spattered. A homunculi head rose up beneath her. Black teeth snapped at her. Gasping, she hit it, twisting aside. Still more hands groped at her, raking her sides, grabbing her hair. Strands ripped from her head. She screamed, but when she did another coughing fit seized her.

The end of the hallway was so far away, maybe five whole feet. An eternity.

Hands grabbed her ankles. She tried to kick them away. They grasped her tightly. Began to drag her backward. More hands found her. One seized her wrist. Another a breast. Another a thigh. One gripped her cheek, seeking purchase on her skull.

And then they all pulled . . . *in different directions* . . .

She screamed. Horror and pain filled her. She would be torn apart like a rabbit to wild wolves.

Then, a silhouette, standing at the end of the hallway.

"Ravic!" she said.

"Katya!" the figure screamed. "Fuck!" It wasn't Ravic. It was Heather. Cursing. She stood, shoulders hunched against the cold air, wooly orange blanket draped about her shoulders for warmth, bottle gripped tightly in one hand.

"Heather!" Black claws tore at Katya. Pain burned through her.

Heather started to take a step forward, to run to her rescue.

"No!" Kat screamed. "Your blanket! Throw me your blanket!"

It took a moment, but Heather's drink-addled brain got it. Thank the gods! Heather unwound the blanket that draped her shoulders and, hanging onto one end, tossed Kat the other. For a life-long instant the end hung, suspended, in the air. Then it fell.

With her one free hand, Kat caught it.

Heather tugged.

Grunting and straining, cursing like a sailor, Heather pulled Kat from the grasps of the homunculi, and Kat clung to that blanket grimly, crying and cursing and bleeding. At last Heather pulled her free.

Heather crouched over her and held her tight. Shudders racked Katya, and she cried into the young woman's shoulder. Black snot ran from her nose. She spat out more of it. Both trembling, the girls held each other, and their gasps echoed in the hallway. In the distance, there came the sounds of commotion. Katya's screams had roused the roost. Figures holding candles began to cautiously approach.

"What happened?" someone asked.

Spitting gunk, Katya didn't have the wind to answer.

"One of you woke me up," Heather said. "Said Kat was in trouble, so I went out looking. Heard her scream, and saw Vivia come out of the homunc hallway."

"Magnar!" breathed one of the wait staff.

"Vivia!" snarled another. A chorus of righteous indignation filled the hallway, warming Katya's heart. It was clear Vivia had kept the wait staff oppressed through fear, and they hated her. This might be the perfect moment to rouse them against her.

Then, all of a sudden, before the posse could be formed, before the traitor could be found and put to justice, footsteps pounded down the hall in the direction of the elevator. Katya knew there was a stairwell near the elevator that led to the next floor down. These days it was the only way other than the elevator to access Ravic's lair.

Breathless, several men and women who must be Ravic's lieutenants stormed into the homunculi hallway, then passed through it recklessly. Nothing stopped them.

When the lieutenants saw Katya, Heather, and the collection of employees of the Factory, one said, "What's this? Can't you see we have important business! Get out of the way!"

The group moved back or scattered, and Ravic's lieutenants swept by. Even in the dim light, Kat could see that they wore grim faces. Anger and fear had hold of them as they stomped into the main room. "*Ravic!*" one shouted. "Ravic, we need to speak with you! There's an emergency!"

Katya forced herself to her feet, Heather supporting her, and staggered after them. What was going on? She had a bad feeling about this.

In the throne room stood Jack, shaking his head, his face wet—wet, but somewhat restored, the flesh smooth, the lines retreating.

"What is it?" he said.

'Shit!" said one of the men, the one who had called for Ravic. He was a big man with a proportional belly. Acne and boils pocked his face, but he had grown a great curly black beard to cover them, and it fell over his chest, beautifully combed. Somewhat more disorderly black hair fell over his face. Kat had seen him around a few times, and she thought he ran one or more of Ravic's gambling dens. Max the Max, she thought he was called.

"It's Loqrin!" Max said. "He's attacking! *Fuck!*" Sweat beaded his well-combed beard, and his eyes blazed. All the other lieutenants seemed in a similar state of agitation.

"Attacking?" Jack affected an innocent look. "What do you mean?"

"I MEAN HE'S FUCKING ATTACKING! *SHIT!*"

With infuriating leisureliness, Jack lit a cigarette. "Can someone tell me what Max means, more specifically?"

With somewhat more calm, a short woman with large hands said, "Loqrin's attacking from every direction but east. A bunch of his boys, in autos. Usin' grenades and repeaters. A lot of our men've died already."

Concern entered Jack's face. An act, Kat thought. "We have to do something."

"That's why we came here!" shouted Max the Max.

Jack drew on his cigarette. "I see."

A red-faced man said, "They're attacking from the west, mainly."

That's where Ravic's defenses were the weakest, Kat remembered. Because Jack had advised it, then told Loqrin to take advantage of it. She opened her mouth to speak, to betray him, but Jack shot her a dark look that caught her off-guard, and she closed her mouth. Her mind spun. What would happen if she did speak up? Likely no one would believe her, and Jack would have an excuse to kick her out on her ass. She had to stay here, had to be of some use to Ravic.

"We have to pull everyone back," Jack was saying. "Have to consolidate our power. If Loqrin wants a war, we'll give it to him."

"BY THE GODS WE WILL!" roared Max, pounding a hammer-like fist into a meaty palm.

One of the other lieutenants, a slender fellow with a curly mustache, shifted uncomfortably. "Shouldn't this be Ravic's call?"

"Yeah!" Max said. Then, more softly: "Where is he?"

"Get Ravic!" another lieutenant said, and more agreed.

"Of course," Jack said. "You're right. For a moment I thought this was the old days."

"Fuck you," said the red-faced man. "I know who you are and what you did. You'll never get those days back."

Something crossed Jack's face. "Very well. Hold on a moment while I get Ravic."

"Fuck that," said the short woman. "Let's all go."

They surged up the throne room, Jack leading the way. Katya had half expected Ravic to come storming out, drawn by the noise, but strangely he didn't. Something fearful itched at the back of her mind, and she remembered her dreams and her premonition, but she ignored it.

"Come on," she told Heather. "Let's go."

Heather nodded. With her still half-supporting Katya, they followed Jack and the other lieutenants. More came out of their rooms, yawning, throwing on clothes, asking questions. In angry, frightened voices, the ones that had come from below told them. The members of the wait staff, looking worried, stayed in the throne room as the men and women who were highest in Ravic's counsels bustled up the hallway toward Ravic's bedroom. Katya and Heather trailed along behind. Katya almost felt well enough to stand on her own. Her lungs still burned, though, her head still spun, and the floor was very cold against her bare feet.

Someone banged on Ravic's door. When no one answered, they repeated the gesture, then harder, shouting curses as they did.

At last they kicked the door in.

They poured inside, crying angrily. The noises cut off abruptly, however, and a cold silence fell over the group. Like a collection of pallbearers, they gathered around Ravic's bed and stared down at it.

"Well, fuck," said Max.

Katya's heart beat fast and hard. Cold sweat coated her face. Breaking away from Heather, she stumbled forward, elbowing her way through the line of lieutenants. At the sight of what lay on the bed, she gasped and fell backward. She tasted vomit in the back of her throat. Before she could fall, one of the women caught her.

"No . . ."

Ravic lay on his bed, mountainous and graying, the hope of Lavorgna, the king of Lavorgna, he who would form a union and defy the Guild, quite dead, a knife handle protruding from his chest right over his heart.

Chapter 13

Something died in Katya.

"No," she said again. "No . . ."

As if asleep, she walked over to the bed and felt his pulse. Nothing. Of course. His gray-green eyes stared blankly upward. His mouth hung partly opened. With trembling fingers, she closed first his eyes, then his mouth. She tugged at the knife, but it was firmly wedged.

The lieutenants cursed and struck fists into palms. "WHO?" Max shouted. "WHO DID THIS? I'LL GUT THE FUCKER!"

Several angry men and women turned toward Jack, who looked just as shocked as the others. Katya felt a great swell of anger build in her, and she wanted to stab a finger at him and condemn him as the murderer. It was all it would have taken, she knew, to rouse the men to kill him. He was suspicious enough already. He had been awake, dressed and more or less composed when they had come across him. And the lieutenants would believe that it was a man, not one of his waitresses or concubines. Only a man could kill *such* a man. That's the way they would think, anyway.

Katya opened her mouth to speak, to get Jack killed like he deserved, but suddenly she stopped herself. Jack hadn't done this. She knew that. He hadn't had time. He'd been calling for a servant even as Vivia carried Katya out of his room. It would have taken him some minutes to reattach his head to his body. Shit, Kat hated to admit it, but he had probably been on the way to help *her* when the lieutenants came across him.

It had been Vivia. It had to be.

As soon as Katya thought it, she knew it, and shame overwhelmed her. She had forced Vivia into it. As soon as Vivia had heard her screams, she had known the occupants of the floor would be roused against her, and she'd had to act, had to prevent Ravic from mobilizing against Loqrin.

Katya had done this. Just as if she'd wielded the knife herself. She never should have confronted Vivia, never should've entered Jack's room. That one act had killed Ravic. *She* had killed Ravic. Vivia was just the weapon she had used.

She was so absorbed in her own thoughts that she almost didn't notice the angry men and women gathering around Jack, and Jack backing up into a corner. In a high voice, Jack said, "I didn't do it! I swear! I had no idea! Hells, you think I would really—"

"You tried before!" one of the men growled.

"He did!" another said.

"No, no, I . . ." Jack waved his hands, placating. "I would never! I mean, I know that once I *thought* about it, but really I would never . . ."

"Bullshit!"

"Get him!"

Angry murmurs swept the room.

Large hands seized Jack and hefted him up. A fist punched his gut. Another struck his face. Feeling both guilty and satisfied, Katya watched. Jack deserved it, she told herself. He deserved it a thousand times over. Ravic would have raised up the common man of Lavorgna, given him rights, freedoms. Jack was just a deceitful hanger-on, a sham prince.

But then, slowly, watching Jack get pulverized, the guilt got the better of her. *He had been coming to rescue me.*

Only half believing what she was doing, she rose, standing up on the bed straddling Ravic's huge bulk as if to prevent vultures from feasting on it—a pose like that was bound to get their attention—and shouted, "Wait! Stop! Jack didn't do it! *He didn't do it!*"

At first they continued pummeling Jack. He was on the floor now, bloody, his clothes ripped and torn. One of his dry, withered ears lay on the floor beside him. But then, slowly, a few of the men stopped, then a few more, as Katya continued to scream.

One of the women among the lieutenants said, "Stop! Stop, guys, let's hear her out!" She was a tall woman with purple-dyed hair and a tattoo of a monkey on her cheek. When the men had settled down a bit, and Jack lay, moaning but alive on the floor, the woman turned to Katya and said, "Honey, what do you have to say?"

Curious eyes turned to her, Jack's among them. Sweaty-faced men kept Jack pinned down with their feet.

Kat swept the sea of faces. She knew she looked awful, with torn shift, black snot and black gunk caking her mouth, homunculi material coating her limbs, her fingers, tangling her hair, and she tried to think of something that would satisfy them. "Jack and I were fucking," she said at last. It was simple, to the point. It caught their attention. "He couldn't have done it."

The purple-haired woman frowned. "Bullshit. When we found you, you were . . . well, I don't know what you were doing, but it looked like you had tried to enter the homunc hallway. Unsuccessfully." She sort of grinned, and there were some chuckles.

For a moment, Katya almost abandoned her plan, almost told the truth, which would surely have condemned Jack, who probably deserved it. But she reminded herself that Jack hadn't known Vivia was going to kill Ravic, and he had been on his way to save her while Vivia had actually been doing it.

She took a breath. "We were fucking," she insisted, "then we had a fight. He wanted to marry me, I told him to eat his dick. We yelled at each other for a while, then I stormed out and was going to run away." She snorted. "The homunc hallway put an end to that idea."

The purple-haired woman mused on that. The rest of the lieutenants looked at her, as if waiting to see what she would say. "Why didn't you have any bags with you, even a purse, and why weren't you dressed?"

Katya shrugged. "It wasn't the best-laid plan, I admit. I guess I kinda hoped Jack would chase me and stop me from leaving. I think he was. That's why he was right there when I came out of the hallway."

Jack stared at her, disbelief but also something else in his eyes. Admiration? Gratitude?

The purple-haired woman rubbed her cheek. She and the large-handed woman exchanged glances. At last she nodded. "Fine. You and Jack were fucking. So who killed Ravic?"

Katya very much wanted to shout Vivia's name, but how to explain that she knew it had been Vivia without getting Jack killed?

Before she could think of a solution, Vivia herself appeared in the doorway, face flushed and breathing hard. At the sight of Ravic stretched dead on the bed, she screamed and ran to him. Angry eyes pierced Katya, but Vivia didn't say anything to her. Vivia nearly knocked Katya aside when she reached Ravic, then knelt over him and beat at his chest, tears coursing a river down her cheeks. "No! No! No!" she screamed, pulling her hair. "No, my love, you can't leave me! Nooo!"

It was a bit much, and Katya was tempted to spit on her. The lieutenants glanced at each other uncomfortably. The purple-haired lieutenant frowned.

"You can't die!" Vivia continued to wail. "You can't be taken from *meee*!"

A throat cleared. Eyes turned to regard Jack, now standing and straightening his garish pink-red tie. He spat out a tooth. Placed his ear in a breast pocket. "Actually," he said, "he doesn't have to stay that way."

"What?" Vivia demanded, looking shocked and angry. Fierce daggers flew from her eyes. *"What?"*

He seemed calm. "His brain is intact. If we hurry, we can get him to Dr. Reynalt in time for him to be brought back."

"You're fucking insane!" Vivia said. It was all but a snarl. A clear warning blazed in her eyes.

"She's right," the red-faced man said. "You're mad. The Doc's an enemy of the Guild. No one sides against them. Well, except him."

"'No one' is going a bit far," Jack said, "especially these days, with the Brotherhood and all. But I don't think they're going to be able to do any worse to Ravic after finding out that he's been for a visit to the Doc than has already been done to him."

They parsed that sentence, then the purple-haired woman said, "I'm not sure about that. Remember the black cells."

Katya wasn't listening. Hope blossomed inside her, reawakening whatever had died when she'd seen Ravic lying there. "Yes!" she screamed. "Yes, yes do it! Take him to the Doc! Reynalt will fix him!"

Max pulled at his well-combed beard. "I vote we do it. Fuck the Guild. I mean, that's why we're Ravic's people, right?"

The purpled-haired woman nodded. "Just don't come looking for me when this backfires."

More agreements came, but disagreements too.

"The Guild will be pissed," the red-faced man repeated. "I don't want any part of it."

"Fine, then you can just resign your commission," Jack said. "Maybe Loqrin can hire you."

"Maybe he fuckin' can," the red-faced man snapped. "If you ain't forgot, he's rippin' up the whole Ward as we speak."

As if to punctuate this, a bust of gunfire came from outside.

Jack wiped a trickle of grayish blood from his lips and flicked it away. "Gather all our men. Consolidate them here at the Factory."

"Gather 'em in this madhouse?" Max snorted. "You don't know what it's like out there! Loqrin's turned the Ward into a warzone."

"That's why we have to strike him hard and fast, with all our strength, while his men are occupied here. It's the perfect time," Jack said. "Cut off the head of the snake while the body's away. Don't worry, Ravic and I talked it over before he . . . before this happened. We have a plan."

A plan, Kat thought. Ravic had mentioned a plan. Could Jack be part of it? But no, that was impossible. He was a traitor. However, traitor or not, he meant to help his brother, in defiance of Vivia, and that was all Katya needed for now.

"You don't understand," the short woman said. "It's crazy out there, all our men fighting in scattered pockets. It could take *days* to round them up into one force."

Jack stared at her. It was clear he had taken over. One minute the lieutenants were beating the shit out of him, the next they were taking his orders. Katya was impressed despite herself. "I'll give you till sundown tomorrow," Jack said. "Gather here in the Factory parking lot. Then we'll drive en masse to Hollows, right down Ratagat Road, it goes right in. We'll storm in and tear Loqrin to shreds."

Max nodded, grinning evilly. "That'll be a sight."

The red-faced man snorted. "And if you don't make it? If you bite it on the way over to the Doc's?"

"Then leave without me," Jack said. "Max'll be in charge. Five o'clock tomorrow. That's when our army leaves. When Loqrin goes down."

They nodded angrily, but happy that they had a purpose. Max's eyes gleamed.

Katya shared a look with Heather, who looked blank as usual. Katya wasn't blank. Her mind spun. If Ravic had had a plan, and if Jack shared it somehow, however unlikely that seemed, it couldn't be as simple as just driving in one great convoy over to the Hollows and shooting the place up. There must be more to it. She had no time to think on it, though, for Jack said, "See to it. I've got to go. Ravic has to reach the Doc before the rot in his brain is irreversible. See you at sundown."

Katya hadn't noticed it, but Ravic's bodyguards, including Gunnerson and Syd, had joined the gathering, and now at Jack's instruction they hefted up Ravic's great bulk, slowly and carefully, and followed Jack down the hall.

"Wait!" Katya said. "I'm coming with you."

"And me," said Heather, following Katya.

"And me," added a feminine voice behind them, and Katya's blood ran cold.

The elevator doors clanged shut. Katya and Heather huddled in the corner under the wooly orange blanket, which was streaked with homunculi material. Heather clutched Katya's hand tightly. Katya shook with stress and cold.

In the middle stood six of Ravic's bodyguards, Syd and Gunnerson and four others, with Ravic on their shoulders. All six were strong men, but even so they sagged under their

Boss's weight and their faces purpled. It was strange to be in the elevator with Ravic without his personality dominating everything. It was like a void had opened up somehow instead, sucking at the life of the others.

Jack stood near the buttons, and on the other side Vivia lounged against the wall, smoking a cigarette, her eyes murderous. Often they strayed to Katya, and Katya wanted nothing more than to blurt out *Vivia killed him! Get her!* Only Vivia could have gotten so close to Ravic with the knife, probably in her waistband, without him suspecting. But Kat knew it would be hard to convince the others, and Vivia's own knife—it was a hunting knife, Kat saw—was back in the sheath on her fishnet-stockinged thigh. Ravic had probably encouraged her to wear it. He'd probably gotten a kick out of it. Now, however, all she had to do would be to pull it out and plunge it under Ravic's jaw and into his brain. Then he wouldn't even have the slim chance that he had now. And Vivia would do it, too, Kat was convinced. If Vivia was found out, if the others believed Kat, than Vivia's reaction would be to do as much damage as she could before she went.

The elevator stank of piss, vomit and sex, and it was crowded and uncomfortable. Worse, it was cold. Katya's belly clenched when she saw the Pit Room spread out before her, dark and deserted, with a few lights still blazing, far far below. Click click click. The elevator's machinery sounded rusty, strained. Her one reassurance was Heather's grip. They often exchanged tense glances. With the shared blanket, heat slowly allowed Katya to stop shivering, though she wished she'd had time to run to her room and throw on some shoes and clothes, maybe wash up. She still spat gunk and occasionally coughed. She wanted a cigarette to get the taste out, but she refused to bum one from Vivia.

The elevator did not slow as it reached the floor.

We're going to crash!

Instead, the elevator slipped right through the floor. The trapdoor slammed shut above, enclosing them in darkness. A moment later, lights blazed, flickering and unsteady.

The elevator thumped to the ground, and Jack yanked the door open.

"Let's hurry," he said.

Without a look back, he led the way out into the small underground parking garage. Kat marveled at all the expensive autos. Jack led to one particular vehicle, huge and thick, with armor plating and a grill like silver teeth. Spikes jutted from its wheels, grill, bumper and top. Four homunculi with spiked collars listed on the running boards, seemingly dead, but at Jack's approach they straightened.

Ravic's limo, Kat thought, staring at the massive, armored, spiked monstrosity. It could be no other.

The bodyguards carefully hefted the Boss into the rear cabin, lying him flat on the floor between the two seats. Syd climbed behind the wheel, and most of the bodyguards piled in the front section. There wasn't room for all of them, so Gunnerson entered the rear, keeping watch over his master. Vivia sat beside him.

Next Jack entered, sitting across from Vivia, and Katya and Heather hunkered by him. Katya put as much distance between herself and Vivia as she could. *Bitchbitchbitch.* Katya wanted to lunge across the space, grab Vivia's cigarette and plunge it into her eye.

She gnawed her lip as Syd fired up the engine. The limo lurched to life, passed through the guard station at a blur and then out into the night. There was no time to waste.

As soon as they were out, Katya saw what the lieutenants had been saying. It was war. Autos lay crumpled on the road, flaming. Shops burned, and gunfire ripped the night. Katya saw a middle-aged woman run across the road toward an open doorway, where people, presumably family members, gestured frantically. She reached the doorway, slipped inside, and the door slammed shut behind her. Katya could imagine the frantic locking of doors, the dragging of furniture. Reminded of the Hollows, she shivered.

"I'm scared," Heather said.

Kat wanted to say *I'm right there with you*, but with Vivia glaring at her she would admit to no weakness, so she just squeezed Heather's hand and said "It'll be okay."

Down one street she saw an auto zoom around the corner, with two other autos in pursuit, guns blazing. A man leaned out the window of the fleeing auto and she thought she recognized one of Ravic's men but wasn't certain. He fired a shotgun at the lead pursuer. The car swerved and smashed into a shop front. Glass erupted. Flames licked out. The two autos whizzed around the corner, still firing at each other, and were gone.

Not a minute later Kat saw a small fire engine speed the opposite way, and she wondered if they rushed to douse the shop-fires or one of the other innumerable blazes that pocked the Fifth Ward.

It was chaos.

Police autos and horse-mounted patrols wandered here and there, helping where they could, but this was a war of Bosses and Kat knew they would mostly stay out of it.

Thinking of Loqrin, of what he was doing to the Fifth, she scowled at Vivia, thinking, *This is what you wanted. You did this.*

As if reading her mind, one corner of Vivia's mouth twitched upward.

The limo raced on. Gunfire rattled, near then far. Often Katya's gaze strayed to Ravic. He just looked so . . . *dead*. She didn't allow herself to cry. She noticed that Vivia kept looking at Jack, sending him silent questions. He made his face hard and did not answer. No one spoke, except occasionally Gunnerson, who would say, as if to convince himself, "He'll be alright. He'll be alright. He's tough as stone, that one." The engine roared, the tires squealed, and chaos exploded all around them.

Katya could immediately tell when they left the Ward by the diminishing sound of gunfire. Unconsciously she breathed a sigh of relief. Beside her she felt Heather relax.

The limo rolled into an area known as the Commons. Kat had never been here, but she knew of it. Its name had come about because no one Boss could lay claim to it. Instead it was where several Bosses' territories, Ravic's included, met, and as such it had historically been heavily disputed. The people that lived here were freer, because they owed allegiance to no Boss, but they lived in a constant state of fear. It was here that Dr. Reynalt made his home, where he would have to pay homage to none.

"There it is," Jack said. A huge mass loomed ahead—a great block of brownstones, dark red brick, covered in lichen. Countless scars twisted on the sides of the structure. Sections of it sagged. "They call it the Warren," Jack went on. "Bombed to the Seventh Hell during the war. The residents that survived had to move out. The Doctor took over the building, renovated it. It's all changed now. He's built libraries, ball rooms, great dining halls, all out of the rubble. And, of course, his laboratory."

Gunnerson swore. "Gives me the creeps. Thinkin' of all those dead things, livin' in there." He looked at Jack and made a face. "Beggin' your pardon, sir."

"Is it true Dr. Reynalt *makes* the dead things?" Heather asked. From her tone it was hard to tell if this pleased her or frightened her.

"Remakes them, more like," Jack said.

"But not with clockwork?"

"No."

"And . . . his creations, they're free?"

Sadly, Jack nodded. "Yes."

The tires squealed, and the limo trembled as it jerked to a halt before the Warren's main doors. Thick and metal, they stood at the head of a short flight of steps.

Gunnerson opened the door. Cold air washed in. "Well, let's get him up."

Jack hauled him back. "Not so fast." He indicated the Warren's roof. There figures with naked rifles crouched, and, as Katya watched, several shifted their weapons so that they trained on the limo. Several had already done so.

"It's not safe," Jack added needlessly.

Gunnerson grunted. "Well, what then?"

Jack didn't answer. Silence fell over the occupants of the limo.

On the floor, Ravic rotted.

"Well, I'll do it, damn it," Katya said.

Before anyone could stop her, she opened the door and slithered out. Jack cried out, and so did Heather. Katya looked back to see the other girl offer her the blanket. After a moment, feeling the cold, shuddersome wind, Katya accepted and wrapped it tight about her. Not wasting another second, she marched toward the Warren. The orange blanket fluttered, taking some of the wind's blast. Above, snipers targeted her, and she stared up at them, feeling her legs shake.

"Hell with it," she said.

She forged up the stairs, grabbed the brass knocker and smashed it against the heavy metal doors. Once. Twice. Thrice. BOO-OOM. BOO-OOM. BOO-OOM.

The eye-level panel scraped way and a pair of mismatched eyes glared out. One was green, the other red. "Yar, what is it?" The eyes ran up Kat and down, narrowing. Kat knew she looked terrible, a small young woman wrapped in a black-smudged blanket, with black smears beneath her nose and around her mouth.

"Yer a sight," said the man behind the door.

Katya pointed to the limo idling on the curb. Steam billowed off the engine. "In there is someone important, and if you don't bring him back to fucking life Loqrin Mars will win and the Fifth Ward will rip itself apart."

The eyes blinked. The panel closed, and for a heartbreaking moment Katya didn't know if the door would open. Then came a series of pops that must be bolts sliding, and the door swung outward with a creak. Katya jumped aside. The owner of the eyes stepped into the gap. He was a medium-sized man with long stringy hair, a long nose and a sharp protruding chin. The skin of his face seemed to be composed of two or three sheets of slightly different-colored skin, and his left hand and right hand were of different sizes. One had webbing between the fingers.

"I'm Maynard."

"Katya Ivreski at your service, and the good-looking corpse behind me is none other than Boss Ravic."

Maynard's mismatched eyes widened. He whistled. "Not sure if the Doc'll operate on a Boss. Could be bad business, that. Still—couldn't hurt to check. Big money in Bosses. Better get the stiff inside before he freezes to death." Maynard chucked to himself.

He stepped outside and signaled to the snipers. Grateful, Kat turned to the limo and gave two thumbs up.

Almost instantly, doors banged open and Ravic's bodyguards dragged their captain from the interior and up the steps, staggering and panting as they went. Jack, Heather and Vivia followed behind. Maynard showed them inside, down a hallway guarded by homunculi on chains, then to a stairwell. One way led up, the other down. On the upper level stood a group of strangely-attired men and women looking tense, carrying guns, hammers and blades. They stank of death. Returners.

Well, Awakened, to be more precise, Katya thought. Returners that had been brought back successfully. The

Doc's minions, as some would have it. Dressed in odds and ends, usually bits of formal wear, the Doc's people had heard the fighting and were prepared for war.

"It's alright," Maynard said, waving them away with his webbed hand. "Jus' a customer." With a bleak look back at Ravic, he added, "Mayhaps." He started down the descending stairwell, lighting the way before him with one lantern-bearing hand and waving Kat after him with the other. They came to another metal doorway, and another panel. After verifying Maynard's identity, the man on the other side of the panel let them in.

"Come, come," Maynard grunted, leading the way in.

As Katya stepped into the laboratory, her jaw fell open.

Chapter 14

Towering machines spitting sparks rose high overhead, and other vast machines chugged and hummed, some belching smoke or flame. Returners, or Awakened, swarmed all over the place, twisting gears, punching buttons, shoving carts of alchemically treated wood over to a furnace. It all stank of death and lightning. Despite the heat, Kat felt chills. She was surrounded by the walking dead. Yet she felt no malice, no threat. They might as well be normal people almost. Of course, some had three arms, or four, or radio antennae sticking out of their skulls, or tubes sticking out below their lower mouths in place of a lower jaw, or metal plates covering half their heads, or . . .

"This way, this way," Maynard said, and slouched over to one corner of the room, only half shielded at the moment by a sliding glass wall. Kat saw strange gasses issue from vents overhead, bathing a mound of—

Her stomach dropped.

It was a mountain of corpses. And parts of corpses. Arm, legs, heads, torsos, and all manner of pieces, stacked halfway to the ceiling high overhead, kept chilled and fresh by the gasses, Katya realized. Gooseflesh covered her arms, and only partly because of the cold. To her relief, Heather caught up with her, and the two huddled together as they approached the mound of jigsaw death.

A tall, manic figure stood before it, his servants all around. From his obviously mortal appearance to his domineering personality, it could be no one but the infamous Dr. Reynalt himself. Tall and thin, eyes blazing, he had thick black hair, black eyebrows, and a sharp curved nose. His dark eyes, set under those impressive eyebrows and over that beak of a nose, gave off a hawkish air, and when he suddenly wheeled and stared at Kat, she jumped.

"What's this?" he demanded. "Can't you see I'm busy?" He had a cart before him stacked with body parts. As if the visitors had bored him already, he turned back to his minions, rubbed his chin, then pointed at a severed foot sticking out from the mound. "That one! And hurry! We don't know how long power will last with the fighting, and our generators won't go forever."

A dead man retrieved the foot and set it reverently on the cart. Staring at the contents of the cart, Kat felt sickly all of a sudden. *He's making someone*, she thought, transfixed by the notion. But not for profit, obviously. He'd grown wealthy and influential reanimating the corpses of beloved family members for the well-to-do, but that did not seem to be his current task.

Maynard coughed. "Doc, if I may?"

"Yes, what is it?" asked Reynalt, half turning around. He and Maynard seemed to share an easy familiarity, though it was clear which was the employer and which the employee.

Maynard nodded toward Ravic, who lay over the shoulders of six sagging and purple-faced men. Breath escaped their mouths in ragged bursts.

"More spare parts?" Dr. Reynalt said. "Excellent! I'm sure these men know I pay a more than reasonable rate for choice parts."

"These are no *parts*!" Katya said.

The Doctor looked at her condescendingly. "A beloved father, then? Well, I'll have you know that I will treat him with respect. And his . . . beloved pieces . . . will go toward creating new life, or bringing back old life. I am sure it is what he would have wanted." It seemed a practiced speech, likely one given many times. As if to accentuate this, he offered a canned smile.

Jack stepped forward. "Actually, no. We've come for an Awakening."

"Then you've come at the wrong time! Can't you hear the fighting? The power could go off at any—" Up until then, the doctor's face had seemed bored with them, preoccupied. But suddenly his eyes widened. "Why, is that—Rupert, could that be *you*?"

"I'm known as Jack these days."

The Doctor smiled, brightening his hawkish face up considerably and almost making him seem likeable. With a different energy animating him, he stepped forward and clapped Jack on the shoulder. Jack returned the gesture.

"So it's going well then?" Reynalt said. "I see you've continued the regenerative treatments. Excellent! So many of my patients disregard my instructions or don't adequately—" Something about Jack's demeanor silenced him. Slowly at first, but then suddenly, his enthusiasm drained away, to be replaced by dread. "My friend, what is it? Wait, don't tell me . . ." His gaze drifted slowly to Ravic. "Magnar! Could that be . . . ?" He all but ran over to the corpse. Studied the face. "It is! Gods be reamed, it is!" Frantically, he spun to his minions. "Well, don't just stand there! Fire up the equipment! We have a Boss to Awaken— and a guild to screw to the wall."

In the distance, guns cracked. Sirens wailed.

Syd lit a cigarette, and Katya bummed one. It was a Hellfire, and it made her cough miserably. Nevertheless, she smoked, grateful for the nicotine. She reclined against a wall and smoked while Heather went off to find something to drink. The Doctor and his people swarmed about, tinkering with equipment, sorting through body parts, thawing a torso, strapping Ravic down onto a sort of slab. Katya twisted uncomfortably when she saw Reynalt's people first shave Ravic's skull in spots, then bore holes in it and insert tubes. The tubes were hooked up to machinery that slowly began to chug.

"They're soaking his brain in regenerative solution," Jack told her. He had come to stand beside her.

Katya swallowed her disgust. "Guess you had to go through that too."

"They put my whole brain in a bath, actually. Ravic's lucky."

Katya looked up at him. Genuine concern filled his face, and he did not seem to be able to take his eyes off his brother. *Then why did you betray him, asshole?* "Do you . . . remember anything?"

"You mean before I was Awakened? No, nothing. Just being . . . well, the axe . . . then waking up here."

She took a hit on her cigarette. "So you don't think there's any . . . you know, anything after death?"

He smiled humorlessly and shook his head. "I don't know."

Silence passed. Gunfire in the distance. Heather had found a bottle of something and sipped on it noisily. She offered Katya a sip, and Katya accepted without much thought. It burned her throat and warmed her belly. She took another.

Ravic's people occupied themselves on the sides. Someone had found a pack of cards and they were playing in a desultory fashion, trying to ignore the goings-on in the middle of the laboratory, where Dr. Reynalt was sawing at Ravic's chest and plugging tubes into his chest cavity. In a corner, the severed torso recovered from the mound was bathing in some sort of thawing solution. When it was ready, Dr. Reynalt supervised the removal of the heart. Katya couldn't watch.

Vivia meanwhile was in and out of the room. Occasionally she would disappear upstairs, and Katya had no doubt she was contacting Loqrin via phone, or trying to. *Probably telling him Ravic's plans.* Katya had tried following her in order to prevent this, but the Warren was an easy place to get lost in and Vivia had vanished into it easily.

Currently Vivia paced up and down the room, smoking furiously, stalking back and forth, back and forth, like some jungle animal in a cage. The similarity was heightened by her long sleek fur coat, high-piled red hair and knee-length black boots, high heels clicking on the concrete floors like martial drumbeats. It was clear she didn't want to be here, and why would she? Dr. Reynalt was trying to undo what she had risked her life to do. And Jack, her supposed accomplice, had instigated it!

In the distance, scattered gunshots still punctuated the night, and to Katya it almost seemed like the Warren was under siege. At least she'd been able to clean up a little.

Gunnerson found a radio and turned it on. A harried yet professional voice filled the room, and the bodyguards lowered their cards.

" . . . and the police are saying to remain in your homes if you're in the Fifth . . ." (static) " . . . no telling when the violence will be . . ." (static, hissing; Gunnerson slapped the radio) " . . . Police Commissioner James Vance is quoted as saying, 'This is a mob war that has been brewing for some time. The animosity between Boss Mars and Boss Ravic has long simmered . . ." (static, squelching) " . . . war is like a pocket of gas exploding. Let it burn itself out, and stay out of its way in the interim.' Critics are saying the Commissioner's hands'-off policy is yet more Guild influence, but supporters remind us that Vance was the anti-Guild candidate. This reporter thinks that such a distinction is . . ." (hissing, squelching, another bang from Gunnerson) ". . . just in, another fire on Marble and Hafferstrug. Any residents in the area are advised . . ."

The voice spoke on, and Katya listened intently. It was as if that one voice plugged her into the greater world beyond the Warren. A curious sort of energy filled her. The world wasn't all shit. There were still good people out there, fighting the good fight.

Heather nudged her.

"What?"

Heather pointed to a far wall, where Katya could see what looked like a depression. And a balustrade . . . She frowned, her annoyance forgotten. "A stairwell, going *down*? But we're already underground!"

Heather nodded. "What could it mean?"

"It goes to the Below," Jack said.

Kat raised her eyebrows. "Why would any normal person want to go down there? I mean," she amended, "in as much as the Doc can be called normal."

Jack leaned back against the wall, crossed his arms over his chest. "The Doctor goes on periodic sojourns down there, or sends one of his minions to do it for him. Usually he goes himself."

"Why?" asked Heather.

"For many reasons. One being that the Doctor studies the ruins of the Elders. He tries to understand them. He also looks for pieces of their technology that he can use, or—and I know this is his dream—to find an Elder corpse to reanimate."

"*That's* creepy," said Heather.

Jack shrugged. "He is Doctor Reynalt. But just think what could be learned from such a thing. All the Elders' secrets, their knowledge, laid before us at last. Some say they could twist time, or travel between the spheres, that they could commune with the Outer Lords."

Kat and Heather shared a look. Kat felt a chill. "Look," she said, "I don't know about all that. All I know is nothin' good ever came of fuckin' with the Elders' stuff."

Jack inclined his head, once to the left, once to the right. "Perhaps, perhaps not. Some say the Doctor's techniques for reanimation were inspired or extrapolated from their texts. He's made a great study of them. That's another of his purposes in going into the Below. To find their engravings and tablets, make copies. They say he spends long hours trying to translate them, understand them. Many of his crew are tasked with various related projects. Some are probably in the Below right now, making transcriptions. I've heard it said that no one outside the Guild knows more about the Elders and their ways than the Doctor. Of course, he was once *of* the Guild, which might explain it."

Katya scratched her cheek. "Maybe he can help us figure out what Loqrin's up to."

"Perhaps."

"Why are *you* helping us, anyway?"

He lifted a single eyebrow. In a lower voice, he said, "Why would I not?"

Heatedly, she said, *"You know why."*

He sighed. "Not all is as it may seem, Katya. I advise patience. And no more heroics, please. The plan is still in motion. A somewhat major deviation, yes, but it will still work."

"Deviation? Yeah, a fucking hell of one."

"Language," Heather said. She seemed to have forgotten about her earlier bout of cursing.

Gunfire crackled outside, distant but steady. Katya was almost used to it by now.

At last the activity around Ravic's body began to break up. A sweaty and obviously exhausted Dr. Reynalt staggered over to the group of Ravic supporters, wiping his brow as he went. Kat's heart beat faster as he neared, and she climbed to her feet excitedly. The others gathered round as well. Gunnerson killed the radio.

"How's my brother?" Jack said.

"I have done what I can," Dr. Reynalt said. "Even now my crew is finishing up the procedure—stitching, removing tubes and the rest. It is my hope that your brother will make a full recovery. And by *full* I mean *alive*. He will require none of my machinery or alchemy to sustain him. He will, in effect, not be a true Awakened."

"That's wonderful!" said Katya.

"His heart had been destroyed and his brain had undergone some injury due to lack of oxygen, but I have replaced his heart and renewed his brain. It will be some time before he wakes, and he will need several days' bed rest when he does, but I predict a successful outcome."

"*Great*," said Vivia, in a voice that could have ground glass. As she spoke, she shot Jack yet a venomous look.

Jack swallowed, but it was clear he was relieved. "Thank you very much, Doctor. You've served my brother and I well yet again. I hope there won't be a third time."

Dr. Reynalt's thick eyebrows lowered. "I serve no one."

"Pardon me."

The Doctor swept his sweat-drenched hair back from his high forehead. "I'm famished. While I've been working, my people upstairs have prepared a meal for us in the dining hall. I would be honored if Boss Ravic's brother and friends would join me . . ."

Jack bowed. "We would love to."

Dr. Reynalt, preceded by some of his Awakened, mounted the stairs and vanished up above. "Come," Maynard said, the last of the Awakened to follow.

"I could eat a bull," said Gunnerson.

"Wouldn't that be cannibalism?" said Syd.

The bodyguards began mounting the stairs after the Doctor and his people. Katya looked to Vivia and didn't like the look in her eyes. She was staring at Ravic and grinding her teeth.

"Why don't you let a lady go first?" Katya said, holding two of the bodyguards back. The other four had already reached the doorway up above. She gestured for Vivia to follow.

All but growling, Vivia mounted the stairs, her boots click-clacking on the concrete like gunfire. Shrugging, the two bodyguards followed. Katya smiled to herself. Sandwiched between the bodyguards, Vivia would be harmless. Heather started after them, then Katya, and Jack brought up the rear. Katya realized she was still only wearing a shift, and she looked over her shoulder to find Jack eyeing her legs and rear, then hastily look away when she caught him.

You always want your brother's women, she thought. *Well, too bad.* Of course, she wasn't really Ravic's woman. She was her own woman. And it wasn't as if—

Movement caught her attention.

Vivia had reached the door. In what seemed like one smooth, well-coordinated motion, she slammed it, bolted it, spun around—at the same time drawing her hunting knife from its sheath on her thigh—and slit the throat of the bodyguard following her. Blood jetted in an arc, spattering her face, but she did not seem to notice. Even as the bodyguard slumped against the railing, Vivia hurled the knife end over end. It struck, point first, in the chest of the second bodyguard, who reeled backward, knocking Heather into Kat, and Kat into Jack behind her. They fell in an ungainly heap.

Vivia leapt over them and landed on the other side. Pinned by Heather and the dead man above, and Jack below her, Katya wriggled to get free. She felt Jack's legs kicking beneath her back. She craned her head to see several of Dr. Reynalt's people break off their work on Ravic and stare, dumbfounded, at Vivia. Several of them started to advance on her, tools in hand to use as weapons.

She stalked toward them with the lethal grace of a tiger. Even as she moved, one hand went behind her, under the fur coat, and pulled out a large revolver. Dimly Kat recognized it as Ravic's.

Crack! Vivia shot the closet technician. Brains exploded on the back of his head, spattering two others. *Crack*! *Crack*! Vivia shot them next. Another lunged at her out of the shadows between pieces of machinery. She kicked him away with her sturdy boots and shot his face as he flew away. More blood and brains spattered.

By this time, Jack had wriggled free from under Katya and was lifting himself up. Katya frantically struggled to get out from under Heather, who wasn't moving. Two more shots were fired behind her as she freed herself and climbed to her feet. Looking down she saw a red mark on Heather's forehead and realized the back of the dead bodyguard's head must have struck her as he fell. She was out of it.

The technicians were fleeing into the shadows of the room, which were many. Vivia shot one more in the back, then flipped open the cylinder. Gun smoke drifted up from the revolver. With her free hand, she dug out a box of shells from her fur coat and began reloading as she casually strolled toward Ravic, who lay lifeless and helpless on the slab surrounded by equipment. Vivia's heels clicked like the ticking of a bomb.

A shadow slipped behind her. Death's Head Jack spun her around and dashed the box of shells from her hand.

"Leave him al—"

She slapped him, hard, across the face, and he stumbled backward. She was strong. "I don't know what your game is," she snarled, "and I don't care."

"Sonya—"

She jumped forward and clubbed him on the skull with the butt of the revolver. He tried to ward her off, but her strong arm crashed down again, and again. Jack fell to the floor, moaning.

Katya began crossing the floor. *Shit shit shit.*

"Godsdamnit," Vivia hissed. She was scanning the ground for the box of shells. "Fucker!" She saw Katya. "You! Stay out of my way, slut."

"You don't have to do this," Katya said. She wished she had a weapon. Her rings weren't enough.

"You don't know what I have to do," Vivia said. "How big this really is."

Jack began to stir on the floor.

"Stay down if you know what's good for you," Vivia warned him. Her eyes roved the floor, searching, searching. At last she threw down the gun in exasperation and strode over to one of the machines near Ravic. A great, thick cable led from one machine to this one. She ripped the cable free, and sparks burst from the end in an electric shower. "This should do." Holding the heavy cable in both hands, she pulled it toward Ravic. Still he lay unmoving.

Jack, a groan on his lips, rose to his feet. "Sonya—"

"Stay back!" Vivia shouted. She was only a few feet from Ravic now.

Jack moved toward her, unsteady, a hand to his head.

Katya eyed the cable Vivia was holding, saw where its end met the other machine. If she could just remove that end—

Vivia drew closer to Ravic. Sparks hissed and flared from the end of the cable, driving back the shadows. Vivia visibly had to narrow her eyes against it. Katya could only imagine what the cable's energy could do to Ravic. Reduce him to ash, most likely. There wouldn't be anything left for Dr. Reynalt to bring back in any case.

Katya ran toward the machine that sprouted that cable.

Jack put himself between Vivia and Ravic.

"Sonya, don't—"

She shoved the end of the cable toward him, and he jumped back. His dead face looked pale.

Katya reached the machine. Frantically she tugged at the end of the cable. If she could just unplug the damned thing, Vivia would no longer hold a live wire. Grunting, straining, she pulled. It was mounted firmly.

"Die!" Vivia roared, and plunged the sparking end at Ravic's chest.

"No!" Jack said.

Kat saw what he was going to do, and screamed for him to stop. He didn't.

Not hesitating, he threw himself between the crackling sparks and his brother. The discharge hit him, right in his own chest. He screamed, jerked. Smoke rose from his body. He spasmed on the end of the cable like a fish on a hook.

Katya yanked the end of the cable free.

The sparks died.

Jack fell to the floor. Smoke boiled off him.

"Oh, Jack," Katya said, staggering back and wiping sweat from her forehead. How could she have been so wrong?

"Fuck!" Vivia said, facing her. "You little *whore.* I told you to stay out of it."

Katya had no weapon, but neither did Vivia. Cautiously, she approached the other woman, feeling herself crouch. Soft, downy hairs stood out on her forearms and from the nape of her neck. Her belly clenched. She smelled the stench of burning human flesh as she got closer. *Oh, Jack.*

Vivia glared at her as if Katya were a rat just crawled from the gutter. Her gaze drifted, scanning one of the surgical tables that stood near Ravic. With a cry of delight, she reached toward a gleaming, sharp instrument—

Two shadows lunged out and seized her. The Doc's technicians. Fury and fear lit their faces. They had seen six of their comrades die, and they were *pissed*.

Viva writhed like an eel in their grasp. "Let me go!"

"Hurry!" shouted one of the technicians, whether to Katya or someone else Katya couldn't tell; his eyes were on Vivia. "Get something to kill her!"

Katya looked at the gleaming surgical instruments, then at Vivia's long, lethal legs and heavy boots. No. Too close.

She saw an object under a table and picked it up. The box of shells. With a feeling of triumph, she crossed to the revolver, Ravic's revolver, which lay on the floor, and began shoving shells in one at a time. Her fingers shook, and Vivia's curses in the background didn't make them shake any less.

At last she snapped the cylinder shut. Looked up.

Vivia's thrashes had loosened one arm. That was all it took. Her free hand darted to the face of the technician that still held her. Long fingernails jabbed at his eyes. He shrieked, fell back. The other technician lunged.

Katya tried to take aim, but the technician was in the way, and the lifeless bulk of Ravic was just behind Vivia. Katya circled, trying to get a better shot. Almost there . . .

Vivia grabbed the scalpel she'd been reaching for earlier and sank it deep into the technician's right eye. He screamed and fell away, one hand over the damaged orb.

Breathing hard, eyes blazing, Vivia began to turn back to Ravic—

Caught sight of Katya. Froze.

Katya fired.

Vivia threw herself to the side. The bullet whined off a hanging light fixture, made it sway. Drunken shadows leapt about the room.

Vivia disappeared behind a generator. "Gods damn you!"

Kat laughed without humor. She stepped close to Ravic, saw that he was safe, then looked down at Jack. He lay blackened and dead, smoke still rising from him, on the cold concrete floor. His garish tie had blackened. His eyes were half-dissolved in their sockets. His brain would be no better. A wave of sadness came over Kat. She had done this. Somehow her mistrust of Jack had started this whole thing. But how could she know? He was a traitor! Confusion and anger displaced her sadness.

Gritting her teeth, gun thrust forward in her trembling hands, she stepped around a machine and caught sight of Vivia.

Vivia darted.

Kat fired. Smoke wreathed upward. When it cleared, Vivia was gone.

A skittering noise somewhere to Katya's right. She swiveled, pointed. Nothing. Heart beating madly in her chest, she stepped around another machine, pointed her gun. Nothing. *Damn it damn it.* Where had Vivia gone? Jaws clenched tight, Katya circled the machines, turning and stabbing her gun around every corner. At one point she heard Vivia's laughter, but when she reached the spot the laughter had risen from Vivia had gone. Constantly she returned her attention to Ravic, making sure Vivia wasn't sneaking up on him.

Crash! She started, gasped. Someone was banging on the door above. She realized she'd been hearing it for some time now, but it was growing louder. Dr. Reynalt and his people were trying to ram down the door.

A skitter, scrape.

She whirled to see a dark shape vanish into the stairwell leading down.

"Shit," Katya said. With new urgency, she ran toward the stairwell, pointed her gun. The metal door at the bottom of the stairway banged shut.

"Gods no," Kat said, heart sinking. *Vivia had gone into the Below.*

Thinking quickly, she searched all about for a flashlight. She knew there would be one. Dr. Reynalt feared the loss of power. Indeed, she quickly saw that flashlights were scattered all over the place, perhaps for use during surgery. Shining the way before her with one hand and pointing the gun with the other, she descended the stairs.

Thumpthumpthump beat her heart. Sweat stung her eyes. She blinked it away.

She kicked open the door, leapt into the space beyond. A tunnel. She followed, cautiously, back hunched. The corridor led to another stairway, this one also leading down. At the end stretched another tunnel. Alchemical torches in brackets lit the space. One of the torches was missing. Two homunculi leaned from the walls, connected by chains to their collars. They did not even move as Kat slipped between them. Dimly, and horribly, she realized they were here to guard from visitors *coming the other way.*

They were sentinels of a thick metal door, now ajar.

Kat nudged it open, then slipped beyond, where the rugged walls of a natural cavern stretched into the unseen distance. Hairs prickling even worse than before, so much that she could feel each and every straight-up hair as a tension on her skin, Katya stepped into the hall. Moisture dripped on her from above. The cave twisted, bisected with others. She pressed forwards. Always she followed the trace of smoke. Vivia wasn't far.

At last the series of caves emptied out into one of the great open areas of the Below. Gasping, Kat beheld a great wall of blackness before her. She stood on a road or path that wound along the edge of a terrible chasm that plunged down, miles and miles, perhaps into the very core of the planet. Air wafted up, warm against her cheeks, and somewhere bats chittered. To her right she saw the bulge of what had to be a ruin of the Elders, jutting from the cavern wall and projecting over the edge of the abyss. From the weird angles and unnatural facets, she knew the building could never have been built by human hands. *I don't like this place.*

To her left bobbed a tiny, flickering light, diminishing into the distance.

Kat ran after it.

Heart thumping like a jackrabbit beneath her ribs, she pounded her legs as fast as she could. Her legs burned, her chest burned, and her bare feet slipped and shuffled on the hard rock. Uneven and sometimes jagged, it cut at her. She ran on.

Vivia slowed. Kat felt vengeance flare inside her. She lifted her gun, fired. The gun roared, but the distance was too great. Why was Vivia slowing? It made no sense. There was nowhere to go but . . . down.

Then Kat saw it.

All at once, her blood ran cold, and she almost fell over.

Loqrin's zeppelin drifted silently and darkly through the abyss. Only the lights in his gondola gave away his presence. Perhaps he had been waiting. Just as Katya thought this, Vivia yelled out, her voice echoing long and loud. Almost instantly, floodlights blazed out from the zeppelin, picking out the rock of the precipice, then Vivia.

"Hurry!" Vivia yelled. "I'm being pursued!"

The zeppelin swung close to the edge, and someone, maybe Loqrin himself, dropped a rope ladder that unrolled from the gondola doorway. Vivia seized it and began climbing.

"No," Kat said. The bitch wouldn't get away.

She ran, bare feet slapping on the cold stone. Vivia mounted the ladder, her muscular arms and legs propelling her. Kat could see the glow of the gondola doorway above.

A tall, familiar shape stood there. Hatred coursed through Kat's veins.

At last she reached the bottom of the ladder, or as close as she could get. The zeppelin had already drifted away from the edge, so she could not ascend after Vivia if she had wanted to. She craned her neck. Vivia had reached the top. Clearly exhausted, she climbed up, and Kat heard the strange words "Father, there was a problem—"

Katya started. *Father? What the—?*

She could sort it out later.

Shaking, she raised her gun and pointed it dead center at Vivia's back. The distance was lesser now, but it was still not small, and Kat was anything but an expert marksman.

Rage lent her determination. She squinted one eye, bit her lip, and fired. She fired and fired, until the gun clicked empty.

For a heartbreaking instant she thought all of her shots had missed, but just after the last *crack!* Vivia catapulted forward, right into Loqrin's arms.

There was an awful moment of silence. Then Loqrin threw back his head and roared. It was a primal, prolonged howl, and in it Katya could hear pain and unimaginable grief. But she also heard something more—hate.

A wave of victory swept Katya, and she laughed, jumping up and down on the rim of the abyss. *"That's right, you fucker! That's what you get for killing my friends!"*

Loqrin's roar of loss and fury echoed down to her, and the zeppelin's flood lights swept the rocks, seeking her out. Sudden fear overshadowed Katya's anger and triumph. She turned on her heels and ran.

Just in time. Gunfire obliterated the place she had just been standing, and bullets chased her as she fled.

Chapter 15

Panting, feet bleeding, covered in sweat, hair in disarray, Kat returned to Dr. Reynalt's laboratory to find that Reynalt and his minions had broken down the door at last and were cleaning up the mess. Bodies lay on the ground in rows, and the Doctor and his people moved from one to the next. Katya expected Reynalt to be examining the corpses for parts but instead he seemed to be leading one of the Awakened around, or perhaps simply observing him. The Awakened man wore the silver chain that signified a priest of Magnar, the underground cult that was an enemy of the Guild, just as they had been an enemy of the ancient Qaran Empire. The priest appeared to be blessing the bodies, one by one.

Heather, now on her feet and holding a hand to her forehead, stood with Syd, Gunnerson and the surviving two bodyguards around Ravic and Jack. Someone had been good enough to lift Jack up and place him beside his brother, whose lower half was concealed with a white sheet. Jack still stank of smoke, and Katya tried not to wrinkle her nose when she drew close. His flesh made a faint hissing noise. The two dead bodyguards were nowhere to be seen.

"Jack's dead," Heather said, managing to look both blank and sad at the same time.

Katya nodded, tiredly. "Where's the bodyguards?"

"On ice," said Gunnerson, and spat. "There's a debate. Some think they can be brought back. It ain't for us to decide, though. Boss and the Doc'll have to take that up."

Syd scowled. He indicated Ravic and Jack. "Was it Vivia?" When Kat nodded, he swore. "I never did trust that bitch. Reminded me too much of that other one."

Gunnerson nodded. "Sonya. Those were dark days."

"Fuckin' aye," said one of the others.

Katya decided not to mention that Vivia might well have been Sonya. She supposed it didn't matter anymore. The bitch was dead. And her secrets with her.

I killed a woman. For a moment Katya felt dizzy with guilt, and telling herself that Vivia had deserved it didn't help one bit. *I'm a murderer.*

Movement drew her attention. Ravic's chest rose and fell. She went to him and, surprising herself, lay her hand against his stomach. It was warm.

Syd looked from Ravic to Katya. He lit a Hellfire, and smoke wreathed his long, sour face.

Katya had wanted to tell them that she'd killed Vivia, but somehow, in the wake of the discovery that Ravic was alive, she just couldn't do it. And Ravic's life had come at a cost. Her gaze drifted to Jack, then to the bodies of the Awakened—most of which had been shot in the head and were beyond even Dr. Reynalt's abilities.

For a time the men and women stood beside their fallen, and gunfire crackled in the distance. Vaguely Kat was aware that it must be dawn or later. That meant that in about twelve hours or so Max the Max would be leading Ravic's host into the Hollows to smash Loqrin for good and all. Except . . . except that Vivia *knew the plan.* Knew it, and had most likely told Loqrin, who would have prepared for it.

"Pardon the interruption," Dr. Reynalt said, coming over. "I know now is not a good time, and I'm very sorry for your losses. I did not know the two other gentlemen, but I was well acquainted with Jack—Rupert, as I knew him. You might even say I feel a parental grief for his passing. But that aside, it has been a long night, and the food has grown cold above. I know you must all be hungry, even if part of you does not feel like eating. Please, if you will join me. You can do nothing for Ravic now. He will rouse when he is ready."

Katya nodded. The others agreed limply.

Saying little, they all accompanied the Doc and some of his people upstairs. Two flights up, a massive set of richly-engraved doors gave way to a sprawling dining room. Katya raised her eyebrows when she saw the long, darkly-stained table. It looked like it could seat *hundreds*. What seemed like thousands of glittering plates and serving-ware heaped upon it. A beautiful crystal chandelier hung from the ceiling, and the leaping candle-light it emitted made the crystal glow and dance. More candles lit the table, red wax pooling around their bases. Expensive oil paintings of dreary yet fantastic landscapes adorned the walls.

Dr. Reynalt sat himself down at the head of the table and gestured for his guests to sit close to him. Someone provided Katya and Heather with men's dining jackets to cover their nightclothes. When he was comfortable, Dr. Reynalt rang a bell, and trickles of his people shuffled into the room. They issued from different hallways until at last the great table was fully occupied, and Katya had to stop herself from staring. There *were* hundreds, and one and all were undead. Not just undead, but assembled from pieces of different corpses, so that one half of a face might be a different color from the other half, or one hand black and one hand yellow, and so on. And many . . . well, many had been *altered*. Kat saw a man with an arm sprouting from his head. Another had an iron lower jaw grooved with sharp teeth. One man had four arms, one woman four breasts (Kat wondered if they were a couple). One man literally had eyes in the back of his skull. And on and on. But they were not slaves or victims; all were willing and in agreement with their modifications. That part struck Kat as bizarre as the rest of it.

Their smell wasn't as bad as she would have thought. Dr. Reynalt had obviously treated the bodies with a combination of alchemical substances to retard or even eliminate rot. Also, there were numerous scented candles and bowls of potpourri to reduce even the faint odor that was present. Katya wondered if the Doc could even notice the smell after so long working in it. Probably not. And yet he deferred to his guests.

Servants appeared bearing trays full of savory food, or food that had been savory an hour ago. It was fairly cool now. Still, it was delicious. Kat broke a stick of fluffy white bread and used it to mop up the brown gravy that covered her smothered steak, then munched contently. Beside her Heather drank glass after glass of wine.

No one said much, but there was a din of glasses and cutlery and chewing. From time to time the Awakened would speak among themselves, but they too were subdued. They'd lost six friends, after all. And in the distance, even through the thick walls of the Warren, all could hear the occasional rattle of gunfire and sirens spilling out from the nearby Fifth Ward.

Kat tried not to think of Jack as she ate, but it was hard. *I'm so sorry, Jack. If only I had trusted you . . .* Of course, the question remained: should she have? She kept trying to piece it all together. Why had he been conspiring with Vivia, then betrayed her? It just made no sense.

At last dinner ended, and Dr. Reynalt rose from his seat. He gestured to Syd, Gunnerson, and the other two bodyguards, Katya thought their names were Lowell and Franklyn. "Gentlemen, it is my custom to smoke a cigar after such a feast. Would you join me? I get so few guests."

"Sure," Gunnerson said. "Why not?"

"I like an occasional cigar," Syd allowed.

The others agreed, too, and they stood to follow the Doctor. Katya had no doubt they went to discuss the current situation and start planning what to do about it.

Katya cleared her throat. "Excuse me, but why aren't Heather and I invited?"

Dr. Reynalt turned. Blinked. "Do you women . . . smoke?"

Men. "Why not?" Katya said. "But more than that, I can talk, and we've got some shit to talk about."

"Such as?"

Moving closer to him, she lowered her voice. "I'm Ravic's spy, Doc. I've been to Loqrin's camp, and I know what's going on. If anyone's going to talk about important things, it's me, and *you* are going to listen."

"Young lady, I hardly think—"

"It's true," Gunnerson said. "The girl's right."

Reynalt frowned. He gave a loud sigh. "Come, then."

Heather strolled up behind, wine bottle in hand. It looked empty. "Will there be something to drink?"

"Nice," said Syd, puffing around his cigar.

Dark and cozy, lined with books and beautiful oil paintings, the smoking room smelled of leather and cigars. Low flames crackled in the fireplace. Dr. Reynalt, clenching his cigar between his jaws, sunk into a plush burgundy armchair upholstered in fine leather and gazed at the flames while his guests finished lighting their own smokes and got comfortable. Heather found a decanter of something on a stand and commenced to drink, smoking at the same time. Katya's own cigar made her cough, but Heather breathed it in like air.

The men adopted attitudes of lounging around the room in comfortable chairs or couches. Heather sat on the stool next to the bar, and Katya, staying on her feet, leaned against the wall near the fireplace, relishing its heat.

"So, people, before we get into Ms. Ivreski's debriefing," Dr. Reynalt said, "I was hoping you lot could fill me in. I live such an isolated life these days, just me and my associates. Any mortal interaction I have is typically in the form of a client-service relationship. Perhaps you can tell me why there is war between the Hollows and the Fifth Ward. I had thought an agreement had been reached."

"Some agreement," Gunnerson grunted.

Syd shrugged. "Boss and Loqrin've always hated each other. Some Bosses get along, but those two . . . they just rub each other the wrong way."

Dr. Reynalt sniffed. "Loqrin Mars! Ravic is right to despise him."

Kat leaned forward. "Yeah? Why?"

A dark look crossed the Doc's face. "Suffice it to say that I have memories of him, or his legacy, from my days with the Guild."

"Is it true they threw you out for fucking with the dead?" Lowell said.

Flame-light bathed the Doc's face. "They did not *throw* me out. I . . . escaped, if you must know. The discoveries I had made, the advancements . . . the Guild wanted them. I knew I could not let them have my techniques for reanimation—they would not have used such techniques for good purposes—and had I stayed they would have forced the information from me, so I had no choice but to flee. For a time I went underground, and when I was strong enough I rose again. Now for the Guild to attack me . . . it would be too costly. I have my own army. As for my old brethren, the Guildsmen, they have their own ways of cheating death, at least for a time, and schemes for greater deeds. That's their imperative, you know, along with the craving for absolute power—to discover a path to immortality. Loqrin thought he had found it, long ago. Perhaps he did. But it drove him mad."

"What do you mean?" Katya said. The way Reynalt said *long ago* sounded very long ago indeed. "And why do you know him through the Guild? When I was . . . well, spying on him, this Minister guy, I think his name was Tully, called Loqrin a Minster, too. I don't get it."

Dr. Reynalt looked at her with new interest. "Spying on the Guild, were we? Tut tut tut." He chuckled, and his expression warmed.

"Well? What does it mean?"

He took a puff on his cigar, tasted the smoke and blew it out. "Loqrin is not his real name."

"What's this?" said Syd.

The others leaned forward eagerly.

Cigar smoke crowned Dr. Reynalt's head. "Long ago there was an Archminister of the Guild. Horqrin Kan. A brutal tyrant, but not unintelligent. Quite the opposite, in fact. He made numerous advances, both in alchemy and in personal manipulation. All Guildsmen feared and respected him. Well, when it was his time to go, he recruited several Ministers that had become disciples of his and instructed them in his secret arts. This was hundreds of years ago, before the alchemical compounds that have been invented since, the compounds Guildsmen use to extend their lives nowadays. Since those were not available, Horqrin had his disciples—using the techniques he had invented—remove his brain and insert it into the skull of another, a strong young man. Now Horqrin called himself Morwed Janc, and the first thing he did was murder his disciples and flee. He'd learned all he could from the Guild—hells, he had become their teacher—and had decided to move on. He set himself up as a Boss, and when things between he and the Guild cooled off years later, they reconciled and became allies. Horqrin, or Morwed if you prefer, was a powerful Boss and one of the Guild's few friends in the underworld at that time. This was long before they controlled most of the Bosses like puppets, and is one of the main reasons why they were finally able to do so. Well, every fifty years or so Horqrin would teach his arts to a select few, who were desirous of learning the ways of immortality. He would swap bodies, murder his apprentices, and re-introduce himself to the mob community. He evidently enjoyed being a Boss more than he did an Archminister, as he kept at it, generation after generation. Of course, time has had certain unfortunate effects on his brain. The alchemical preservatives we have now weren't available until the last fifty years or so. Consequently, he is quite mad."

Katya's cigar smoldered forgotten between her fingers. "You mean to tell us . . . Bullshit! Loqrin can't be . . . not hundreds of years old . . ."

"I believe it," Heather said. "It explains some things. Like, he would always talk about things that happened long ago. I thought he was just, you know . . ." She twirled a finger beside her ear.

Katya slumped back against the wall. She took a puff on her cigar, coughed. "Well, you know, I wondered how he'd got all those Returners. I mean, he must've had thousands, all packed in those Arches. *That's* how he got them. He's been killin' people for hundreds of years."

"Killing them and worse," Dr. Reynalt added.

"Fuck," said Gunnerson.

Lowell and Franklyn muttered in awe. The fire crackled, and the log popped. In the distance gunfire rattled.

Katya collected herself. She had to use this opportunity. "You wanted to know why Loqrin's attacking the Fifth?" she said.

Reynalt looked at her. "Yes."

"Well, partly it's because Ravic's trying to organize a union. The Underground Brotherhood, you've heard of it?

Well, that's it. Or will be. And Loqrin's trying to stop him. Now I know Loqrin used to be an Archminister, I guess that part makes more sense. But there's more to it than that. Jack and Vivia were feedin' him info. He knew Ravic was on to him, after him, and he meant to take Ravic out."

"Wait a minute," Gunnerson said. "Jack wasn't—"

"Shut it!" Katya said. "We're talking here." Gunnerson opened and closed his mouth, then fell silent. Dr. Reynalt looked impressed.

"You were saying," he said.

"Well, that's why Loqrin's attacking, but that's only part of it. He wants victims. See, Loqrin's been abducting people and giving them to the Guild. Tully and his boys've been doing tests on 'em in the Below. Some sort of translation chamber, I think they called it."

Dr. Reynalt sat up sharply. "Dear gods! Are they mad? Do they know what they could unleash?"

"I think they've unleashed it," Katya said. "Loqrin's been making haunts."

Firelight reflected in Dr. Reynalt's eyes. His face was still and tight. "Tell me everything."

Quickly, Katya did, leaving little out. Dr. Reynalt grew paler and paler as she spoke, and his lips compressed into a tight line. When at last she finished, the fire had died down to embers, and Kat had thrown away her cigar and replaced it with a cigarette, which she found much more palatable. Dr. Reynalt didn't object.

"What could they be doing down there?" Katya asked.

Dr. Reynalt had been staring into the glowing embers. Now, pale and sweaty, he looked up. "They can be doing one thing only. That chamber is a device the Elders used to project their consciousnesses through time and space, sending them into other dimensions to commune with beings there. Some believe they could even leave their bodies behind entirely and exist as a living consciousness on other planes, or even possess the body of another. It would be this last possibility that would intrigue my former brethren. The eternal search for immortality. They would want to project their consciousnesses, their souls, if you will, into another's body, thus eliminating messy surgery and its side-effects. Besides, Horqrin's techniques have never been replicated, save by me. However, to project one's consciousness, one must *cross out of this plane*. One must travel through others." A faraway look came into his eyes. "There are planes out there, beyond the spheres, planes of pure consciousness, where there is no matter, and the beings there are beings of thought. Some are great and terrible, and live in vast seas of psychic energy. Dark, awful beings . . . My brethren must be mad to risk arousing such things."

"But what about all those men and women, the factory workers?"

"Guinea pigs, as you surmised. My former brethren know little of the outer spheres and the other planes. Who besides the Elders do? Thus they would experiment on translating the consciousness of another, and they would test myriad planal frequencies to find the right dimension and angle . . ."

"And the haunts?" Katya pressed. "What can they be?"

He frowned. "You said you saw an altar? And a machine?"

"At Loqrin's place, yeah. He mentioned the name of something, a god maybe. The Leviathan, he called it."

Dr. Reynalt's eyes sprang wide. With a jolt, he leapt out of his chair. Katya gasped, and so did some of the others. Heather dropped her drink, and it shattered loudly on the floor.

The Doctor strode up to Kat and loomed over her, his eyes blazing. "Are you sure about that name, girl?"

She nodded.

"But that's . . . that's impossible . . ." With frantic energy, he began pacing up and down before the glowing fireplace. "There's only one being in those seas known as the Leviathan . . ." His voice filled with fear. "Os'ulyth . . . No, please no. Can it be?"

She summoned her courage. "What is it?"

Jaws bunching, he said, "Remember the planes of pure consciousness I told you about, and the seas of psychic energy? Well, there are beings there, great and powerful beings, with minds so vast you cannot imagine. There are many races there in the Seas of Nug'eb—the Mu'gesh, the Curub'nagath, the Ri'u, I don't know them all. But from the engravings of the Elders I have learned that dreaded name. Os'ulyth is . . . well, a great and terrible being, ancient beyond words, the Leviathan of the psychic seas, worshipped and feared as a god by many races. Perhaps . . . perhaps it *is* a god."

Katya's mind reeled. She staggered over to the bar and helped herself to a drink. Heather was finding herself another glass. Both their hands shook.

"The Elders believed that Os'ulyth had grown mighty enough to reach out its mind and connect with other planes, other spheres. It has discovered the dimensions of flesh, like ours, and it desires to cross over, to become flesh and enjoy fleshly delights. If it ever accomplished this goal, there would be terrible results. It would destroy and transform any world it entered."

"Damn," said Kat. "And you think Loqrin . . ."

He wiped sweat from his brow. "Yes. You see, for eons Os'ulyth has been checked in its desire. Fortunately for us and countless other beings, its consciousness is simply too vast to cross over. It would need to anchor itself in a being in our world to cross here, in effect to possess someone. But our minds are too small, much too small, to contain it."

A dark shadow rippled over his face. "Yet I fear Horqrin has found a loophole."

"What do you mean?" Katya said.

Dr. Reynalt looked at her tensely. "*Horqrin has been bringing Os'ulyth over in pieces.*"

Chapter 16

Gunfire rattled outside. No one noticed it. Every eye was riveted on Dr. Reynalt.

"What . . . what do you mean?" Katya said, and downed a sip of liquor.

Dr. Reynalt's eyes blazed. "These haunts, they aren't ghosts at all. *They're pieces of Os'ulyth.* Horqrin is bringing It over, *one brain cell at a time.* Don't you see? *That's* what the haunts are, if you will—individual brain cells of the Leviathan. With Horqrin aiding It and sabotaging the Guild's machines, Os'ulyth has been possessing these test subjects, inserting a little bit of Its great mind into each one. The effect, of course, is to radically alter the victim, to change them into what we have come to call haunts. However, Os'ulyth is a being that feeds on psychic energy—his subjects in his own plane feed him constant sacrifices; he writhes in a great orgy of psychic blood—and the haunts are especially vulnerable to starvation, living as they do in a plane not their own. Thus they feed from the minds of men, off our psychic output. It's the only way they can survive, to feed from intelligent minds."

"They eat brains," Gunnerson breathed.

Dr. Reynalt shook his head. "They don't *eat* brains. They eat *consciousness.* Souls, if you like. When Os'ulyth crosses over, humankind will become cattle for it."

Katya trembled. "Last night Loqrin rounded up a bunch of factory workers. Strikers. I think he means to make haunts of them all."

Dr. Reynalt nodded. "It's happening right now, I'm sure of it. Even as we speak, Horqrin is bringing this . . . this *thing* over, bit by bit, brain cell by brain cell. Once enough cells are gathered, they will congeal. I don't know how many minds it would take to hold Os'ulyth. Thousands, millions maybe. But perhaps if a substantial part of Itself were here, It could, so to speak, wedge Its toe in the planal door and open it for the rest to follow."

Feeling faint, Katya said, "How many would it need?"

Dr. Reynalt shrugged. "Who am I to say?"

"Guess!"

"If I had to—to guess at how many minds would make a toe! the absurdity!—perhaps . . . maybe a hundred or so."

They stared at each other hard. "I don't think he has that many," Katya said, thinking quickly. "There were maybe a dozen haunts before last night, maybe a few more, and he rounded up maybe forty strikers. But . . . in all this chaos . . ."

"Yes!" Sweat flew from his brow. "Yes, *that* must be why he's launched this attack! To cover his kidnapping of scores of people . . . vessels for the Mind-Eater . . ."

Katya grimaced. "It's all my fault. He only ramped up his game after I escaped. I forced him into this. But if what you're saying is right, then that means . . ."

Dr. Reynalt was pale. "Yes. He's ready. It's all ready."

"He must mean . . . the crazy fuck must mean . . . he's going to bring Os'ulyth over tonight!"

A long moment of silence passed in the room. The fire crackled. A police siren wailed in the distance.

Just then, there came a knock at the door. They all jumped. Cautiously, a woman's face peered in.

"Yes, Carol?" Reynalt said.

The woman swallowed. Evidently she had heard their raised voices and had hesitated to enter. "It's Ravic, sir. He's awake."

The next few minutes were a blur to Katya. Heart thumping, fingers shaking, she rushed along with the others down the flights of steps to the laboratory. Her mind spun with images of great, blasphemous gods destroying the world, transforming it, feeding on people as if they were cattle. Why would Loqrin Mars be doing this? She found it hard to believe, even as mad as he was, that he could worship such a thing as this Leviathan.

But all these thoughts vanished, or at least slipped to the rear of her thinking, the moment she saw Ravic.

He lay huge as life on the slab, each limb as thick as a tree trunk, scars seeming to mark each square inch of him. Sometimes where the hair grew out over them, the hair was white. In some places it was white anyway. An even whiter sheet covered his legs and groin, but his huge feet stuck out. His great chest rose and fell, bare and hairy. New scars, freshly stitched and sitting amid a mass of bruised tissue, ran around the area of his heart. The incisions were so fresh Kat could see where the flaps of flesh met and were tied together by stitches.

And then his head, his great, leonine head. Currently it rested on a pillow. His mass of hair and beard still enveloped it like a mane, but it was faintly ridiculous now. A half dozen patches had been shaved, and the skull itself was bruised and stitched in the bald spots. Nearly half his hair was gone, and the remainder thrust out in irregular locks.

But Kat almost didn't notice these small details when his huge, lantern-jawed head swiveled, and his gaze fell on her. A burst of lightning coursed through her, and she felt a strange smile contort her face.

"Boss!" said Gunnerson, clapping Ravic's hand and shaking it vigorously. Moisture gleamed in the man's eyes.

"Not so rough," Dr. Reynalt said, laying a hand on Gunnerson's shoulder. "He has much recovering to do."

Excitedly, the bodyguards greeted him.

Ravic's gaze swept his visitors, and he frowned. In a strained voice, he said, "Where . . . is Jack?"

Silence fell. The bodyguards looked away. Jack's body must have been put into storage, as he was nowhere in sight.

At last Katya spoke up. "He . . . he died. Vivia, she tried to kill you when you were sleeping. He stopped her, but she killed him for it."

A groan escaped Ravic's lips, and his head sank deep into the pillow. "Jack . . . Rupert . . ." Then anger crept into his voice, and his eyes changed, burned. "Vivia! I'll kill her! *I'll gut her like a fish!*"

Katya laid a hand on Ravic's forearm. His flesh was hot. "I'm sorry, but I already killed her."

"Yes?" The word came out in a breathless rasp.

"I shot her. She'd run into the Below, Loqrin was waiting for her, in his zeppelin. Before I shot her, she called him Father."

"*Father?*"

"I didn't know Loqrin had any kids," Heather said. "I mean, he never let us have any. And when we got that way . . . and you don't want to know what he did with the fetuses . . ."

"Was she Sonya?" Katya said. "Jack called her Sonya."

"Yes," Ravic said, his face hard. "It was her. In a different body. She hid it well, with all that hair. You couldn't see the scars. But it was Sonya's brain, all right. Her diseased, evil little brain."

"That's some shit," Gunnerson said.

"The women I know get into enough trouble with one body," Syd added.

"Loqrin must have raised her to hate me," Ravic said. "Brainwashed her against me."

Katya nodded. "Then he sent her to you, and she became your girl. She tried to get Jack to betray you, and he went along with it. She wanted to bring you down, that was her mission from the beginning. Maybe even to take over your territory for Loqrin."

"Then when she was found out . . ."

"Back to Daddy. But when they learned Jack had come returned, and thought he might still be in love with her, they put her in a new body and sent her back. She confessed to Jack who she was and tried to do it all over again . . ."

Ravic grinned bitterly. "Jack didn't take the bait, though. He came to me as soon as she told him. Together we were working her, feeding Loqrin false information, sometimes some real info to string them along."

She stared. "*That's* why he encouraged you to defend the east side. Because she was right there watching! *Listening.*"

"That's about the size of it."

"Damn! If only I'd known . . ."

His other hand reached around and grabbed hers, enclosing it firmly. "Thank you for killing her."

Tears burned her eyes. "You said you wanted a killer."

Ravic looked regretful for a moment, but before he could speak Dr. Reynalt cleared his throat, drawing their attention. "I think that's about all for today. We need to let Ravic rest."

The bodyguards nodded, grumbling, and began to turn back. Heather touched Katya's arm and said, "Let's go."

Katya shook her head. "I'm staying."

"But—"

Dr. Reynalt had overheard. "Everyone out."

"Boss and I have things to discuss."

Dr. Reynalt started to protest, but Ravic said, "She stays."

"Very well," Reynalt said. "Everyone else, follow me."

Someone had placed thin, silk Zanshinese partitions around the slab to give Ravic some privacy. They were colored red and purple, and butterflies and giant salamanders stood out on them. Dr. Reynalt stepped around the partitions as he left. Heather patted Katya's shoulder and followed him.

Feeling something quiver in her stomach, different from before, Katya turned back to Ravic. He was regarding her strangely.

"What did you want to talk about?" she said, then, when everyone else had gone, she bent over and kissed him, right on the mouth. Startled, he almost pulled away. He overcame his surprise, though, and returned her kiss. His lips were warm and slightly rough.

Smiling, she pulled back and then climbed onto the slab. She straddled him, right around the waist, and stared down at him. He looked up at her, amazed.

"Kat . . . what's got in to you?"

"Nothing yet." She smiled impishly.

"Really, is this the best place, the right time? I mean, *Jack* . . . dear gods . . ."

She thought of the Leviathan crossing over tonight. "There might never be another place, another time. Besides, now *you're* the one that's helpless, and *I'm* the one with the power. When is that ever going to happen again?"

"Kat . . ."

Slowly, gently, she ground her hips against his. His lower half was still covered by a sheet, and it was soft against her. She wore only a silken shift and a man's dinner jacket. No underwear. Slowly, rhythmically, she rubbed him, and it wasn't long before she felt a stirring, possibly despite himself. Her fingers traced the scars in his chest, ran through his hair. Almost reluctant at first, his large hands massaged her thighs, cupped her buttocks. His hands were warm, almost hot.

A couple of Dr. Reynalt's people came through the Zanshinese partitions to check on Ravic. They gasped.

"You've gotta pay for admission," Katya said. "Otherwise get out!"

They glanced at each other, blushed, and retreated.

Ravic looked up at her. Sadness touched his eyes. "I'm sorry I made you kill Vivia."

"You didn't make me anything. She deserved it. Now shut up unless it's sexy."

Afterwards, she lay beside him, curled up under one huge arm. For awhile she drowsed, and when she woke up she found him looking at her. She smiled. She could feel his heart, his new heart, beating against his ribs.

"Well, that wasn't so bad, was it?" she said.

"No." He stroked the small of her back. "So am I going to have to die and get resurrected every time for you to . . . do what you did?"

"I don't know. We'll take it as it comes. No pun intended."

He murmured something unintelligible.

"By the way," he said. "I meant to tell you this earlier, but I never . . . well, I did what I promised."

"What do you mean?"

"I had Sedic and his gang arrested."

Katya blinked, then smiled. "Really? Wow. That means . . . I'm free. I mean, at least I don't have *that* to worry about. Shit! When this is over, if it ever is, I won't have to look over my shoulder for that fucking creep."

"Nope. He has a lot of years in prison to look forward to, instead."

She laid her cheek against his chest, careful where she put it. Sudden fear overcame her, and she let out a breath. It was one she had pent up since her conversation with Dr. Reynalt.

"What is it?" Ravic asked.

"Loqrin Fucking Mars. You're not going to like what I've found out." Briefly she told him what she and Dr. Reynalt had surmised, about Os'ulyth and the haunts. Ravic said little, and his face was largely impassive, but it grew tighter and tighter as she spoke, and he blinked a lot, slowly.

At last, when she had finished, he said, "Dear gods . . . what is Loqrin *thinking*? Bringing something like that here?"

"I don't know, but that's not all of it." She proceeded to tell him about the gang war.

"Fucking bastard! I'll strangle him with his own guts!" Ravic started to sit up but screamed in pain and collapsed back to the slab. He lay, trembling, breath coming out of him in ragged bursts.

"I don't think you're going anywhere," Katya told him. When he seemed to be all right once again, she said, "But what can we do? Jack told Max to round up your people and gather at the Factory. They're going to drive right into the Hollows at sundown, guns blazing, and I just know Vivia, or Sonya, whatever, told her daddy all about it. She was upstairs on the phone while you were under."

Ravic nodded soberly. "That's what Jack and I wanted. He even mentioned the street he wanted Max to drive up, didn't he?"

"Yeah. Ratagat. Why?"

Ravic grinned. "Good thinking, Jack. A cool head even then. He meant to go through with the plan."

"I don't get it."

His grin faded. "We were trying to get Loqrin to ambush us."

"*Why?*"

"So that we could ambush his ambushers. We knew he'd ambush us anyway. One of his look-outs would have notified him as soon as our convoy crossed into the Hollows, and he'd set up an ambush, but we wouldn't know where or when. This way we control it. Deal with it. Eliminate the last of Loqrin's forces still in the Hollows, then move on to him."

"Not entirely stupid, I guess."

"Jack or I would have led the charge into the Hollows, but in secret the other would lead a smaller group to set up position at the most likely ambush spot, Ratagat and Livath, that's where the streets are narrowest and there are the fewest cross-streets to escape down. We'd pounce on Loqrin's ambush party when they revealed themselves. The raiding party would roll right on through. But now Jack's gone and I can't go anywhere. I trust Max to lead the raiding party, but there's no one to lead the ambush party, and no party to lead. I guess Jack intended to do that after he'd seen to it that I was safe, but . . ." He balled a fist. "We're fucked. Loqrin will bring that . . . that *thing* over tonight, and we can't stop him. Can it really have come to this? The end of the damned world?"

Katya pushed herself up and swung her legs underneath her. "Maybe not," she said.

He fixed her with a hard glare. "How?"

"I think I know a way. But I'm going to need wheels. And a driver."

Concern touched his face. "What do you mean to do, girl?"

She forced herself to smile boldly. "I'm going into the Hollows, and I'm going to stop that motherfucker."

Chapter 17

Syd's swears traveled even through the partition of the limo, and Katya rolled her eyes. Ravic had ordered him to help her and even given her his limo for her purposes, and he didn't seem to appreciate it. She smoked one of Syd's abominable Hellfires and blew the smoke out the window. Tires ground on asphalt below, and the expensive engine purred like a cat. Up ahead, Syd cursed.

She wished Heather could have come with her. Gunnerson and the others had refused to leave Ravic's side, and Dr. Reynalt had been preparing his people for retreat into the Below in the event the Leviathan crossed over. He did not believe Os'ulyth could be defeated through force. *We might die like rats*, he had said, *but we will not die like cattle*. Thus Katya supposed she was Lavorgna's only hope, maybe the world's, and she could have used some company. Heather, however, had been passed out drunk.

The sun blazed brightly overhead, and Katya relished its warmth, feeling it soak into her skin. On the other hand, the time was just after two o'clock. About three hours till Max led Ravic's men into an ambush and got them all killed. She had to act fast.

As the limo rolled along, she saw burned-out buildings and blackened cars to all sides. Sirens and the occasional bout of gunfire still echoed in the distance, but the violence had faded during the daytime. That only deepened her suspicion that one reason for the attack was to cover more abductions. Even now Loqrin would be at that strange Elder building in the Below, and there would be a line of poor doomed factory workers and random citizens trailing from the translation chamber down the hallway. They would be bound and hooded and frightened, and Loqrin's Returners would be marching up and down the line of them, striking any that acted too boldly. The stink in the air would be one of misery. The men and women, even children, would be sobbing, praying to their own gods, even as Loqrin used them to bring *his* god-thing over, piece by fucking piece. *But why?* Katya kept thinking. *What does he have to gain from it?*

She expelled a long stream of awful black smoke and smoothed her dress down. At least Dr. Reynalt had found her some clothes. They belonged to a young woman whose body he had bought for spare parts some weeks ago. She had been ground beneath the hooves and wheels of a horse-drawn carriage, and there hadn't been much left of her for him to use, but what *had* been left had been clothed in a simple black dress, and that's what Kat wore now. The girl had been younger than she was, and the dress was tight and itchy. She had torn it off above her knees to allow greater movement, and she wore the dead woman's small black slippers on her feet. They pinched. Over her shoulders she still wore the man's dinner jacket she had been given last night. Despite the sun, it was early autumn, and the wind blew cold up from the south.

Ravic's revolver rested on the seat beside her. Spare cartridges snuggled in her jacket pocket. She hoped she would not need them but knew how unlikely that was.

They left the Fifth Ward and entered the Hollows. Syd crested a great hill, passed the mansions and factories on the ridge, then rolled the car down the other side, toward the Sink. Familiar listing buildings loomed all around, forlorn and decrepit in the daylight. Lines of laundry swung in the breeze. A few pasty men were patching up a crack in one of the building walls. A girl with asymmetrical eyes jumped rope by herself.

"This place needs new management," Katya said to herself, and punched a button. "This'll do."

Syd pulled over, and she climbed out. Rapping on Syd's window, she said, "I need a hand."

"It never ends."

Grumbling, he climbed out from behind the wheel and accompanied her down an alley.

"There," she said, pointing overhead to the fire escape. "Gimme a boost."

"Usually people go down those things, not up."

Still, he boosted her onto his shoulders, where she stood precariously until she had a grip on the fire escape, then hauled herself up, grunting and straining. Her new dress wasn't quite so new by the time she was up and staring down at Syd.

"Am I to wait for you, then?" he said.

"Yeah. I don't know how long I'll be."

He shrugged and lit a cigarette. "Take your time. I've got a full pack."

Sweat beaded her pores by the time she reached the roof. A quick search of the pigeon coop revealed nothing, not a note, not a scrap. She knew Reddin's band used various drop spots to communicate with each other and their customers, and had been told this was one of them, but there was nothing there. Sighing, she crossed over a creaking wooden plank to the sagging rooftop next door, then scampered over another plank to the next one. Her stomach flipped with every crossing, and she chanted prayers beneath her breath even as the wood creaked and groaned beneath her. Soon she came to a second pigeon coop. This one had a bit of scrawled writing that was the code-word for a particular drop-spot. Only one of Reddin's associates would have been able to read it. Fortunately Aqa had taught her some of the code-words.

Sweating and dusty and spitting pigeon feathers, Katya made her way down the inner stairwell of a certain building. Though it was cooler in here, it stank of cabbage and strange spices. The Hollowers really were terrible cooks. In the boiler room was a certain cranny reserved for messages, and in this one was crammed the name of yet another drop spot.

"Shit," Katya said. Reddin's people were being *very* cautious in the wake of Loqrin's attack last night.

She found the next drop spot in an all-but-abandoned laundry room ten blocks over. Syd drove her. Under the corner of a certain laundry machine lay another message. *This* one disclosed an actual location, not a drop spot.

"Thank the fucking gods."

A few blocks over, she entered a building through a back door and crept down a dark stairwell into what had at one point been a spa room, but it had been long abandoned. A narrow doorway led to another set of stairs. Somewhat creeped out, Katya descended, feeling hungry and disoriented. She made her way through a system of tunnels, just knowing she was lost, then along the sewer for a while. Here and there graffiti marked the walls, and she recognized several symbols Aqa had taught her. They hinted that she was going the right way.

Two dark shapes lunged out at her.

"Who are you?"

Startled, she jumped back and raised her fists. "I'm Katya, and I want to see Reddin."

They laughed. "So do we."

One grabbed her under the arm and jerked her into a dark, shadowy corridor. It stank of rat piss and vomit. She didn't struggle. She was pretty sure they were Reddin's men. *Pretty* sure. She kept her fists bunched just the same.

They led her through a large archway and into what seemed like a natural cavern. Braziers stuffed with flaming coal lit the chamber and provided some warmth, but not much. Ragged figures huddled around them, and Katya recognized Reddin's men. Tattoos, piercings, strangely colored hair, the occasional mutation. Relief washed through her.

The two sentries dragged her toward a certain cluster, where the carnie-types were gathered around a tall speaker silhouetted by the fire. Katya couldn't see the figure's details, but even framed by the fire her green tattoos glowed like burning jade.

"Aqa!" she said.

" . . . just have to hold out," Aqa was saying. When she saw Katya, she stopped and said, "You!" She moved forward, and now Katya could see her face. Anger filled it, and her eyes were wide with fury. "You *bitch!*"

"W-what? W-what's wrong?"

Aqa stomped forward. "You little cunt, you disrupted the meeting last night. If you hadn't done that, none of this would have happened!"

"Oh." Kat dropped her gaze to her feet. "Yeah, sorry about that. I, ah, made a mistake."

"A mistake!" Aqa stepped even closer. Kat could feel Aqa's breath on her forehead, and for a moment she thought Aqa would strike her. "Is that what you call a *mistake?*" Her voice was shrill, unreasonable.

Katya swallowed, forced herself to look Aqa in the eye. "I know what I did screwed things up. But I don't think it's what got those men caught. Loqrin used his Returners to flush 'em out, and his men—"

"Fucking slut! Think you know everything, do you? Well, maybe you know where *Reddin* is! Do you, bitch? *Do you know where he is?*"

"He's not *here?*"

Aqa clenched her fists. Then her anger seemed to give way to fear, and she looked away. "He never came back last night. We don't know where he is. He could be bleeding, dying in some gutter. If it weren't for the confusion caused by your little scene, we would have left together. We never would have gotten separated."

"So that's why you're pissed."

Aqa snorted. "If Reddin doesn't return, I don't know what we're going to do."

"*You* could lead them. They look up to you."

Aqa finally returned Katya's gaze, and Katya saw sadness in her eyes. Grief. Deep grief. "Maybe, but what about *me*?" In a small, quiet voice, so that none but Katya would hear, she said, "I don't know if I can go on without him."

Slowly, hesitantly, Katya reached out and squeezed Aqa's arm. "It will be alright. Somehow."

Some of the tension left Aqa, and she stepped forward suddenly and hugged Katya to her chest. Aqa was much taller, but that didn't matter. Kat could feel her shaking. A lump formed in Kat's throat.

"I'm sorry," she said. "I'm so sorry about last night. I was wrong about Jack."

Aqa shook. She was obviously trying not to sob. "I know, sweetheart. I know. I . . . I didn't mean to yell at you. It's just . . . I'm *so* worried. What has taken him so long?"

Katya patted her back. "It'll be alright, I promise." She started to say something about Loqrin, about needing Aqa's help, but held back. Now wasn't the time.

"I could use a drink," Aqa said, stepping back and wiping at her eyes. "Want one?"

Katya nodded. A long bar ran along one side of the room, and the rotting remains of a liquor cabinet hung behind it. Stalactites shoved down from above, and Kat and Aqa wove through a forest of stalagmites. Firelight lit them in red, rippling light, making them glisten and burn, and sending their shadows like black teeth across the floor.

"What is this place?" Katya asked.

Rooting through the liquor cabinet, Aqa said, over her shoulder, "Used to be an old underground drinking den, seventy, eighty years ago, back when spirits were illegal."

"Underground. I get it."

"No, kid. Really." She found a bottle, two dusty glasses, and poured them both a drink of sherry. "This place was illegal. City-wide crackdown on drugs and alcohol. A conservative backlash against the rise of the industrial age, the looseness of morals. There were wild parties down here, though. Music and dancing and drinking among the stalagmites. You can almost hear it, can't you?"

"Hear what?"

"The music. Laughter. High heels on stone."

All Katya could hear were bats chittering somewhere, and the plink-plink of water. That and crackling flames and muted, depressed conversation. But she nodded noncommittally. She saw there were only two entrances to the room, the natural archway she had entered by and, on the opposite side, an arch that passed into a smaller natural cavern beyond. Gods knew where it went.

She and Aqa drank for a while, and Aqa seemed to relax a bit. Some of Reddin's people approached and they bullshitted for a bit while Katya mostly stayed silent. How could she turn these folk into the soldiers she needed them to be? Maybe this whole thing had been a mistake.

Just as she was about to ask Aqa for help, knowing she would refuse (*No suicide missions for us, kid. We're profiteers, not martyrs*, she could almost imagine Aqa saying), sudden commotion erupted from the archway Katya had entered by.

"Reddin!" someone shouted. *"Reddin's back!"*

The change that came over Aqa was instant and incredible. Her eyes lit up, and a white smile split her dark, green-inked face. She all but leapt over the bar in her rush toward the scene of activity. Cheers and rough shouts rose up all around.

Smiling, Katya followed. *Finally*. She knew that Reddin would help her, at least. He hated Loqrin and would do anything to stop him. Also, he was an ally of Ravic and had secretly been helping him organize meetings of the Brotherhood.

Reddin's men swarmed about a dark, medium-sized figure, clapping him on the back and exclaiming loudly. "You're back, boss!" "Good to see you back!" "Thank the gods, we thought we were fucked!" "What'd we do without you, boss?" "Three cheers for Reddin!" "Hear hear!"

The figure that must be Reddin just walked forward, slowly and awkwardly. Katya wondered if he might be hurt. She noticed that he moved in odd little jerks and twitches. They reminded her of something. Doubt gnawing at her, she approached. She could see his features now, pale and rough, the red-glowing tattoo of an eye on his forehead.

Aqa reached him and embraced him tightly, rocking him back and forth. She planted kisses on his forehead, right over the glowing eye.

"Oh you stupid man! Where *were* you?"

"No . . . where . . ." Reddin croaked.

"You must be hurt," Aqa drew back and looked at him with motherly concern.

Katya drew close now. She could see the lines of worry, but also happiness, on Aqa's face, could see the blank and lifeless look on Reddin's. Something was wrong, terribly wrong.

And then Katya heard it. She had to strain her ears to hear it, but she was suspicious and she did.

Tick. Tick. Tick.

A cold wave trickled down her spine. *"Get out of the way!"* she shouted, yanking her gun, which hung from the holster Gunnerson had given her. "Out of the way, Aqa! He's a clockworker!"

Aqa turned. Others did likewise. Reddin merely lifted a hand, pressing something on his side.

Katya pointed at his head. Fired. Her gun roared, and brains exploded out of the back of Reddin's skull. He flew backward to the ground.

Even as his body was still sliding across the ground, Aqa, insane with grief, rage and confusion, pulled out her own gun and pointed it at Katya's face. *"What did you DO?"* Aqa trembled visibly, but her gun stayed remarkably still.

The muzzle of that gun seemed to swallow the world, and for a moment Katya forgot how to speak. Very gingerly, she replaced her pistol in its holster. Shuddering, at last she said, "L-look at him. *Look* at him."

Aqa, teeth bared, clicked the hammer of her revolver back. "You're *dead*! Do you hear me, you're *dead*!"

"J-just look at him. *Please.*"

Others were pointing their guns at Katya as well. Still shaking in anger and horror, Aqa turned slowly and stared down at Reddin's body, really *looked* at it. Katya did, too. She saw the holes she had punched with her gun, saw broken clockwork gears spinning, scraping against each other.

Something halfway between a sigh and a moan escaped Aqa's lips. "No . . ." She shook her head, denying it. "No, no . . ." She did not try to stop the tears now but sank to her knees before Reddin and held his limp carcass in her arms. "Oh, my beautiful man, what did Loqrin do to you? What did he *do*?"

The others lowered their guns and stared. Kat breathed a sigh of relief, wiped cold sweat from her forehead. Her legs shook. But something was still wrong. The tick-tick-ticking seemed to have *increased* in pace, not wound down. She remembered Reddin punching something on his side—

Shit.

She stepped forward and tried to pry Reddin away from Aqa. It wasn't easy. When she partially succeeded, however, she saw through one of the holes. What she noticed was a bundle of wires, and several long red sticks.

Tick tick tick.

"It's a bomb! A bomb! RUN!"

She bolted toward the far side of the cavern. After a moment of confusion, a few others followed. Over her shoulder, Katya saw Aqa examine the body. Then she let out a curse, jumped to her feet and ran after them. The rest of the crowd followed her lead, and just in time.

BOOOOOM!

The blast shook the cave. Stalagmite shrapnel rained over the cavern, slicing tender flesh. Several of Reddin's men flew to the ground, dead. The ceiling rumbled. Cracked. A section of it caved in and crushed a group of men and women. The roar was terrible. Kat felt the vibration in her bones, in her eardrums. The blast nearly knocked her off her feet. Dust choked her lungs.

When Aqa reached where Katya huddled by the far archway, she ran on, through the tunnels, and everyone poured after her, a tide of panicked, screaming people. Katya allowed herself to be swept up in the wake. A column of smoke and dust chased her, and the walls collapsed around her as she ran.

At last, coughing and trembling, she emerged into the sewer, and for once she was glad to be there.

Cursing and shaking, Reddin's people gathered around Aqua, who looked as if she had moved past grief and embraced sheer, raw fury. Her eyes were wide as saucers.

"I will *get* him!" she thundered. "I don't care what it takes, I will make Loqrin *pay!*"

Katya, coughing and wiping dust from her face, staggered forward, pushing people out of her way. "I think I know a way," she said.

The sun sank in a ball of fire to the west, bathing the horizon in blood and sending the listing shadows of the Hollows tenements creeping east like the limbs of some nightmare being. Cool wind stirred Katya's hair. Together with some of Reddin's people—Aqa's now—she crouched in the shadow of the needle that sprouted from the building's roof. In the distance, dim at first but then loud, she heard the roar of engines. Dozens, all driving fast, deep into heart of the Hollows.

"Right on time," she whispered. "You go, Max."

On the other side of the spire, out of sight of Reddin's people crouched a line of Loqrin's men in suits and hats. They clutched bombs, grenades and sniper rifles. Katya had seen them before, when she peeked around the edge, but she did not wish to peek again for fear of alerting them. There were similar teams on adjacent rooftops, and on rooftops across the way. But there were similar teams of Reddin's men, as well.

Max's convoy of autos rumbled down Ratagat, growing louder and louder.

Katya risked a peek. Loqrin's men tensed, brought rifle scopes to their eyes, readied to tear pins off grenades, held alchemical bombs overhead . . .

The autos grew closer.

"*Now*," she whispered. Aqa had given her command of this crew.

The biggest carnie, the one with spiked red hair and a tattoo of a lizard on his arm, turned to the others. "Do it!"

It was clear they respected his word more than hers, and she couldn't blame them. Who was she to them?

Instantly, they sprang out from their hiding place and fell on Loqrin's men. Kat sprang, too, aiming her gun as she went.

Loqrin's men spun. Bombs dropped to the rooftop. Hands reached for pistols and knives.

Katya fired, shooting through one man's shoulder and tumbling him backward off the roof. He screamed as he went. She fired again, and again. All around her Reddin's people fired their own guns, running toward Loqrin's men as they did. When their ammo ran out, they cast their guns down and fell on Loqrin's men with blades and lead pipes. Kat saw one man go down with a crushed skull, another man take a knife to the throat. Sputtering and bleeding, he too fell backward off the roof. He did not scream.

Shaking, Katya reloaded her gun. Her fingers trembled. Only five bullets left, she saw. *Fuck*. She had to save them for Loqrin.

She shoved her pistol back in its holster and rushed forward into the fray, fists raised and sharp rings gleaming. Before she got two steps, a hurtling body knocked her off balance, and a fist smacked her cheek, hard. The next thing she knew she lay on her back, gasping, the world spinning above her. Slowly, groaning, she rose to her knees, then her feet.

The rooftop stank of gun smoke. On nearby rooftops she saw similar fighting taking place, dark figures surging against each other, guns blazing, knives glimmering. She saw a green-tattooed figure kick a man off the building and turn to face another, blade flashing. The buildings echoed to the sound of gunfire and screaming.

At last it was over. Loqrin's men sprawled dead on the ground, their blood and brains streaming in thickening rivers. Kat couldn't look.

"It's over," said the man with spiked red hair. He had a fresh cut on his cheek and held one of his arms gingerly. Several of his comrades had died, and his face was grim.

Katya nodded. "Thank you. Thank you all."

Still weak, she staggered over to the rooftop and looked down. Alerted by the sounds of gunfire, Max had stopped the convoy. Armed men gathered around the autos, pointing their repeating rifles and shotguns upward. She saw one huge figure with a black bristling beard, shotgun clenched tight.

"Max!" she screamed. "It's okay!" Her voice drifted down, echoing from building to building.

The figure below put a hand over his eyes. "What's going on?" he roared.

She smiled, not that he could see it. "Just wait."

She made her way to the fire escape and climbed down. She still tasted bile in the back of her throat from the violence. *How many men did I kill?* The question gnawed at her. She thought she'd killed three, but it might have been two, or four. Her mind had been spinning so fast, and everything had been going so crazy. *Shit*, she thought. *What am I becoming?*

Sweating, she at last reached the ladder, kicked it down and jumped to the cracked asphalt below.

She panted as she made her way to the head of the alley and found Max's men aiming their guns at her. She hesitated, but forced herself on. She was almost becoming used to guns being pointed at her. The line of idling autos crouched, engines steaming in the cold night. The sun had set, and only the ghost of a glow lit the road. Darkness gathered, forming huge pools of darkness. Black clouds swept in from the south. The air reeked of ozone. Katya shivered in a sudden cold breeze.

She trotted over to Max, who looked even bigger and uglier now, shotgun in hand, black beard bristling, overcoat cloaking his huge body, making it seem even huger.

"Who are you?" he demanded. "What the fuck's going on?"

Warily, his men tensed around him, some aiming their guns at Katya, some at Aqa's people above.

Katya stopped before him and smiled as brightly as she could. "Don't you remember me? From last night at Ravic's place? I was the girl in the hallway."

Confusion, then recognition lit his eyes. A lusty laugh came out. "You were the hussy stood up for Jack! Yeah, I remember you! I didn't know the Boss liked such little fillies, but I can see why he might've made an exception for you."

"Fuck you," she said mildly.

He laughed. "What're you doin' here, and just what in blazes is going on?"

"Long story. Short version: Loqrin tried to ambush you, I ambushed him back. Well, *we* did, and now you're safe to kick his ass. Only it might be too late. Loqrin's down in the Below, doing fuck-all. You wouldn't believe me if I told you. Good news is if I can beat him, now there's some of Ravic's men left to put the pieces back together afterward. If Loqrin'd gotten you, we would've been fucked."

He scratched at a hairy, boil-covered cheek. "I don't understand half the words comin' out of your pretty mouth, darlin'."

"That's okay. Listen, I think I left Syd about ten blocks over. I need to get to the Sink, and fast. Maybe you can give me a lift. I don't know when, but sometime soon Loqrin's gonna come out, and when he does—"

The worst possible sound split the night.

Sirens.

Long, wailing, gut-wrenching sirens. At the sound, Katya's insides twisted, and she felt a cold claw skitter down her back.

"Damn!" she said.

At the noise, Max and his men hunched their backs and aimed their guns all around. "What's going on?" he demanded, spittle spraying from his thick lips.

The sirens continued to wail.

Katya shook her head, running shaky fingers through her hair. "Fuck fuck fuck!"

"What is it?" Max said.

Kat, get ahold of yourself. "One of Loqrin's goons must have radioed him during the attack just now. Now Loqrin's trying to fuck us so we can't stop him."

"How, girl?"

She didn't need to answer. She heard the scraping, the shuffling. Hungry moans rattled up from rotting throats. Dreading what she would see, feeling cold and scared, she turned slowly about. Dark, hunched forms slipped from an alley, approaching the convoy. Than another alley, and another. She saw a naked man with no genitals but an exposed rib cage. She saw a woman with teeth made of razors. Another Returner only had skin on the left half of his body. The stench of the creatures' rot rolled before them.

"What in the Nine Mouths of Zug?" Max said.

The Returners swept down on the convoy, a tide of death. Max's goons lowered their shotguns and repeaters from pointing at the rooftops to pointing at the Returners. Fired. *Rat-rat-rat.* The shotguns *boomed.* Max blew off the head of an approaching Returner, pumped the slide, blew off another. Katya aimed her revolver but realized she couldn't fire it. She had to conserve her bullets. *Only five. Shit.* Returners swarmed toward her. She needed to get to the Sink, need to get there *now.*

She grabbed Max by the lapels and with all her strength jerked him around to face her. "Max! I'm on a mission from Ravic! You believe that, right? I mean, I just saved your ass!"

Boom!

Max nodded, irritated. "Yeah."

Moan, scrabble.

"Good," she said. "Because I'm not done yet. I need to get to the Sink. Do you think you can take me there?"

"Godsdamnit, I'm a little busy." He broke free to smash one Returner in the head with the butt of his gun. *Crunch.*

"Too bad!" she shouted. "You're driving me, or you're gonna have to explain why not to Ravic."

He turned to her strangely. "You mean—"

"That's right! He's alive!"

An oddly boyish smile lit his craggy, boiled, hairy face. He laughed. "Alright, girl, for that I'll take you anywhere. Hop in and I'll drive you myself."

She climbed in the back of the auto while he squeezed behind the wheel. Thinking that they were supposed to, his guards jumped on the running boards, firing their guns as they did. Katya pined for Ravic's auto, sitting just a few blocks away. Armor-plated, spiked and protected by homunculi, it would have been the perfect vehicle for her purpose. Sadly, this smaller, clunkier specimen would have to do.

The engine roared, and Max plowed over three Returners in the first few seconds; Katya could feel them being ground beneath the wheels. One beat its fists against the undercarriage, and she winced. *I hope that wasn't one of the dolls.*

The filthy things pressed in from all sides. Max's men blasted their guns, then clubbed the Returners when they ran out of ammo. Kat saw one young man dragged from the running board and ripped apart in a shower of blood. Drops of it hit the window.

A rotting hand struck the glass on the other side, spattering blood across the window. Shocked, she jerked back.

The auto surged forward, knocking over Returner after Returner. The men on the running boards had long since spent their ammo, and they crawled in through the windows, which Katya frantically rolled down for them. Sweating, breathing heavily and bleeding in numerous places, they gazed wide-eyed at each other, then to the swarm of Returners outside. Rotting hands reached in through the open windows. Frantically the men rolled them up.

Kat's heart beat hard and fast in her chest. All she could hear was the moan and groan of Returners, the scrape of their nails on glass, and the roar of the engine.

At last Max broke free. The auto lurched forward and rounded a bend. The ragged horde diminished behind. But they weren't far away.

"That way!" Katya shouted. "Left!"

Max swerved, and Kat's stomach lurched.

"There! To the right!"

The auto sped onward, and in the distance sirens wailed. Katya imagined countless Hollows residents locking themselves in, bolting their doors, barricading themselves in. How could people live like this? Loqrin was a monster.

"There!" she said suddenly. "There it is!"

Before them gaped the immensity of the Sink.

Max jerked to a halt, almost throwing Katya forwards. She caught herself, breathing heavily.

"Thanks." She slipped around one of the gunmen, shoved open the door.

"Wait!" said Max. "What do we do now?"

She climbed out and went to Max's window. Sweat streamed off him, matting his thick beard. He blinked his eyes repeatedly. His huge chest rose and fell. Kat noticed that Returner filth streaked the windshield, and Max had the wipers going. *Squank squank squank.*

"Should we wait for you?" he asked, rolling his window down.

"No. Go on. Find Aqa, she's the leader of Reddin's folk now Reddin's dead. She's the one that saved you. Fight off the Returners. And . . ." She scratched her head. "Round up the Hollowers, get 'em outta here. Some bad shit's about to go down, and you should get them away from it. Do that. Round 'em up, get 'em outta the Hollows—oh! I can't believe I forgot. The dolls!"

"The who?"

Katya pointed upward at a distant arch. "Loqrin's harem—prisoners! There's still a few left. Get them out. The top of the middle Arch. A few Returners guard them, but they shouldn't be any trouble for you. Got that?"

He paused, but only for a moment. "Got it."

She strode over to the observing platform that projected far out over the Sink, the same platform she had first met Loqrin on. It was only a few nights ago, she reminded herself. Not even a week. It seemed like an eternity.

She stared over the side, into the gaping maw of the chasm. Blackness met her vision.

"What will you do?" Max called from behind her.

Suddenly, the darkness stirred below her. By the lights of the moons, she saw a long, gleaming stripe, rising toward her. The zeppelin! Shit, Loqrin wasn't wasting any time. He'd been waiting for nightfall, nothing else. Os'ulyth must not like daylight.

"What will you do?" Max repeated.

The zeppelin rose, higher. Katya made out the bright lances of its floodlights. And beneath it, Kat could see something. It was only a glimpse, only a hint, but by the zeppelin's lights she thought she saw movement. A great roiling blackness . . .

The zeppelin rose . . .

Kat twisted her rings so that they faced inward. Then, shucking off her uncomfortable shoes, she climbed the balustrade of the visitor's platform and poised directly over the zeppelin. Wind blasted her, and she swayed.

"Girl, damn you!" Max shouted. "What are you doing?"

Kat turned, just once, and flashed him a grin. Her blood buzzed like fire. "I'm going to kick Loqrin's ass!"

Without another word, she spun about—*and leapt.*

Chapter 18

For an eternal moment she hung, weightless. The blackness rushed all around her. Wind filled her ears, whipped her hair, stung her eyes. The zeppelin grew huge below her.

Then—*whump*

The impact drove the breath from her in a whoosh, rattled her teeth in her skull and nearly knocked her out. She thought it might actually have for a moment, because the next thing she knew she was sliding backwards. The fabric of the zeppelin scraped her face, rustled against her dress and burned her knees and arms.

"Shit!"

Frantic, she clawed at the tight fabric with her ringed hands. Her rings bit deep, sank home. Slowed her slide. Long jagged tears followed her. At last, before she shot out into space, she stopped. Gasping, cheek and legs and arms burning, she clung to the zeppelin for dear life. It rose and rose under her. She saw the lip of the Sink pass by. Then she drew even with the tenements. Then they too began to fall below.

Her stomach clenched as she thought of the long drop below her. *Heights*, she thought. *Why does it have to be heights?*

Dark clouds swept in overhead, lightning flickering in their midst. Rain flung down, drenching her. She spat out water and cursed.

"I hate rain." *Rain, heights, and Loqrin*. Her three biggest hates all together.

The water turned her purchase slippery. Heart thumping, wet and cold, she clawed her way down to one of the struts that made up the zeppelin's skeleton and latched on tight. What now? She couldn't claw her way down to the gondola, couldn't climb on the underside of the bulge. She wasn't a *fly*.

She turned over her options as the zeppelin reached a certain height and stopped its ascent. She felt the airship shudder, and the propellers clanked, changing direction. The rudders angled. Below her she heard the spark and roar of machinery. She could see lights in many colors shooting out of what must be the gondola, though she couldn't see the gondola itself. Loqrin would be striding back and forth, yelling orders to his tamed, halfway-intelligent Returners, who would be throwing switches and levers on the strange machines just as Katya had seen them do before. What were the machines for, anyway? Something to do with the haunts, most likely. He had been *herding* them.

At last there came a series of ticks, then a sound like radio static. Then: a *hum*. A deep, throbbing noise, as if some sort of equilibrium at been reached.

The zeppelin moved.

It caught Kat by surprise. Jerked her. She dug in. Rain pounded her, sticking her clothes to her, getting in her eyes, her ears. Lightning struck to the north, outlining leaning buildings.

The zeppelin swung away, out over the tenements, and when it drew some distance away Katya turned her head and saw what it had been hovering over, what its machines had been dealing with. Turned, and stared.

Her blood ran cold.

"No . . . no . . ."

She had wondered what the dark, roiling object had been, the thing that had been below the zeppelin in the Sink, and now she saw it in all its splendor. It was a great, black sphere, more or less, rippling like water, like smoke. Huge, maybe two hundred feet in diameter, it hung high above the Sink, crackling, shifting. It wasn't always a sphere. Sometimes it stretched, elongated, or bulges protruded from it. Sometimes it appeared more amoeba-like than anything else. For a moment Katya thought it was just a big black *thing*, just blackness and nothing else, but then she noticed movement inside. Lights. No, not lights, *flames*. Tiny (from her vantage point) blue flames drifted from outer parts of the black mass, seeming to swim against fantastic currents toward the center. There many flames had already gathered. Katya couldn't see it all the time, because shadows rolled across the surface, and maybe in the depths, too, but when the shadows shifted, she saw a great, burning blue fire in the core of the mass.

She knew she was witnessing something out of this world—alien, horrible. Her hairs prickled, and she felt cold all over, a cold that had nothing to do with the rain. Lightning flashed, and thunder crashed, but she barely noticed. All her attention was focused on the ball of darkness.

The lights, the flames . . .

Haunts, she thought. Loqrin had made gods-knew-how-many haunts over the course of the day, and they had congealed into this one mass. Perhaps *he* had congealed them, with his strange machines. Perhaps that was their purpose.

The flames drifted toward the center, the core of the object. She wondered if each flame still enveloped a human body, or at least a head. They fed off psychic energy. Did that mean that the core was stuffed with floating corpses, or maybe just their skulls? Or were the rules breaking down now, realities shifting as the thing grew in power, as the Leviathan took form?

Like will-o'-wisps, the blue flames migrated toward the core of the mass, and shadow-currents moved, and Katya realized it was aligning itself, making itself, *birthing* itself.

How long before it was finished, before Os'ulyth was born? She had to act fast.

She slashed at the zeppelin with her rings, tearing a strip away. She poked her head inside. There was a huge cavity. Hanging in it was an equally huge bag. Gas, she guessed. Helium, hydrogen, she didn't know. Struts and girders contained it, and there were catwalks, walkways . . . Some seemed to lead down, toward the gondola.

This was it. With one backward look, she crawled inside. But in that backward glance she saw a dark thing rising toward her, drawn out of the shadows of the town below. Gelatinous and radiating cold, and yet burning at its heart with a blue flame, it flew to her. Black tendrils stretched toward her skull. Hairs stood up on the nape of her neck, and she was too frightened to scream.

But not too frightened to act. Quickly she made the sign Loqrin had made. Fist to the heart, spiral before her face. The haunt shuddered and passed on by. Rain beat in, and lightning flickered.

Breathing heavily, Kat saw others. First one, then two, and three quavering shadows drifting up from Lavorgna. Drawn by Loqrin's machines, no doubt. He had made many haunts over the course of the day, but there were still others out there, prowling the town for victims. He was drawing them to him, to Os'ulyth, trying to collect all the scattered pieces of the fractured god.

"Fuck," Katya said. A chill coursed through her.

Wet and shaking, she climbed down the girders and struts that surrounded the gas-bag, made her way to one of the cat-walks. Metal rattled under her feet, and lightning blasted somewhere outside. The zeppelin trembled.

Trying not to make too much noise, she stepped down from walkway to walkway until she stood on the lowest level, looking up at the huge bag of gas. How many gas bags were there? Two, three? She didn't know, they were hidden by partitions. She just hoped the zeppelin wasn't hit by lightning. Then again, maybe that would be for the best.

Frightened, all too aware of the coalescing mind of Os'ulyth not a mile away, she crept down the walkway toward the ramp that led down into the gondola.

Sounds ahead. Loqrin shouting. Machines belching. The blare of static, the hiss of steam or gas. Also, smells. Smoke, ozone, mercury, the stench of rotting flesh.

I'm REALLY in over my head, Katya thought.

She drew her pistol. Five bullets. Great.

She made her way to the ramp, started down. Lights of many colors, red and yellow, green and turquoise, shimmered up from the gondola interior—shimmered, then changed. No color stayed constant, not for more than a few seconds. And the smells changed too, from ozone to sulfur, from mercury to iron. What bizarre machines had Loqrin built?

She crept down the ramp, toward the bridge. Shadows before her, the mad shadows created from the light of all those glowing, flaring machines. Twisting, leaping, contorting shadows. Then she saw what caused them, the Returners, lurching and limping from engine to engine, just as she'd supposed, stabbing buttons, wrenching wheels, pulling levers.

Loqrin strode among them, shouting commands. Tall and handsome, haughty and mad, Loqrin's face twisted in savage glee, and passion lit his eyes. Kat saw that he wore a parachute pack on his back. With lightning and bizarre, alien machines all around, things that could grow out of control and explode if mishandled, and gas bags above, Loqrin was taking no chances. He was a man obsessed with immortality, after all.

"No, you fool! That button!" he shouted. Irritated, he shoved a Returner out of his way and depressed a knob himself. "There! Now start the sequence! Yes, yes, good!"

Laughing, he marched toward the front of the bridge, where Katya saw a large wheel and some levers and buttons that had nothing to do with the strange machines. He grasped the wheel, pulling it gently. The zeppelin turned. Beyond the great windows the wheel was mounted before, the skyline of Lavorgna changed. Kat saw another wispy, gelatinous shadow glide up. It spun around the gondola, and Loqrin shouted orders to his crew. Machines chugged and sparked, and the haunt flew-swam toward the great mass of Os'ulyth ahead.

So he does control them, Katya thought. *Amazing.*

The Leviathan looked even more massive than it had before, swollen and pulsing above the Sink. Down below, she saw great activity on the streets. People running, fleeing, scrambling from their listing tenements. She imagined the Hollowers joining forces with Max and his men, together with Aqa and her carnies, cutting their way out of the Returner-infested Hollows. *Good,* she thought. *Run fast, run far. I don't know if I can do this.* There were over half a dozen Returners in the gondola, plus Loqrin. She only had five bullets. *Fuck!*

She took a deep breath, let it out, and strode down the rampway.

A nearby Returner lifted his head. Saw her. He looked puzzled.

Suck it up, Kat.

She shot him through the nose. Brains and blood flew out the back of his head, and he slumped against the machine he had been operating, sliding through smears of his own blood on the way.

At the noise, the other Returners spun toward her. Loqrin stopped in his tracks and whirled around. The shocked expression on his face was priceless.

A Returner flew at Katya, a wrench gripped in his hands, meaning to bash in her skull.

She pulled the trigger. The Returner flew backward, brains spraying. Another lunged at her. Boom! It crumpled to the floor, writhing. Smoke drifted up from her revolver. Ravic's revolver.

They were undeterred. More fell on her, howling. She blew out the back of one's head, then shot another in the chest.

No more bullets left! Damn.

Hopefully they didn't know that, though. It was a six-chamber gun, after all.

With a trembling hand, she pointed the revolver at Loqrin. "Call them off!"

They advanced on her, warily. One lifted up the wrench from its fallen companion. The reek of dead bodies made her nauseous. Strange lights flashed, and she smelled aluminum and, strangely, hazelnut, but only for an instant. It was replaced by a smell that reminded her of crushed ants.

They stepped closer. Closer.

For a moment Loqrin looked resolute, as if he would rather die than give the order for them to back off.

Katya cocked the gun. Click. The gun pointed right at his skull. Right at his ancient, diseased brain, a brain that had seen the insides of many hosts.

"Give her space!" Loqrin barked, mumbling something under his breath.

Grudgingly, beating wrenches or knives against open palms, the patchwork undead obeyed. Glaring at her, the Returners stepped back. It was clear they would spring on her at the slightest provocation.

Katya drew in a deep breath. How was she going to do this? There were four Returners, plus Loqrin, and no bullets. *Shit shit shit.*

Stalling for time, she waved her gun at the Boss of the Hollows, then gestured to the god-thing forming over the Sink. "What are you up to, you demented fuckbrain?"

Anger contorted his devilishly handsome face. She wondered if the man it had originally belonged to had been a good man. "I am bringing to the world something it has sorely needed. Transition."

She made a face. "Transition from *what*? *To* what?"

He shrugged eloquently. "To *control*. More specifically, *my* control."

"You're insane! It won't be under your control, it'll be under Os'ulyth's!"

"Ah, so you know. Interesting. Well, but that is where you are mistaken. Look around you. See these machines, these glorious machines? I built them, ostensibly to control the haunts. Os'ulyth even helped me design them, for He knew His various essences would be without central command and would need guidance once in our plane. However, in secret I improved on the designs, enhanced them. Now, when He crosses over in all His majesty, *I* will be able to control *Him*! I will wield the power of a god!"

She would have shot him right then if she'd had any bullets. Anger consumed her. "You idiot! You sick, demented *idiot*! You won't be able to control that Thing. You think these tinker-toys will be able to stop a god? Your diseased little brain must have degenerated worse than I thought—and I *thought* you were pretty runny in the head already."

As she had been speaking, she had become aware of his eyes leaving her, swiveling to look at something over her shoulder . . .

Was it a trick, or—?

A skitter behind her.

She spun, gun raised, for use as a club if nothing else.

A shadow lunged at her. She had expected something on her level, but the shadow came from above. A long knife glittered in the darkness.

Katya stumbled back. The blade flashed where her throat had been.

A monkey-like screech reached her ears.

The shadow hit the ground, coiled and lunged—

Before it did, she saw what it was, and her mind reeled. It was a monkey, or maybe a chimp, she wasn't good with apes. Undeniable intelligence shone in its eyes, but the intelligence wasn't native. Its skull had been opened, and there in its skull cavity sat not a small monkey brain but an oversized version of the organ, what must be a human brain, encased in glass and surrounded by fluid. Whatever it was, the creature must have been in the back, checking on the gas-bags, or maybe in one of the cabins toward the gondola's rear, while Kat had crept up on the bridge.

Before she could digest all this, the monkey leapt at her again. The knife flashed. She struck the blade aside with her gun. Both gun and blade spun to the floor.

Gibbering and screeching, the monkey lunged at her, knocking her over. Strong hands tore at her throat. Her ringed fists smashed it in the face. Once. Again. Blood spurted.

Howling, the monkey grabbed her by the shoulders and dashed her against the floor. Her skull cracked, her back flared.

She punched it again, hard, this time right in the brain-case. Glass cracked. A thin slice of greenish fluid burst out. Screeching in panic, the monkey tried to draw back. She grabbed it by the arms and rolled. Rolled, smushing it under her, rolled again, toward the bridge doorway. Smack! They rammed up against the bulkhead. She half-lifted herself, pulling the lever that opened the door.

"No!" Loqrin cried. *"Sonya, my darling!"*

Sonya?

The door popped open. Wind tore at Kat, sucking her toward it.

She and the monkey wrestled before the open door. Kat's mind spun. Dimly, even as she punched the ape in the face and felt hands tear at her arms, she realized what must have happened. The Tick-Tock Doc had put his daughter's brain in a monkey skull, until he could either repair her old body or find her a new one.

Monkey fangs flashed toward Kat's throat.

She smashed the glass cover of the brain again, and the monkey paused, threw up its hands to protect its head. Kat used the moment to gather her feet to her chest—

"Your brain was never your best feature, anyway," she said.

—and kicked.

Screaming, the Sonya/Vivia-monkey flew out of the open doorway and vanished into the night.

Breathing heavily, Kat yanked the lever, and the door shut. The wind stopped. Gasping, she leaned against the hatch for a rest.

Loqrin didn't give her a chance. Fury gripped him, transformed him. Back rigid and face hard, he strode to a rack of what looked like black metal spears on the wall and tore one loose.

"Oh shit," Kat said. She recognized the devices the Guildsmen's pet homunculi had used against the haunts at the translation chamber. Loqrin must keep some handy for emergencies.

Grinning like a maniac, he triggered the black lance, and a blue, crackling energy burst from its tip.

"You killed my daughter!" he screamed. "My bride! I had almost readied her new body! Oh, so beautiful, and only just flowered!" Hate twisted his face. "Now you will DIE!"

He leapt at her. Stabbed his lance.

She rolled aside, desperate.

An explosion behind her, right where her head had been.

She climbed to her feet and ran toward the rack. A Returner lunged at her, but she ducked his clumsy grasp and stomped—hard—on the arch of his foot. He howled and fell back.

She snatched one of the black lances, depressed the button that activated it, and whirled just in time to block a thrust from Loqrin. Blue light exploded. She danced aside. Struck at him. He dodged, snarling. She brought her lance down on his head. He blocked her, shoved her back. Thrust at her middle. She blocked him. Stumbled back again.

A Returner leapt at her, wrench gripped in hand.

She struck him in the chest. An explosion of blue, and the crackle of radio static. The Returner flew backward, smoking. It hit the floor, slid, and did not rise.

Loqrin came on, snarling, cursing. He was taller and stronger, but he favored one of his arms. She remembered stabbing him beneath the shoulder blade.

"How's the arm?" she shouted.

Lightning smashed nearby, and the accompanying clap of thunder rocked the gondola.

Growling, he stabbed at her head.

She dodged, and the tip of his lance erupted on the wall behind her. The stench of burnt metal filled the air.

Behind him the black mass of Os'ulyth grew larger. The zeppelin had been circling it, gathering strays, but now with no one to steer it, the zeppelin swung off course, buffeted by the wind. It was headed straight toward the mass.

Loqrin, breathless, sweat streaming down his noble face, struck at Kat, again and again. Her arms ached. Even with his injury, he was just too strong.

A Returner darted in at her, and she danced back, letting him take the blast of Loqrin's lance. As Loqrin stepped over the smoking corpse, Kat jabbed at his middle. He blocked her, angling his lance upward so that her lance tip flicked past his face and over his head. Before she could draw it back and angle for another strike, he stabbed at her, right at her face.

She leapt back, off balance.

Something behind her. A corpse. Her heels caught it. She tripped, went sprawling. Her back struck hard. Air burst from her mouth. Her head cracked the floor.

Grinning, victorious, Loqrin loomed above her.

Her hand groped for the staff . . .

"And so it ends," he said, raising his lance, point down. Blue energy crackled on the end of it. He would drive it right down into her chest.

Kat's fingers found the staff. "No," she said. "I don't think so."

She swept her legs into his ankles as hard as she could, knocking him off balance. He wobbled. A look of fear seized him.

She gritted her teeth, grabbed her lance, and thrust it at his crotch. There was an explosion, a scream, and Loqrin flew backward.

Gasping for air, feeling her blood rush like fire, Kat climbed to her feet. She smelled burning flesh. Good. Another Returner rushed at her back, but she spun and blasted him in the throat. A flare of blue, and he flew backward, truly dead. That was it. The last Returner.

Wiping sweat from her brow, she turned and stalked toward Loqrin, who lay smoking and writhing on the floor, his hands gripping his destroyed manhood. Mewls and grunts escaped from his lips. Fury and horror danced in his eyes. His black lance lay some distance away, tip crackling. She kicked it even further away.

"No," he gasped. "No."

"Yes," she said. She kicked him in the face, hard. He groaned, went limp.

Working quickly, she knelt over him and removed his parachute pack, then slung it on her own back. She took a moment to familiarize herself with it, then marched over to the gondola's steering wheel.

The black mass of the Leviathan throbbed ahead, even larger now. The blue flame that flickered in its core flared even brighter now, limning the various shadow-currents that drifted through it. Dark wraiths circled it, joining it one by one. The blue fire in the center grew even brighter, an almost painful blaze, like a blue sun in all that blackness. And, just vaguely, Katya could see shapes inside the sun. *A doorway*, she thought. The sun was some sort of doorway to Os'ulyth's own plane. Even as she watched, the door was opening, and the Leviathan was dragging itself through . . .

She must hurry.

She saw that the zeppelin would just miss the black mass. Grinning fiercely, she spun the wheel, and the zeppelin pointed right at it.

"No," Loqrin, who had evidently woken up, groaned behind her. "You don't know what you're doing! The machines will be destroyed, and fields will collapse. Os'ulyth will be forced back! Our chance to change the world will be gone!"

She hesitated. "Change the world?"

"Yes! You know how bad this world is, Katya. You've seen it with your own eyes. The corruption, the darkness. Now is our chance to make a *difference*, to make it better."

She lifted her lip. "It's people like you that make it so bad, you son of a bitch. Without you, I'm thinking things'll be a damned sight better."

"No . . . no . . . there can still be a way. We can work together. Find me a new body, set ourselves up as *kings*. Only just do this one thing, girl. Work with me, not against me, *and we will rule the world.*"

"Thanks," she said, "but I'm good."

Os'ulyth loomed very close now. Its black, writhing protozoan mass filled the window. The blue sun inside it throbbed. Swelled.

She crossed to the doorway she had ejected Sonya/Vivia from. The wind roared, louder and louder.

Over it, she heard Loqrin try one last, desperate tac:

"We could be gods!"

"I'm glad you like gods so much, you son of a bitch," she said. "You're about to meet one! Say hello for me."

Without another word, she jumped. Wind rocked her, and rain blasted her, but her blood rushed like fire and she barely felt it. The ground grew closer and closer before her. Her belly tightened, and she felt her gorge rise. She *hated* heights. Frantically she found the cord, the longer one. Pulled it. Her chute shot out, ballooned, caught the wind. Her stomach lurched.

She cheered and swung from her ropes. Drifted down toward the ground.

She craned her head. The zeppelin barreled toward the seething, churning mass of the Leviathan, a great torpedo into the heart of a god.

"Go!" she shouted, flipping her middle fingers at them both.

The zeppelin struck.

For a heart-breaking moment, nothing happened, and Katya felt colder than she had before. The zeppelin simply disappeared into the black mass, swallowed by it.

Nothing happened.

"Shit," she said.

Then, suddenly, the burning blue flame at the darkness's core flickered, went out, and there was an explosion of orange and white as the gas tanks erupted. If there were any bodies or brains still in that bastard, they burned to a crisp just then.

WHUSH! There was a suck of air—a great, electric inhalation—as if the black mass was breathing it in, and then the horrible, amoeba-like thing collapsed in itself. There was a roar, and then an explosion of blue flame and black shadow swept outward, filling the sky with unearthly fire. Katya rode the strange winds all the way to the ground.

At last she hit the street, rolled, and came to a stop.

Laughing, clapping her scraped hands, she disentangled herself from the parachute and stood there in the rain, watching the weird lights in the sky spread outward from the central hub, the place where the Leviathan had hovered. But was now no more.

The ground rumbled beneath her. Her stomach lurched.

What was this?

The ground rumbled again.

"Oh, no . . . please no . . ."

But it was.

"Shit."

The explosion, right over the Sink, must have destabilized the Hollows, an already unstable region to begin with.

"Shit shit shit."

And in the distance, she could hear the moan and howl of Returners. She hoped the residents had evacuated successfully.

She wouldn't have time, she realized. The ground shook, trembled, nearly knocking her to her feet.

"Fuck."

It could go at any moment. She didn't even have a cigarette.

At least I killed Loqrin, by the gods!

All of a sudden, wheels squealed, and headlights swept her. She blinked against them. A huge, spiked, armored car rolled to a stop before her. A window rolled down, and Syd bellowed, "Get in, kid! This whole place is goin' down!"

Laughing, soaked to the skin, she climbed in the passenger side of the front compartment and slid in next to him.

"Floor it!" she said.

He needed no encouragement. The engine roared, and the limo shot off.

"I've been following that damn airship ever since I saw it," Syd said. "I knew you'd be up there if you were anywhere. I didn't know how you'd come down, but I was hoping—shit—"

A wave of Returners, glistening in the rain, appeared around the next bend. With strange howls and gibbers, they surged toward the limo.

"Brace yourself," Syd said. "This is going to be rocky."

Kat grabbed the door handle with one hand and the dashboard with the other. Syd hit the gas, and the limo bowled into the filthy, ragged ranks of Returners. Kat felt the bump as one, then another, ground beneath the wheels. The spiked hood of the auto impaled one, who still moved, slapping at the hood. The spikes skewered others, layers deep. Returners pressed in from all sides, smashing the glass, scraping it with their nails. The eerie, mindless, hungry groaning of the creatures filled Kat's ears and sent shivers down her spine.

Below her, coursing up through the tires, she could feel the ground shake. It wasn't quite a sound but a vibration, rattling her very bones.

It grew stronger. Stronger.

Syd broke free of the mass of Returners. The auto lurched forward, careening madly around corners. Returner gore sloughed off the hood, streaked the windows. Kat hit the windshield wiper button. *Squank squank.*

Behind her she heard a great roar. Not an animal sound, but a roar made by the very earth. She turned to look. Syd had lowered the opaque glass partition between the two compartments, and she saw tenements collapsing behind her. Clouds of dust and masonry erupted into the sky. *The Sink was spreading, and the Hollows were collapsing into it!* The collapse spread and spread. The listing tenements fell, toppling into the abyss they had resisted for so long. Kat saw one great tenement, huge and scarred by the war, leaning crazily, then even crazier as the ruin approached, as its downhill neighbor gave way. For a moment, it teetered on the edge, defiant even now. It wobbled, cracks veining it, bricks spraying as pressure tore it apart, and at last it surrendered, falling into the abyss with a great grinding noise, section by section. Laundry lines that connected it to the buildings on all sides snapped and waved in the wind, then fluttered upwards, trailing above it as it vanished into the abyss.

And there were others. So many others, a great circle of devastation, like the world itself had grown a mouth and was devouring them scores at a time.

The collapse came closer, closer.

The ring of destruction spread, growing ever nearer to Kat and Syd. Syd pushed the pedal to the floor. The expensive engine growled. The auto strained forward.

The destruction spread, fast. Faster.

Worry gnawed at Kat. "I sure hope Max and Aqa got everyone out in time."

Syd didn't answer.

Loqrin's Arch collapsed into the widening hole, and her worry was joined by a sense of vengeance fulfilled. *Godsdamn bastard.*

Tenement after tenement fell like dominos, as well as the mansions, the factories. The destruction was vast, changing the very face of the city.

To her relief, it generally looked deserted, empty. Max and Aqa must have done it.

At last Kat and Syd were clear. The destruction slowed, then stopped, and the last teetering mansions on the ridge stood. Panting, Syd stomped on the brakes. Together he and Kat watched the cloud of dust billow up from the ruins, dampened by the rain. Occasional tenements on the rim of the destruction wobbled, fell, sometimes slowly and a piece at a time.

"Damn," said Katya, flushed. Rain thrummed against the roof. She wiped sweat from her forehead and tried to get her breathing under control. "I need a smoke."

Syd gave her one. She inhaled gratefully.

"You really need to get your own pack."

"Yeah," she said, expelling the smoke. "I really do. Oh, by the way, be on the lookout for monkeys with knives."

"I always do."

Syd lit a cigarette himself. Thunder rumbled in the distance, and lightning struck like a lizard's tongue.

"Let's drive," Kat said, throwing her legs up on the dash and sticking her cigarette in her mouth, free hand behind her head.

She took a deep breath. It was done. Loqrin was dead. The Leviathan sent back. Ravic lived, and the Underground Brotherhood would continue on.

And tomorrow?

She supposed she would figure it out then. She didn't know where she was going. She didn't know if she would keep being an assassin, a spy, or maybe something else. For the moment she didn't care. She just smoked her cigarette, flipped on the radio, and watched the lightning pound down.

Syd shoved the auto into gear, and they rolled forward into the storm.

THE END

Stevrin narrowed his eyes, trying to peer through the veil, but whoever or whatever was following him remained hidden.

Fuck this. Wrapping his hand around the knife he carried in his jacket pocket, he hurried on, down one alley, then another. Lit a cigarette to steady his nerves. He would lose whoever was after him soon enough. No one knew these streets better than he did.

Who could be after him? *What?* A fifteen-year-old orphan was easy pickings in this city, of course, but he wondered if it could be . . .